Nothing left to lose

My thanks to PW for all his encouragement with this project and to CDM and RAM to whom Lisa owes so much. Finally thanks to my editor Leah, who took my draft and turned it into a novel; any mistakes remaining are mine alone.

Chapter 1

I saw the tree 200 yards ahead as I rounded the bend on the dual carriageway. It was set back on the grass verge ten feet or so on the in front of the office of some rural estate building. I found myself looking at it and wondering how fast I would need to hit it to end my misery. I didn't want to live without Jane, the only woman I have ever truly loved; without her life was bleak and pointless. With a trunk about a foot thick, would the tree be enough to write off the Saab and me with it? Ultimately, I was a coward. I might have nothing left to live for, but if I was going to do it, I didn't fancy making a hash of it, seriously injuring myself and still surviving. I cursed that I was driving a Saab, not a two hundred pound Vauxhall Nova. Looking forward I saw the concrete support of a bridge, a far better option, but metal crash barriers had been erected to thwart that possibility. Despite the air conditioning, my palms became greasy with sweat on the wheel and then the shakes set in; that had been very close.

Perhaps I'd better explain. My name is Ian West, I'm a 52 year old teacher and seven days ago, my wife of thirty years had told me it was over and she was leaving. Popular myth has it that news like this is like a blow to the pit of your stomach; it's not, it's higher than that, just under your ribs; a blow wears off, this is more like a hand twisting and tearing at your insides and it doesn't stop. To say I was a mess would be the understatement of the year. Our relationship had been in trouble for some time, but self-delusion had always been my strong suit. What I had thought to be cracks in our marriage, were yawning chasms that were unbridgeable for my wife. Jane was not just my wife, she was my best friend; she did not know it, but she meant everything to me, I had just never taken enough trouble to tell her, or show her. Without her I felt helpless, for over thirty years Jane had been the foundation on which I had built my world and now she was gone and my world was disintegrating around me. She wanted things to be amicable, which they would be; we had too many years together and the kids to think about, for it to be anything else.

Nevertheless, I was devastated, a failure as a husband and as a person. Life seemed to have little to offer; the future looked desolate and solitary. Lucy, my daughter, lived in Manchester, where she was studying for her Masters in Political Science. She had been sympathetic enough on the phone, but her way of dealing was to distance herself. Rob, my son was touchingly concerned. He wanted to be there for me, but he had gone travelling his girlfriend, prior to going to university. He wanted to come home from New Zealand to be with me, I refused to countenance it. Staying away from this mess would be the best thing for him. I was damaged enough; I did not want my son to be. What had been driving the car that day, was a few pieces of me held together by the tranquillisers and antidepressants prescribed by my sympathetic GP.

Still deeply shaken by my near miss, I pulled on to the drive of my soon to be ex-home. Not only had I lost Jane, but I was losing my home too, the prospect of life in the sort of house I had started in thirty years ago, merely served to rub salt into the wound; I had nothing left to lose. Still shaking I got out of the car and locked it. I went in, an empty man into an empty house and turned on the TV to blot out the oppressive silence. Sky News came on, an in-depth interview with Richard Sinclair, the charismatic and appealing leader of the British National Regeneration Alliance. An election was just weeks away and public dissatisfaction and disillusion with all the conventional political parties was at an all-time high, following press accusations of MPs profiteering from expenses and general corruption. The minor parties like the BNRA were expected to be the main beneficiaries at the polls. I looked at the carefully contrived appearance that Sinclair presented; a little younger than me, urbane, smooth and handsome, his mellifluous public school voice made his carefully presented mixture of ultra-nationalism, xenophobia and understated racism seem almost reasonable.

"Great, the acceptable face of fascism, that's all I need." I growled as I stabbed at the remote to change the channel.

I sat and allowed an episode of an American TV cop series to wash over me and anaesthetise my mind; I poached an egg and forced myself to eat. Appetite had been a problem since Jane left and I had lost 10lbs, every cloud has a silver lining. I caught sight of myself in the mirror, six feet tall, only slightly overweight, though less so now, brown hair greying only a little, blue-grey eyes, a reasonably good-looking man, who could have passed for ten years younger, were it not for the watery redness of my eyes. I settled to more mindless TV, before giving up and heading for bed. On my way I stopped off at my study and idly logged on to my Facebook account, needing to see that life was still going on elsewhere. Facebook was my way of keeping in contact with my former students. As the page loaded, there were a number of comments on my wall from various members of my sixth form who had just left. One comment stood out, it was from Lisa, a former student, now in her mid-twenties. I had taught her throughout her school career and had seen her develop from a cute kid into an attractive and intelligent young woman. She was the type of girl who had it all - looks, an outgoing personality and a talented sportswoman, yet with an appealing modesty, never really believing how good she was. Her message was simple.

"I need your help, please read my email.
Lisa x"

I logged on to my email and sure enough there, amongst the spam, was an email from Lisa dated three days ago. I clicked on the message.

"Hi,
I'm home for a few days and could do with a hand with my latest assignment. I called in at school, but they said you were away. Any chance we could meet up so I could pick your brain? You know more about Nazi Germany than anyone I know and I need your opinion on something.
See you soon
Lisa"

5

My first instinct was to decline, I didn't want to face people, but I knew I could spend the day staring at the walls fighting back the tears, or I could get out and do something positive. I emailed her back.

"Hi Lisa,
          Glad to help if I can. How about Starbucks in the Market Square tomorrow at 2.00? Let me know if you can make it.
          Ian"

I began to work through the rest of the backlog of emails, within a few minutes a reply from Lisa popped up.

"Thanks see you then.
          Lisa."

I finished off sorting the email and went to bed. More pills and I fell into a deep but disturbed sleep.

I slept in late the following morning; with nothing to do until 2.00, I lay in bed and read for an hour or so. There was no work for me, the doctor had signed me off and the summer holiday, six weeks of solitude, loomed in a week or so. I got up at 12.00 and showered, As I shaved, I noticed just how haggard I was looking, not the face I really wanted to present to the world – not that I wanted to face the world at all at the moment, a deep dark hole had a greater appeal. I pushed the thought away quickly; self-pity was not an attractive trait. I pulled on jeans and a tee-shirt and a pair of trainers and set off for town.

At two o'clock I walked through the bright July sun across the market square flanked by mediaeval and Georgian buildings. Pushing open the door, I welcomed the air-conditioned chill of the dim interior. I saw Lisa at once, she was quite noticeable, just twenty-five, light blonde hair cascading to her shoulders, with an attractive heart-shaped face and the most remarkable and expressive dark blue eyes, a small straight nose and full lips that were made to smile; she also had the figure to go with it, she was the sort of girl who turned heads in the street. Today she was wearing tight blue jeans, turned up to her mid-calf, and a white clinging top. Her sunglasses had been pushed up on top of her head, where they contrasted severely with the blonde hair that was tucked behind her ears and cascaded down to her almost bare shoulders. She was stunning. I had always had a soft spot for her and the fact she was so easy on the eye didn't made being with her a hardship. As I approached her table she looked up and saw me. With a smile she gave a little wave.

'Hiya, I got you a cappuccino, that okay?' She looked more closely at me. 'Are you okay, because you look like crap! Maybe I shouldn't have bothered you.'

'Thanks a lot! I'm okay,' I said, 'Mental, rather than physical. My marriage has just gone down the toilet and I'm having a hard time dealing.' I bit my lip as the tears welled up in my eyes.

'I'm sorry,' she looked at me with genuine sympathy. 'I know how hard it can be, I saw what it did to my parents when they divorced and they had only been married for sixteen years, nowhere near as long as you. Dad was seriously messed up for two years, and mum won't ever marry again. Is there anything I can do?'

'Yeah, you can tell me how I can help; I really need something to occupy my mind at the moment.'

'Okay, if you're sure. I've got this gig as a researcher for a TV company. I've been looking into Moseley and the British Union of Fascists in the 1930s and I've come across something… peculiar. What can you tell me about the Reichstag fire?'

'Reichstag fire? 27th February 1933, Hitler had only been Chancellor of a minority government for a month. A week before the election the Reichstag building burned down. Hitler claimed it was the signal for a communist revolt, persuaded President Hindenburg to give him emergency powers, through the Decree for the Protection of People and State, which allowed him to arrest the leadership of the communist KPD and their Reichstag Deputies. It gave Hitler's government the power to arrest without

7

trial, search private homes, censor post and telephone calls and restrict the freedom of assembly and expression. Communist and socialist meetings and newspapers were banned. Not surprisingly, the Nazis won the election, though not as well as they expected to. The whole episode gave the Nazis powers that were to become the cornerstone of Hitler's dictatorship. That enough?'

She smiled 'I remember most of that from your A level lessons all those years ago. But what else do you know about the fire itself?'

'Let me see...There's always been some controversy. The fire was noticed about 9.30 at night, apparently it started in multiple locations, implying arson and the building was gutted. A Dutch communist called van der Lubbe was arrested at the scene, confessed to acting alone and was later executed. Some historians have always questioned the convenience of the timing just before the election, allowing the Nazis to take out their biggest rivals. There are theories that the Berlin Storm Trooper leader Karl Ernst was responsible, working under the orders of Goering. An investigation in 1962 in West Germany concluded that van der Lubbe worked alone and there was no plot, but a subsequent investigation in 1970 cleared him totally. The thing I think is most telling is that by 28th February, the following day, the Nazis rounded up and arrested over 4,000 leading Communists. That's a pretty short time to arrange a purge of that magnitude unless they knew in advance and were prepared. Now tell me what this is all about.'

She reached into a canvas shopping bag by her feet and drew out a pink manila folder. Putting it on the table between us she opened it and pulled out a sheaf of photocopies. She passed me the top one.

'This is a copy of the diary of Francis Self; he was secretary and unofficial right hand man to Alexander Raven Thomson. Raven, as he was called, was to become Moseley's Director of Policy and Self was right alongside him throughout. These are the curious extracts.' She handed me the first sheet, an entry in the centre of the page was highlighted.

Tuesday 14th February 1933

Department Z sent a delegation led by Anderson to congratulate the Führer on his accession to power. Arranged to have Miller included in the delegation, due to his longstanding links with the National Socialists from his days with the IFL. Those contacts could prove fruitful for the future, especially if we can emulate what Hitler has achieved.

'Ok,' I said 'So the BUF sent a delegation to congratulate Hitler on coming to office. Not much of a surprise. What's the IFL?'

'The Imperial Fascist League, forerunner of the BUP, formed around 1929 and heavily Nazi in outlook.' She grinned at me. 'Hey, look at me teaching you, how times change. And the story continues beyond the obvious.' She handed me a second sheet, highlighted on it was:

Monday 6th March 1933

Anderson's delegation returned today. From his report it looks as if we will have a firm ally in the Führer, who should be in our debt after the ardent assistance of Miller in the events of 27th February. It is gratifying that our movement should have played such a central role in defeating Bolshevism in Germany.

'Right, this looks a bit more intriguing, but doesn't prove an awful lot,' I said.

'I know' Lisa said 'but don't you see the play on words here ardent... burning? Is it possible that this Miller character was somehow involved in the burning down of the Reichstag? Because if it was, it would make an awesome story.'

'You're going to need far more than this to support that hypothesis' I said 'I thought I taught you better than that about the use of evidence. Yes, you've got an intriguing hint here, but I don't think it's enough for you to go to your bosses with, certainly not if they're a making factual programme rather than fiction. It's interesting, but not sufficient.'

'I know that there's not enough here to hang my theory on, but I'm not finished yet,' she said. 'There's one more page I'd like you to read.' She handed over a third sheet; the top two entries were highlighted.

Wednesday 15th March 1933

I received a full account from Miller regarding his part in the events in Germany. It seems beyond belief that a member of our movement should have played such a pivotal role in, what I am sure will be, a turning point in the history of modern Europe. Sending Miller, or should I call him Hauptsturmführer Miller, appears to have paid dividends. It certainly appears that the Führer is in our debt and he's not a man to forget his friends. I have a meeting with Raven and OM tomorrow and I will ensure that they see this report in its entirety.

I looked up, 'OM? Oswald Mosley himself?'

She nodded 'I think it must be; who else with those initials would be meeting with Raven? But look at the next entry.'

Thursday 16th March 1933

OM and Raven were very impressed by Miller's report. Both agree he could be destined for great things in the Party. I too received my share of kudos for attaching him to Anderson's delegation. OM however is concerned that having members of the movement involved in illegal activities in a foreign country could be detrimental to us if word got out to our political enemies; the Jewish press would have a field day. He has ordered me to destroy the report and make it clear to Miller that his part in this can never be made public. I have my doubts about destroying such a crucial document, only four of us know of its existence, OM, Raven, Miller and I. I have instructed Miller to remain silent on the issue as OM ordered, but the report I will secrete amongst my other papers, hidden in plain sight as it were. I feel that Germany is destined for greatness under Hitler and evidence to remind him of the service the BUF has rendered him may well be advantageous to us in the future.

'Don't you see?' Lisa went on excitedly. 'That report may still exist. These final entries certainly imply that Miller played some sort of central role in events, though I don't quite get the reference to Hauptsturmführer Miller.'

'Mmm, Hauptsturmführer was a rank equivalent to captain in the Allgemeine SS, if it had been an SA or Storm Trooper rank it would have been a Sturmhauptführer. Don't even ask me how I know that, I need to get a life!' I choked up as the irony of these words sank in and I had to take a deep breath to regain my composure. To her credit Lisa pretended not to notice my momentary lapse.

'I think I know where to look to find Miller's report, if it still exists. This would totally prove my theory, if we could find it. My research has shown me that all of Self's papers were left to his nephew when he died in 1953. The nephew had no use for them and donated them to the politics department at Queen Mary's College, London. I've contacted QM and spoken to their archivist. They've still got all the papers, though they've never been catalogued or sorted and apparently there are a lot of them. What I really want to know....' Here she paused.

'Go on,' I said

'No, you've got enough on your plate; it's not fair for me to intrude at a time like this. You got better things to think about than my research into the Reichstag Fire.'

'I noticed the 'if we could find it' earlier. I'm in!' I declared. 'The only other option is moping around feeling sorry for myself. The best therapy is to keep occupied, the problems will still be there when I've finished. At least, that is if you're asking me to help.'

'If you're cool with it, I'd really appreciate your help, especially if there's the quantity of papers I think there might be.

My expenses should run to a week in a hotel in London for you, to save you driving down each day. I've made an appointment to start sifting through the archive the day after tomorrow, if you're up for it.'

'I'll be there.' I said. I did not realise where the road I had just embarked on was to lead me.

Chapter 2

We drove down to London in my Saab on Sunday evening. We stopped off at the M11 services for a burger and then down to the big city. It was dark when I dropped Lisa off at the Hackney flat she shared with her boyfriend James. He was away in Prague on business for a month, but my staying there was out of the question, our relationship was not like that. I checked into the Travelodge in Docklands and was in my standard motel room by 10.00 p.m. A double bed, bland décor, with an ensuite shower and toilet, the room was soulless, matching the way I felt. I picked up the remote from the work surface and turned on the TV to get the news and collapsed on the bed. Once again the news was full of the impending election. With all the fuss over M.P.s' corruption and the general public disillusion with politicians added to the recession and unemployment situation, the election due in September was unpredictable in the extreme. The government's share of the vote was collapsing fast, the Opposition was odds on to win the election, but their ability to win a majority was very much in doubt. With the Liberal Democrats no more popular than Labour or the Conservatives, it appeared that there was a real possibility of minority parties gaining significant numbers of seats in parliament and becoming very influential; hence the fascination with Sinclair and the BNRA, who had become increasingly popular. The TV was covering a speech he was giving in Luton:

'In the past few years, the tired old parties have failed to protect the interests of the citizens of this country; they have allowed us to flounder in a morass of Human Rights legislation, political correctness and multiculturalism, where we have become ashamed to be British. We are more concerned with the human rights of terrorists and illegal asylum seekers, than with the rights of the law abiding majority of our citizens, whose forbearers did so much to make this country great. We must ensure that British jobs are given to British people, who will be the vanguard of making this country great once more. I call upon the good people of England, Scotland and Wales to send a loud and clear message to these parties of the past, who have feathered their own nests whilst failing the country, to the politicians, who like so many Neros have fiddled whilst Rome burned – We have had enough! It is time for something new, to reconstruct where you have destroyed, to succeed where you have failed, to make us proud to be British.'

The news cut back to the studio, where the newsreader looked at the latest polls which indicated the likelihood of the BNRA winning up to forty seats, if their vote held up until the election. If they were right then the BNRA could be left holding the balance of power, any party seeking a parliamentary majority may have to do a deal with them. The BNRA could be the tail that wagged the dog. The news moved on to the latest British casualty in the war in Afghanistan.

'I can't believe people could fall for that,' I thought aloud to myself.

Surely the electorate could see through the meaningless rhetoric, to the divisive and racist principles that underlay the BNRA message. If it was not for Sinclair's smooth presentation and respectable, charismatic image, the BNRA would get nowhere; he was the beard behind which his party hid.

Turning off the TV in disgust, I readied myself for bed and settled to some background reading. Picking up the first volume of Kershaw's mammoth biography of Hitler, I re-read his account of the Reichstag fire. He certainly didn't see any Nazi plot, just an opportunistic exploitation by the National Socialists to settle accounts with their communist opponents. Maybe Lisa's theory was nothing more than a red herring, but as I thought about it, I realised what an important red herring it was for me. Today was the first day since Jane had left that I had not needed tranquilizers to get through. For the first time in ages I fell into a natural sleep.

The next morning, I showered, breakfasted and made sure I took the all important antidepressant. I walked along East India

Dock Road in the morning sun, and took the Dockland Light Railway from All Saints to Tower Gateway. A brief walk took me across to Tower Hill tube station and on the underground to Mile End. I walked down the Mile End Road, until I saw the Peugeot dealership, on the other side of the road that Lisa had told me to look out for. I was waiting for her as arranged outside the large blue steel railed gates that marked the main entrance to the campus. It was just before 10.00 and within ten minutes I was joined by Lisa. The blonde hair in a pony tail, she was wearing a revealing strappy blue top and tight jeans – I tried not to notice too much.

'Hi,' she greeted me, 'did you have a good night?'

'Yeah, surprisingly good,' I answered. 'What now?'

'We've an appointment with Mark Bell, the archivist I spoke to last week.'

'I see you've dressed to impress the poor man, you should be able to wind him round your little finger, unless he's gay,' I teased.

She coloured slightly.

'Well it never does any harm; a bit of cleavage can get a whole lot of co-operation. It always worked on you,' she retaliated.

This time it was my turn to blush, working with attractive young women, one tries hard not to notice, but you're only human, besides, I was more than old enough to be her father.

We walked through the pedestrian gates; the security guards only seemed interested in checking vehicles. The campus she led me across was fairly deserted, the summer vacation having started for undergraduates the month before. The campus was open and light, with Regents Canal running down one side. Lisa led the way through the student accommodation buildings, turning left we entered a pleasant square with trees planted regularly around the perimeter. She walked to a large modern L-shaped brick building fronted by a steel and glass awning-like structure. We were stuck at the turnstile that needed a card to be scanned before we could be granted entry. Eventually Lisa managed to attract the attention of a young woman at the help desk and asked for Mark Bell. After a few minutes wait he appeared, a tall, slightly stooped

15

young man in his late twenties. Lisa presented her credentials to him and introduced me as a colleague. He produced two cards and used them to scan us through. Then he gave each of us a card with a barcode on.

'These will give you access for the week, but please don't lose them. You also need to scan yourself out at the exits. It's the Self papers you're interested in isn't it?' He was having difficulty in addressing anything other than Lisa's chest. I watched with amusement as he struggled to maintain eye contact. 'They're in our store rooms upstairs, I checked the records, you're the first people to access them since we got them in the sixties.'

He led us through the silent library; there were just a few students, mostly postgraduates from the look of them, working at tables between the tall shelves of books. He guided us up the double staircase and turned right to a small room that had a central table and several chairs.

'I'll bring in the first boxes. I'm afraid they're in no sort of order. What exactly are you looking for?'

'We're trying to assess the part played by Self's boss, Thomson, in the development of fascism in 1930's Britain.' I lied smoothly. He left, only to return a few minutes later wheeling a small trolley stacked with three large cardboard boxes. Each box was a two foot cube, and was clearly heavy from the effort it took him to hoist the first one on to the table.

'When you've finished with these, there are another eight in storage, just let me know when you want them. We're open until nine each night, but closed at weekends. Enjoy!' With that he left.

Lisa looked at me in dismay, 'Eleven boxes, this could take us forever. We don't have that sort of time. I've a deadline of three weeks and we could search this lot for that long and come up with nothing.'

'Well, the sooner we start....' I said opening the box. It was full of papers, some typed, some hand-written, none of them appeared to be in any form of order. The first five documents ranged in date from 1928 to 1939. This would be a long job.

'I suggest we sort them by date. One pile for the twenties, as that doesn't concern us; another for anything after 1935 and individual piles for each year from 1930 to 35 and one more for undated material.'

'OK' she said 'let's get started'

We worked in virtual silence, reading and sorting the papers. By lunchtime we were halfway down the first box. The date related piles of paper were growing, but there was nothing of interest. All the campus eateries were closed. We walked out on to the Mile End Road. A hundred yards up the road was the New Globe, a dingy Victorian brick pub that was painted a powder blue colour. It didn't look too promising, but it was a better option than the fried chicken and kebab shop next door. I led the way in. Inside the pub was surprisingly modern, belying the spit-and-sawdust impression given by the exterior. We ordered, then settled on the chrome framed seats around a table. We sat watching the traffic and ate sandwiches that were really quite good, no alcohol; beer, antidepressants and historical research don't mix. We discussed what we had found, which made it a short lunch and an even shorter conversation. Then it was back to work. We began to recognise Self's handwriting at a glance and discard those papers. What we were looking for would be either typed or in a different hand. At three thirty we reached the bottom of the first box, loaded the papers back into it and began on box two. At twenty to five Mark dropped in on us.

'How's it going guys? I'm off duty at five, but you can leave your stuff in here overnight, if you're carrying on tomorrow. Have you finished with this one? I'll get rid of it and get you another before I go.'

At 7.30 we reached the bottom of the second box, with no luck. Both Lisa and I were topped out and we decided to call it a night. We ate in a generic Italian restaurant in Spitalfields Market, making only desultory conversation as we were so tired. As I pushed the food around my plate, we spoke briefly of her career, caught up on some of her peers and my colleagues, but she was careful to avoid the subject of my failed marriage.

The next morning we met at nine for a full day of research. The three boxes supplied by the ever helpful Mark were emptied, but nothing was achieved. We parted frustrated outside Queen Mary's at 8.45 pm.

Wednesday was not a good day, I was having a serious wobble, I felt empty and worthless, a hollow man. I now knew what it meant to be "gutted". I could not keep my thoughts away from the future. A future that heralded retirement in just a few years, followed by a solitary existence, I had always envisaged Jane and I growing old together, in fact I had been quite looking forward to us spending time together with no work to get in the way. The thought of growing old and dying alone terrified me. I could not see me going out and finding a substitute for Jane, there could be no substitute for Jane. Anyway, I really could not see me going out to meet women and dating. I was alone and that was how I would stay. The tears were close to the surface again, I didn't know if they were for her, for me or for what might have been. I gave in and popped another pill.

I had read somewhere that sunshine and exercise were good for depression, so I walked in the morning sun, past All Saints to Limehouse station. The mile and a half walk in the morning sunshine helped, or maybe it was the tranquillisers. Whichever it was, I had a grip of myself by the time I arrived at Queen Mary's. Lisa was not there, she phoned my mobile to explain she had been called in to the office for a meeting. I ploughed on alone. The research was more tedious without her company. She joined me apologetically just before twelve and we took an early lunch.

'It really is good of you to help like this Ian,' she said, 'are you certain that you want to continue with this fruitless search? You could go stay with Lucy, it's very clear that you need some support to get you through this. You don't look good at all. I'll be honest, you've got me quite worried.'

'Thanks for your concern,' I muttered, embarrassed that my fragile state should be so apparent, 'but this is the only thing that is stopping me from falling apart totally. I know I'm not myself, but believe me I've been a lot better since I started this project, it's been really therapeutic and I'll always be grateful to you for putting it my way. You've saved my sanity.' Now the embarrassment ran both ways and we lapsed into silence.

Work began again at one; two hours later we struck gold. Half way down box number seven, I came upon a document that was dated Sunday 12th March 1933, but more importantly it was in a hand that was very different to that of Self. I flicked to the last page of the document, it was signed W.H. Miller.

'Bingo!' I said. Lisa ran round to table to look. We sat and read it together and despite what we already suspected, it was astonishing.

Chapter 3

Sunday 12th March 1933

Dear Mr Self,

Following our return from Berlin, I am writing in confidence to report on the events that occurred.

I was attached to our delegation to Berlin because of the contacts I have made there in the past few years and my being bilingual, speaking German like a native. I knew Sepp Dietrich, an SS Gruppenführer and I was also well acquainted with Viktor Lutze, the police president designate in Hannover. I regarded Dietrich, in particular, as a friend, despite his being fifteen years my senior.

We arrived in Berlin on February 16th. I was, as you know, the only member of the delegation who had no specific duties. On the following evening, I made contact with Dietrich, being invited to his home for drinks. Over the next few days we had many discussions about the Führer's rise to power. Dietrich is a very useful contact to have, as he has now risen to the rank equivalent to Lieutenant-General in the SS, and since Hitler came to power he has taken command of the SS Watch Battalion, Berlin. He has a particular brief for Hitler's personal safety and meets with him on an almost daily basis. Thanks to the good offices of Dietrich, I was able to meet with the Führer a few days later. I presented him with the letter of congratulation from the Leader and added my personal best wishes. The Führer was gracious enough to hold a conversation with me for some time. With the forthcoming election, Hitler was obsessed with finding a way to negate the political power of the Reds before the ballot.

The way the National Socialist government in Germany works is curious by our standards. It seemed to me that Hitler was less involved in the day-to-day governing of Germany, instead he made general declarations and those around him were left to devise ways to make them happen. I had been in Berlin a week, when Sepp contacted me, inviting me to an important, if somewhat mysterious, meeting. He declined to state either the venue or purpose of the meeting. The following day a car picked me up and took me to the Party headquarters, a huge five-storey building. I was shown into a conference room, where I was met by Dietrich. He asked me if I was prepared to undertake a potentially hazardous mission to secure the future of the National Socialist Reich and help destroy communism. Having assured him that I would give my life to the cause of stopping communism, Dietrich left. I was joined instead by a tall aquiline man in the uniform of a senior officer of the SS, who introduced himself as Reinhard Heydrich, the head of the SD. We have nothing like the SD in our movement, not even in Department Z. He explained they were responsible for the internal security of the party and counterintelligence. I did not realise at the time that I was being interviewed by the deputy head of the SS.

Heydrich outlined a plan that was already underway, which would give the Führer excuse to deal with the Reds once and for all. He was involved with planning a joint SS/SA mission with Karl Ernst, which would lead to the destruction of the Red scourge for good. He could not go into any details at that time, but on Dietrich's recommendation, he wanted me to take part. He explained that the mission, if it misfired, had the potential to be a catastrophic embarrassment for the Führer, and could even lead to his removal from office. He hoped that by utilising me instead of SS personnel, he could distance the Party and especially the SS from the event. He explained that if the SA were found to be involved, it would be awkward, but not a disaster, everyone knew the SA were the wild men of politics, and the Führer could blame a rogue element acting without orders. However, the SS, with its close personal connection to Hitler would not be so deniable. I, on the other hand, working as an agent of the SS, could be denied. I assured Herr Heydrich that I was willing to take part. He then adjourned the meeting until the next day.

The following afternoon I returned to Nazi HQ. I was taken to the same room, where Heydrich was waiting for me, as was Reich Minister Goering. Goering shook my hand and thanked me for my assistance in this vital enterprise, assuring me that the Party would always be in my debt. Then he left the rest of the meeting to Heydrich, who explained that Ernst was unwilling to see the SA as the only organisation involved and insisted that an SS officer should be involved. To my surprise Heydrich then swore me in as a member of the SS and presented me with the uniform of a Hauptsturmführer. He explained that the SS were the German elite, all of pure Teutonic blood, but because of my German mother and Anglo-Saxon father, I qualified. I was surprised how much he seemed to know about me. Sepp later told me that Heydrich is one of the most powerful men in the Party, due to the intelligence to which he has access; he knows the darkest secrets of all the Nazi leadership.

Dressed in my new uniform, I attended a meeting at SA headquarters with Heydrich. I was introduced to Karl Ernst, SA leader in Berlin and two SA men: Hans Gewehr, who was to command the mission and Adolf Rall, both were members of SA Sturm 17. They now let me in on the 'enterprise'. They planned an arson attack on the Reichstag building; evidence would be fabricated to blame a communist conspiracy to overthrow the state. President Hindenburg could then be panicked into giving the Führer the powers he desired and the KPD would be finished before the election took place.

We were told that an ideal scapegoat had been found. An unbalanced Dutch Communist called van der Lubbe had been found three times in the previous week trying to set fire to government buildings, the Gestapo had arranged his release each time. Rall had been given the task of befriending him and winning his trust. We were to meet with him that night in a bierkeller in Tiergarten where Rall was to introduce him to me. Our task was to encourage him to *make an arson attempt on the Reichstag on the evening of Monday 27th.*

That night, we travelled to Tiergarten on the tram dressed in workman's clothing. In the bierkeller we had to wait for our victim to arrive. Eventually a stocky, round faced young man with a shock of unruly brown hair came over to us. Rall was using the alias Hans Muller and introduced me as his cousin Josef, who had been sacked from the railway for communist agitation. This appeared to satisfy van der Lubbe, who struck me as an intelligent, but unstable young man. He had a strange way of peering at me as if he was having difficulty seeing. In heavily accented German, he explained his eyesight had suffered permanent damage working on a building site. It was not difficult for Rall and I to suggest the attack, whilst making it appear that it was van der Lubbe's idea. We finally agreed to meet again on Friday at the same place.

'Bloody hell, this is dynamite,' I said looking up at Lisa, 'before we go on we should get copies that we can take away.'

'Good idea,' she said, 'I'll see if I can find Mark.' She left the room and I collected up some other papers so it was not so obvious which ones we really wanted. She returned with Mark.

'I can copy those for you, but you'll have to pay, I'm afraid,' he said.

'No problem,' said Lisa handing him a ten pound note, 'is that enough?'

He assessed the small pile of paper I was holding and thought for a second. 'Yes, that should be more than enough.' He led the way to a photo copier and scanned a plastic card. 'There you go.'

Lisa gave him a dazzling smile of thanks and distracted him, whilst I made two copies of the Miller document and one or two other pages. I made sure that the top copies were irrelevant pages, so that even Mark did not know what we had found. Thanking him for his help we returned to our room.

'I think we should hide the original at the bottom of this box,' Lisa said 'then we'll know where to find it, if we need it again, but it would be difficult if anyone else should search for it to try to steal our credit....' She tailed off, as she saw me looking at her with raised eyebrows. 'Sorry, but you've no idea how competitive this business is.' We put the original away and stacked all the other papers in the box on top of it. 'OK,' she said, 'now we can settle down to the rest of the story.' We both turned to our own copies continued reading.

In a meeting the next day, Ernst outlined the plan. Gewehr, Rall and I would enter the Reichstag through a tunnel that led from Goering's residence to the Reichstag building. There we would mix a self-igniting liquid that would start multiple fires after a suitable delay. Van der Lubbe had to be persuaded to break into the building through a ground floor window and as he set his fires, we would exit through the tunnel. He would be left to perish in the fire and be identified later, or captured by the guards, who would be alerted by the broken window. We would then disperse from Goering's apartment, having changed into our uniforms to avert suspicion.

On Friday, as arranged we met with van der Lubbe in Tiergarten. We suggested that in order to improve our chances of success, we should all enter the Reichstag at different places - if one of us was caught, the others might still succeed. Van der Lubbe agreed readily, as we knew he would. He stated proudly that he had firelighters and petrol ready to do the job and advised us to bring the same. We arranged to break in simultaneously at nine o'clock on Monday night. We put it to van der Lubbe that his ideal entry point would be to break in through a window, whilst Rall and I would find other ways in and he agreed to the plan.

At 7.00 we met at Goering's apartment, Goering was not there, providing himself with a suitable alibi, but Hanfstaengl was there suffering from a bout of the 'flu. We were told to avoid him at all costs. We stripped off our uniforms and dressed in workers clothes. Gewehr and three other members of Sturm 17 brought in several large containers of liquid that we moved into the basement and carried through the subterranean passage to the Reichstag at 8.00. Once in the building we mixed some of the liquids together in smaller containers and began to spread them around the building. We paid particular attention to the Reichstag Chamber, I think in all we laid over twenty fires, which once lit would soon merge into one huge conflagration.

We waited until we saw some of our devices begin to ignite and then began to withdraw to the passage. As I went, I caught a glimpse of van der Lubbe; naked to the waist he was running around the corridors screaming and trying to use his shirt as a torch to set fire to curtains and tapestries. We passed quickly through the tunnel and changed back into our uniforms. I could hear Hanfstaengl in a panic on the telephone to Goebbels, telling him to inform Hitler that the Reichstag was ablaze. We split up outside Goering's apartment. I walked towards the Reichstag to join the crowd that was beginning to gather. I could see Inspector Scranowitz restraining van der Lubbe. Then several police dragged him away. Two black Mercedes cars drove through the police cordon. Hitler got out accompanied by Goebbels and Sepp Dietrich. Sepp spoke to a British journalist and ushered him through the cordon. When he caught sight of me Dietrich grinned and beckoned me to accompany him. Hitler was dashing around issuing orders, his black trenchcoat flying out behind him. From his state of panic, it was almost possible to believe that he knew nothing of the plan. Goering, wearing a camelhair coat stood in the entrance. He made his report to Hitler, claiming that a group of communist deputies had been seen there twenty minutes before the fire began and one of the arsonists had been arrested.

On Dietrich's instruction I accompanied the Führer's group as they inspected the damage. We stepped over puddles of water and smouldering debris, coughing in the foul smelling smoke. Someone opened the yellow varnished door into the debating chamber and we could see the inferno within; the fire brigade seemed to be fighting a losing battle. Goering kept emphasising that they (the Communists) had started fires here or there.

Hitler stumbled over a hosepipe and I had to catch him before he fell. By the time we climbed to the first floor, we had been joined by the aristocratic von Papen, wearing a tweed overcoat and homburg hat. Hitler told him that he would crush the communist pest with an *iron fist. Von Papen looked disconcerted by Hitler's rant and excused himself to report on the damage to President Hindenburg.*

By the time the Führer and Goering were giving a press conference, Dietrich had indicated that I should make myself scarce. I returned to my hotel to await events.

As you will know by now, President Hindenburg was persuaded to pass a decree the very next day, which restricted outmoded, liberal civil rights and allowed the SA, SS and Gestapo to round up thousands of Reds from lists already prepared by Heydrich.

When Heydrich met me the following day in his office, Sepp Dietrich was with him. He thanked me for my invaluable service. He told me I would have the right to keep my SS rank and made me an honorary citizen of the Reich. He said that Rall had tried to make a public statement taking credit for the fire, but he had been executed by the SA on Ernst's orders and that all records connecting him to the SA had been expunged. He wished me a safe journey home and reiterated that the National Socialists were in my debt.

This is a full account of my actions and I am sending it to you, for you to share with Raven and the Leader. I shall make no mention of any of this in my report, as I suspect that Major Taylor may have links to the Home Office.

Your obedient servant
W.H. Miller

'Phew, that's amazing,' said Lisa, 'It's exactly what we were looking for. This is going to make an awesome programme. What do you think we should do now?'

'Have you forgotten what I taught you about sources?' I asked. 'We check it, compare it with other known accounts and see if the details that we can check are consistent. It would probably be a good idea to find out who the bloody hell W.H. Miller was. We don't even know his first name for Christ's sake!'

'First thing tomorrow, we start. How about a drink to celebrate?' she asked.

'Not the best idea, with the cocktail of drugs inside me,' I replied. 'Let's call it a day for now.'

'Still bad huh?' she looked at me with sympathy. 'You know, you really need to talk this through with someone. When Dad went through the divorce, he saw a counsellor because he was so messed up. It really helped him too'

'Your dad has more money than me. I don't run my own company, drive a Merc or live in the big house,' I snapped, then paused as I saw her face fall, as she recoiled as if I had struck her.

'I was only trying to help,' she said in a small voice and I immediately regretted my words. 'Look Ian, I've never said this but I owe you big time. If it hadn't been for you, I'd have stayed at home rather than go to uni, because I didn't want to leave that loser Lee. You cared enough to have a real go about me wasting myself and always regretting it. I know I was a bitch at the time, getting stroppy about you daring to interfere with my life and telling me what I didn't want to hear. Well now it's my turn to repay that care and tell you what you don't want to hear.'

'I'm sorry,' I said. 'I'm still feeling very raw and more than a bit vulnerable. I know you were trying to help and I appreciate it, really. It's good to know someone cares. But could we change the subject before I get tearful and embarrass myself?'

We separated on good terms agreeing to meet up again at the Library the next day at nine again. As I sat on the tube heading back to the motel, I thought that Lisa was right; I really needed to seek some help, because I was not coping with the day-to-day stuff, the history was fine, but living a life away from it was a totally different matter.

Chapter 4

I slept badly, tried to force down a little breakfast and left for Queen Mary's. The fine weather had broken and it was overcast, I could feel the light rain soaking through my jacket as I hurried to the tube. Lisa was waiting for me, sheltering under an umbrella.

'What now?' she asked.

'Two things. We go through the letter and see how much we can deduce about the elusive Mr Miller. We also have to look at his account and research to corroborate as much as we can. He might be just a fantasist trying to appear important.' I told her as we scanned our passes at the library turnstile.

Ensconced once more in our study room, I hung my jacket to dry over the back of my chair. 'Let's go through the letter and see how much we can infer about Miller.' We sat in silence reading the letter in minute detail, whilst scribbling the occasional note on pads that Lisa had provided. After an hour we had finished and compared notes.

'Okay' said Lisa, 'I'll go first. British born, with a German mother and English father. Bilingual. BUF member, working for Department Z, which was a sort of intelligence department I think. He's a long standing fascist, as he was with the IFL before the BUF. To judge by the written style, he is reasonably well educated; the spelling, syntax and punctuation show that. That's about it, you got anything else?'

'The degree of detail makes it seem authentic. The only other thing I've got is his age. He says he is fifteen years younger than Sepp Dietrich. I checked up last night, Dietrich was born in May 1892, which would make him thirty-nine at the time of the Reichstag fire, so Miller should be twenty-four, that would make him born about 1909 or so. With a German mother, we should be able to identify him on the 1911 census and get his Christian name, father's name, address etc. That should kick-start our investigation. We need to find out as much about Miller and his parents as we can. We can do much of that on line, so let's start by substantiating the details, whilst we're in a library with access to the books.'

We spent the day searching amongst the texts on Nazi Germany for information on the fire; each of us taking copious notes to compare to the letter. At about three we adjourned to the Globe for a late lunch.

'Well?' she asked, 'What have you got?' She had a look in her eyes that told me she had found something good and wanted to surprise me.

'Right. Most simply tell the story and speculate as to who was to blame without much detail or evidence. Kershaw largely agrees with our narrative, right down to Hanfstaengl reporting it to Goebbels to inform Hitler. Hanfstaengl was a friend and political confidant of Hitler himself. The best source I found was probably was the Monthly Review; they published an article by two American lawyers on the Reichstag Fire Trial. They agree with much of the timeline and confirm minor details, for example, it was Scranowitz who captured van der Lubbe, there was a tunnel from Goering's place to the Reichstag and the fire according to the report started in twenty-three separate places. They also confirm the existence of Rall, though they could find no evidence of his attachment to Ernst's SA brigade. Finally they describe how our arsonist was captured stripped to the waist because he had been using his shirt as kindling to light fires. Pretty supportive on the whole, though there was one German historian who argued very effectively against the whole idea of Nazi involvement, claiming it was a myth. Now come on what have you got, I can see by your face it's good'

'I went on line, whilst you were wading through the books and I found who the journalist was that was at the fire. His name was Sefton Delmer and he wrote for the Daily Express. His description of the aftermath of the fire matches down to the last detail. He confirms what Hitler, Goering and von Papen were wearing, he even confirms the colour of the doors into the Reichstag chamber and says how Hitler tripped over a fire hose.

It's indisputable, Miller must have at least seen the aftermath of the fire, even if the rest's untrue.'

I whistled, 'I'm impressed!' I said

'Well it was you who taught me how to research, so you shouldn't be so surprised. Don't let the blonde hair fool you.'

'I never did,' I said 'you were one of the most instinctive historians I ever taught. It's a real pity you didn't follow it up at university.'

'Let's knock off early and start again tomorrow. Come back to my flat and I'll get us dinner,' she said. We left the pub; it had brightened up, with patches of blue sky peeking out between the clouds. 'You want to walk or take the bus?'

'Walk, if that's okay, the exercise and serotonin are good for me.' We walked along the tow path of the canal, discussing our discovery and where we should go next, as the sun began to come out. We left the canal bank at Old Ford Road and walked for another ten minutes before Lisa led me across the road into Victoria Park. It was a real surprise to find such an open space of greenery and trees in the heart of Hackney. We strolled in the afternoon sun in comfortable silence, each of us lost in our own thoughts. The twenty minute walk in the greenery and freedom of the park lifted my spirits and I could feel my fears recede back into that dark corner of my mind where they lurked. I knew they would doubtless return, but I resolved to make the most of it, while it lasted. I asked Lisa about her boyfriend. When I had known her at school, she had a penchant for chav bad boys, who had an IQ as big as their shoe size; I had often mopped her up after altercations by text or on the phone. Her friends had frequently come to me complaining 'He treats her like shit Sir; I don't know why she puts up with it'. Nor did I, I hoped it was a phase she had grown out of.

'He's awesome,' she told me, 'I love him to bits. He's got a good job in computing in the City. He's funny and caring and thoughtful. He's always buying me flowers and things. I think he might be the one. We moved in together a few months ago and I've never been happier...' she gushed. Then she stopped 'Oh I'm sorry, I'm sure you don't need to hear how wonderful my relationship is, with what you're going through.'

'No problem kid,' I replied 'I'm happy for you.' And I was.

We left the park and crossed the road. Overlooking the park was a terrace of three storey Edwardian houses. Built out of pale brick, now grimed with the dirt of the city, each house had a square bay window on the ground floor beside a white arched entrance. A trefoil of similarly arched windows graced the first floor and two more arched windows stared out of the second floor. Like the doorways, all the windows were decorated with freshly painted white plaster arches over them and supported by pilasters of a similar hue. Lisa unlocked the door and led me up a communal stair way, to the first floor, where she unlocked a second door into her flat. The flat was small, but homely and well kept. The sitting room had a drop leaf table, so it could double as a dining room. A galley kitchen and small bathroom led off to the back of the flat on the left and two doors to the right apparently led to the bedrooms.

'It's a bit of a luxury, having a spare room, but it gives me somewhere I can work away from the chaos of the office,' she said. having seen me looking round. 'but James earns an unbelievable salary and I'm not doing too badly.' She told me what she earned and I whistled; it would take a teacher nearly ten years to reach that wage, even with London weighting.

I crossed to the mantelpiece, where a framed photograph stood on display. It showed a stunning Lisa, in a smart black evening dress that was cut to show off her figure to its best. She was accompanied by a tall handsome man of about twenty-five. He stood considerably taller than Lisa's five feet three inches, I would have estimated him to be at least my six feet, probably taller. He had straight dark hair, regular features, with grey eyes and a dazzling smile. Lisa noticed my attention.

'That's James. That was the first time we went out together, it was his company's Christmas ball.'

'He's a good looking guy. How did you meet?'

'We were introduced by a mutual friend at a pub in the City. We just sort of hit it off at once. One thing led to another and…well here we are.'

'You're well matched, he seems to be good for you, I've never seen you so happy.'

'I am.'

We sat on the sofa and chatted for a while, before she took herself off to the kitchen, rejecting my offers of help.

'Can you turn the TV on? I'd like to catch the news,' she called from the kitchen. I switched on the flat screen TV, the news was just starting. Again coverage of the forthcoming election dominated the news. There were sound bites from the leaders of the three main parties, followed by the latest polls, which showed an increasing degree of support for the BNRA, who had called for a mass rally in Trafalgar Square for Sunday. 'It'll probably be a good idea to steer clear of that at the weekend; I wouldn't want to get caught up in that with some of the people who support that lo,' she said, coming in from the kitchen. 'Steak and salad okay? I'm afraid I haven't had much time to shop recently.'

'Fine,' I replied 'Are you sure I can't help?'

'You could lay the table; the cutlery is in the drawer over there.'

I set up the table and laid out the cutlery. Within a few minutes she had returned bearing two plates loaded with salad and a piece of sirloin steak. She put the plates down and then brought in a basket of freshly cut French bread and some butter. 'Do you want a drink?' she asked. I shook my head.

As we ate, she asked, 'What do we do next?'

I finished my last mouthful of food. 'That was good, thanks.'

'Where do we go next then?'

'I think we need to try and find more about our friend Miller. We need to try to track down his full name to start with.'

'How do we go about that? Where can we look?'

I smiled. 'Got an internet connection?'

'Wifi. I'll go get my laptop.' She left the table and returned with a new Sony laptop. I pushed my plate with its finished meal away from me. I clicked on the internet browser and called up the 1911 census. A search page appeared, asking for first name, last name, year of birth, place of birth and location. I typed in 'Miller', followed by '1909' as the year of birth plus or minus three years either way. Then hit search. There were over 6800 records, which were too many to display.

'Bugger!' I cursed. I thought for a minute then changed the parameters to narrow the search to within a year of his 1909 date of birth. This reduced it to something over 4000.

'Shit!' I cursed again.

'Try typing the initial W into the forename box.' Lisa suggested, but that only gave us names with the letter W listed instead of the full Christian name. I returned to the previous page and hit the 'View results' button. The first page of names came up on the screen, starting with Miller, Abraham, then Miller, Abram.

'Good, they're in alphabetical order by forename, we should be able to jump to the Ws.' I said.

Lisa was looking over my shoulder. 'Try jumping to page twenty-five,' she said, pointing to the line of boxes at the top of the page. I clicked on the number. The list started with Miller, William. I tried page twenty-four, in the middle of the page was Miller, W. Henry.

'Okay, keep a list of these names' I said. Scrolling down the list, I read out - 'Miller, Walter Henry; Miller, Wilfred Henry; Miller Wilfred, Howard…' The list ran on until we reached 'Miller, William Henry' there were eight of them.

'Super,' Lisa exclaimed. 'How do we differentiate these?'

'List them by district and county.' The list continued to grow. By the time we reached 'Miller, Woolfe Henry', we had a total of twenty-three names.

'So how do we know which one?'

'We'll need to buy the detailed results. We're looking for a household with a woman with either a German forename or place of birth - or both. I just hope that our Miller has been listed with his middle name, or this could cost us a fortune. Pass me my jacket.' I used my credit card to buy credits. 'We only need to view the transcript until we find the right one.' One-by-one we called up the entries and our number of credits declined. By the time we got to half way, we had to purchase more credits. At number twenty-two, we reached 'Miller, William Howard'.

'That's it!' Lisa exclaimed. 'Look 'Head of household Miller, Alfred Vaughan aged 32, Army Officer, born Richmond, Yorkshire. Then we've got his wife, Miller, Lisl Marie, 27, born Wedemark, Hannover, Germany. Get the full copy.'

'Got a printer?' I asked calling up the page.

'Yeah, wireless, it's in the box room, just hit print.'

We examined the full copy, 'This tells us his address in 1911 and place of birth. Born in Maidenhead, Berkshire and resident at 30 Lupus Street, Pimlico, London. There appears to be a live-in housekeeper too, so they were not badly off.'

'Mmmm, army officer in 1911, I wonder...' I murmured. Then I went back to the laptop, typed for a minute. 'Yes! Got him, I thought that as a professional soldier, there was a good chance of him being a casualty in the First World War - a lot of professional officers were. I checked with the Commonwealth War Graves Commission and here it is, 28703 Major Alfred Vaughan Miller, 1st Battalion Middlesex Regiment, died 17th October 1917, buried at Tynecot Cemetery, Ypres. So, our Miller's father died when he was eight, which would have meant the family living on an army pension. We might find records in the National Archives in Kew.'

'If I try that tomorrow, you could continue to dig into the mother's background...shit, look at the time, it's nearly 2.00 am! You can't travel back to Docklands at this time in the morning. I'll make you up a bed in the box room.'

'You sure? I don't want to impose. I could call a cab. I mean it's not proper me staying here, when your boyfriend is away.'

'You're staying! You're not my teacher any more, I'm an adult and if I choose to invite a friend to stay in the spare room, it's perfectly proper. James would have no problem, honestly. Unless you're planning to jump on me.' She laughed.

'No, you're perfectly safe; I'm too knackered for that.'

She made up the bed in the small box room. 'You use the bathroom first; give me a call when you're out.'

I washed and went into my room. 'It's all yours,' I called. I closed the door, undressed and climbed into bed. When I turned the light off, I fell asleep at once.

Chapter 5

The morning sun streamed in through the thin curtains to wake me. At first I was confused by my unfamiliar surroundings. Only slowly did I realise where I was. I looked at my watch and was surprised to see it was nearly nine. I rolled out of bed and pulled on my jeans and opened the door into the sitting room. Lisa was sitting at the table working on her laptop.

'Hi, I wondered when you'd emerge, you could sleep for England,' she said, looking up. 'I've left you one of James' tee shirts and some clean socks, I didn't go for boxers, that'd be a bit icky.'

'Thanks.' I went into the small bathroom and washed and showered.

'There's a new toothbrush in the cupboard, I got one when I collected the papers earlier.'

I got dressed, the tee shirt was a bit tight, but otherwise I looked okay. Lisa came in from the kitchen with two mugs of coffee. After a late night and with no makeup save a little mascara, she still looked amazing. Just for a moment, I forgot my situation and my age. Sucking in my stomach, I crossed the room and sat down with her at the table.

'Anything in the papers?'

'Just the usual election stories, there's a whole article here written by Sinclair. He's going on about foreign ownership of British companies, claiming that they protect jobs in their home countries at the expense of British jobs. He makes the same claims about energy companies making more profit from their British customers than they do at home. He calls it ripping off Britain. Of course he doesn't say what he'd do about it. What could he do? Renationalise all the utility companies? Then he reverts to the same old theme of Britons of British descent – i.e. whites – coming first. How does he get away with this xenophobic crap? I think he's a very dangerous man and God help us if he gets any sort of power. One of my colleagues has been looking at links between Sinclair's BNRA and a violent bunch of ultra-right thugs called Storm45, but she could not find enough evidence to prove anything and Sinclair's lawyers were all over us, threatening law suits. There was some pressure behind the scenes too, or at least that was what was rumoured.'

'He seems very sensitive about his image, perhaps because it's all the BNRA have. I agree though, I think he's a deeply unpleasant and dangerous man. I wouldn't trust him as far as I could throw him,' I replied.

After a breakfast of cereal and toast, we left the flat. We agreed to work separately today and to phone each other with the results tonight. Lisa got on the first bus and left with a wave and a smile on her way to Kew. I took the next bus back to Queen Mary's, where I could use a computer. If Lisl Miller was twenty-seven in 1911, she must have been born in about 1884, which would make her 125, if she were still alive, which was unlikely. Therefore there had to be a death certificate, but since she could have died any year since 1911, it was going to be a bitch to find it. I started to search the death certificate records starting with the 1960's when she would have been a septuagenarian. A frustrating hour passed with no joy. Then it struck me, there would probably be a record of the widow's pension paid to her in the archive where Lisa was. I left the library, as phones were frowned upon and called her to ask her to prioritise it. Within the hour she sent me a text, 'Pension paid until 1980.'

I searched the records online and sure enough there it was. I had to use my credit card again to purchase a full copy. Lisl Marie Miller had died in Forest Row, Sussex, cause of death pulmonary oedema. I saved it, then emailed a copy to Lisa and one to myself.

A thought occurred to me, if Miller had continued with the BUF, then it was possible that his exploits could have appeared in the newspapers. I grabbed a sandwich on the run as I took the tube to King's Cross. I walked up towards Euston to the new British Library. Registration was a pain, but at last I got access to their newspaper archive. I confined my search to local papers like the Evening Standard. In the course of the afternoon I managed just two hits. A W. Miller appeared in Bow Magistrates Court, charged with affray, during a BUF march in April 1936. In a second article, William Howard Miller had failed to answer bail on charges under the Firearms Act in August 1939; the judge was told by the police that it was believed he had fled the country. I made notes on both articles then headed for my hotel.

Lisa phoned at six, she had found the service record of Miller Senior, but it had not added much to our investigation. She had read my email and readily agreed that as the next day was Saturday, we would go down to Forest Gate to see if we could uncover anything more about Lisl, as she seemed to be our best bet of picking up Miller's trail again. She would meet me at the hotel at 8.30. My evening without Lisa's company was dull. Not a good idea, I began to dwell on Jane and my defunct marriage. Again the bleak future I envisaged was all I could see. Worse still I began to recall all the good times we had, as a couple, as a family, times that would not happen again. My stomach sank; my hands began to shake like a recovering alcoholic as again I struggled to hold back the tears. I phoned my daughter Lucy, who was very sympathetic and supportive, but she was up to her eyes with her dissertation. She promised to visit as soon as she had a moment and rang off. I turned in early, but found sleep difficult to come by. Eventually I gave up and read until the early hours, when fatigue finally helped me to drift off.

I met Lisa as arranged, still feeling tired after a poor night's sleep. We headed down the A13 before venturing on to the M25. Forty minutes later we pulled in at the services for coffee. Reinvigorated by the caffeine, I drove towards Forest Row. Turning off on to the A22, we passed the unusual sight of a Mormon temple at Newchapel, its tall spire pointing skywards from the rectangular building like the gnomon on a sundial. Half an hour later we reached Forest Row, a pleasant village, where the A22 opened up into a square, with the Chequers, a 15th century inn occupying the left and the church dominating the view ahead. We pulled off the road and drove to a car park. We crossed the road to the church, the Church of the Holy Trinity. It appeared to be built in a late mediaeval style, with a slender tower topped by a steeple. On closer inspection, the stone church dated from the Victorian era. A claret coloured sign confirmed my suspicions.

'Built in 1834,' I said 'the Victorians had a thing about building in a fake gothic style. Let's split up, you start with the grave yard. If the church is open I'll give it the once over, then join you.'

The church was open, but deserted. I pushed open the oak door and entered, finding the cool, dark interior refreshing after the heat of the July sun. With no vault, there was no need to look for memorials set into the floor, so I began to look around the walls. There were a number of polished brass plaques set into the north wall and reading them was not easy in the gloom, but none of them related to a Lisl Miller. I walked round the altar and began to read those set into the south wall. In the south west corner I found what I had been searching for. Set into the wall was a brass plaque about nine by six inches, it had engraved on it:

Lisl Marie Miller

1884-1980

Beloved wife and mother

R.I.P.

This was an interesting find, with her husband dead since 1917; the most likely person to have such an inscription made was her errant son.

The big question was, could we find out any more? I left the church, squinting in the dazzling sunlight to try to make out Lisa in the graveyard. She saw me first; she was talking to a small, stooped, white haired old woman, who was laying flowers on a nearby grave. She shook her head to warn me off. I sat in the sun until the woman left and Lisa waved me over.

'I've found it! It's over here,' she led me to a well-kept grave with a marble headstone. 'What's more I met someone who knew her. That old lady was visiting her husband's grave. I told her Lisl was my great aunt and I was tracing my family history. The old lady said she used to work at The Gables, a rather expensive nursing home just up the hill. Lisl lived there and the two of them became friends. She said Lisl had often spoken of her childhood in Germany and how she lost her husband in the war. Apparently, Lisl suffered great hardships in the 20s and 30s, taking in laundry and sewing to make ends meet. The woman told me Lisl had few visitors. Her big regret was her son, apparently she was always talking about him, she hadn't seen since before the war. He disappeared in France when the war began and was never seen again. That must be our William!'

'Good going Lisa,' I said

'Naah, I just got soooo lucky, I can't believe it.'

'More than luck, I bet the old woman wouldn't have spoken to me.'

'But this doesn't get us much further forward; we already knew that William Miller had gone to France just before the war.'

'Yes, but that bit about her struggles in the depression, it doesn't gel with her spending her declining years in a posh nursing home. Where did the money come from? Who had the plaque placed in the church? If she had not seen William since 1939, it rather buggers my theory that it was him'

'That's a good point; maybe we could visit the nursing home and see what we can find out.'

'Let's go look the place over and then see where we go from there.'

We walked up the hill a quarter of a mile. A sign on the other side of the road read 'The Gables, Private Nursing Home'. Set back in its own grounds behind a privet hedge, was a large Victorian mansion.

'We just can't go barging in there demanding to know how Lisl Miller managed to pay for such a place. Let's go down to the Chequers and have some lunch, while we get our story straight.'

We walked down the hill to the pub, ordered our food and soft drinks at the bar then settled at a table near the inglenook fireplace, which fortunately did not have a fire in on a hot July day.

'Right, how do we blag our way in?' I asked. 'Any ideas?'

'What about we say you're my dad, and Lisl was my mother's aunt. We could invent some excuse as to why we need to know who paid.'

We sat around the table and ate lunch, whilst we concocted our story. Once finished, we left to try it out. We took the car up to the nursing home and crunched up the curved gravel drive. We walked up the broad staircase, which had been augmented by a wheelchair ramp. I rang the bell. The door was answered by a woman in a green nurse's uniform; she wore a badge that said 'Helen, Care assistant'.

'Good afternoon,' I began 'I'm sorry to arrive without an appointment, but would it be possible to speak with the proprietor or the administrator?'

'I dunno if Mrs Coleridge is in.' she said.

'Mrs. Coleridge?' asked Lisa.

'She's the boss. I tell you what, I'll get Sister Thomas, mebbe she can 'elp yer.'

She picked up a phone and summoned assistance. A brisk, middle aged woman with a starched blue uniform and a kind face bustled down the staircase into the reception area.

'Yes, can I help?'

'We'd like to see someone with regard to a former patient, who died about thirty years ago. She was my late wife's great aunt, her name was Lisl Miller. My daughter here had been tracing the family tree and found out that Lisl died here in 1980.' I started.

'I discovered that my great, great aunt had suffered terribly in the Great Depression, but she ended up here.' Lisa continued smoothly. 'I know our side of the family didn't have the resources to keep her here, but I'd like to find out who did. During my researches I've come to be quite fond of Lisl and would like to write to them to thank them for taking such care of her.' It wasn't the best story in the world, but it was the best we could come up with at short notice.

'I'm sorry, our Administrative Manager is not in today. All of our financial records are computerised and I'm afraid I don't have access to them. Even if I did I'm not sure what our policy is on disclosing financial details. So I can't help you.'

'Mrs. Coleridge is the administrator, I believe,' Lisa smiled sweetly. 'I'd be so grateful if you could inform her of my request. Perhaps she would contact me.' She handed over her business card and turned to leave.

'My daughter has a real bee in her bonnet about this.' I said looking at Lisa and putting on an indulgent smile 'I'd be so grateful if you would put in a good word for her, after all, the records in question are nigh on thirty years old. What harm could it do?'

Sister Thomas smiled 'I will see what we can do, as you said, it was thirty years ago, well before my time, I'm sure it would do no harm.'

'Thank you do I appreciate your help. Goodbye.'

Lisa caught up with me outside. 'Turning on the old charm, were we? And you accused me of trying it on with Mark at the library.' I laughed, the first time I had since Jane had left.

It was still only early afternoon, so we continued on to Eastbourne and enjoyed the afternoon sun by the sea. We sat on the pebbly beach eating ice cream and discussing what we could do next. We were dependent on what Mrs. Coleridge decided, until then we were at a dead end. We walked down the promenade with the holiday makers and took a ride on the small train that ran from one end of the prom to the other. That evening we went to a good Italian restaurant sited between the beach and the centre of town, where we went Dutch on a meal. The service was excellent, as was the veal escalope. After that we set off back to London. As we drove through the darkness, we reviewed our progress. We were getting somewhere, but we seemed to be stalled.

'What are you doing tomorrow?' She asked.

'It's Sunday, so not much, I haven't thought much about it.'

'Well, I was thinking, it doesn't seem fair, you kicking your heels in London, all because of me. I've noticed that you get down, when you've nothing to occupy you and I would feel responsible. Anyway, I've not got much to do, with James out of town.'

We agreed to meet the following morning at Spitalfields Market. I dropped her at her flat and returned to my Docklands hotel.

Chapter 6

As I made my way towards Spitalfields, I found myself looking forward to spending the day with Lisa; not in a romantic way, which would be sad considering our age difference. My wife's mid-life crisis was bad enough, without me having romantic intentions towards a girl half my age. No, I was enjoying the friendship and companionship. Just being with Lisa was a breath of fresh air; my problems somehow seemed to dominate my life less. I began to realise how important she was becoming to me.

We met outside the market and had coffee in the new plaza-like square built to replace part of the old Victorian market. The Victorian covered market was coming towards the end of its restoration and we meandered between the stalls that stood beneath the iron framed glazed roof. We left by the exit near the Ten Bells, the pub allegedly frequented by Jack the Ripper and his victims in the 1880s. I pointed it out to Lisa. We then joined the stream of people heading for Petticoat Lane, London's most famous street market.

Lisa frowned, 'That street sign says Middlesex Street, so why Petticoat Lane?'

I recounted the urban legend of how the Victorians were so prudish, that they changed the name rather than have a street named after an item of women's underwear. This made her laugh. We spent an hour wandering happily through the street market. Living in a sleepy East Anglian town, I was fascinated by the cosmopolitan atmosphere. There were stalls selling all manner of things, it was said that you could get anything you wanted at Petticoat Lane market. This was particularly true in terms of clothing; it seemed that you could get everything from 'street wear' to designer goods or last year's fashions. Lisa loved it, weaving between the stalls like an excited child. It made me realise just how young she really was. At twenty five, you think you are all grown up, whereas you were actually just setting out. I smiled indulgently as Lisa bought a brightly coloured pashmina from a stall run by a friendly vendor of Bangladeshi origin. As if to emphasise the diversity of the market, at the next stall she purchased a bag of pot pourri from a typical cockney stallholder.

'Maybe Mr Sinclair needs to come down here and see how well the people of this area get on together. Then perhaps he would stop all that divisive, poisonous crap he spews out.' Lisa commented.

'Quite appropriate really, we're close to where the battle of Cable Street took place in 1936.'

'What was that?'

'Mosley's thugs were thwarted by the local Jewish community and Catholic dockers when he tried to march through the area. Mosley wanted to show his strength and arranged for his fascists to gather in uniform in the East End to be reviewed by him and then attend mass meetings. The government refused to ban the march, despite pleas, protests and petitions from local people. On the day thousands of anti-fascists turned up in the East End. They erected barricades to stop the fascist march in Cable Street, with banners reading "They shall not pass". When the police tried to dismantle the barricades, a pitched battle broke out. Kids were throwing marbles under the hooves of police horses; housewives were pelting them with bottles and rotten vegetables and emptying chamber pots on them from upstairs windows. In the end Mosley's Blackshirts were forced to turn back and leave the East End. They were totally humiliated. After the battle the wearing of political uniforms in public was banned, it was the beginning of the end for Mosley. Sort of fits in with our story line doesn't it? I wonder if Miller was there.'

'Yeah, it fits quite well. Tell you what; let's go up to Covent Garden after lunch.' She said.

'Okay, but lunch is on me. I'll take you for the best burger you've ever had.'

We took the tube to Covent Garden and I led her past the busy old market and along to Garrick Street. There I took her into Hamburger Hero, long rows of tables with seats on either side and a few scattered smaller tables.

'This was Rob's favourite place; it wasn't a proper trip to London, if we didn't eat here.' We ordered cheeseburgers, chips and coke, which soon arrived. The cheese burger was huge and delicious, containing what looked like half a salad and smothered in ketchup; the chips were chunky and filling.

'These burgers are amazing, I don't think I'll ever be able to eat in a regular burger bar again,' she said. Well fed, we strolled around Covent Garden, wandering through the glass covered building and browsing in the fashionable boutiques and craft shops. Outside we watched the jugglers and other street performers in the afternoon sun. Lisa was somewhat freaked out by the mime artists and the performers pretending to be statues and hid her face in my shoulder as we passed them.

As we left the market we heard a commotion away to our left. We turned to see that a group of about twenty-five men were running through the street in a solid phalanx. I protectively pulled Lisa aside. Most of the thugs looked the same, cropped hair and low IQ. They were dressed alike in all black, tee shirts, jeans and boots. One of them seemed different. Although dressed in the same way, he had an expensive haircut and wore handmade brogue shoes. His eyes met mine as he ran past us; there was an intelligence there that was different from the rest. He was obviously in command of the group. As they passed an Asian owned shop, he pointed to it and one of his minions hurled something through the plate glass window. The proprietor looked shocked, but wisely chose to remain in his shop rather than remonstrate with the perpetrators. Premises that were obviously British owned were spared their attention, but every shop or restaurant that could be interpreted as foreign owned was assailed. It was like a scene from the thirties, when Mosley's Blackshirts had run amok in much the same way, though on a larger scale.

'I think they're Storm45,' Lisa whispered 'let's get the hell out of here. They fit the description that my friend gave, before her investigation was closed down.'

Most of the mob had passed us as we turned down an empty side street to get away the trouble. Suddenly Lisa stopped dead as the last of the thugs seized her by the arm and jerked her backwards. He was about twenty, skinny, medium height with short brown hair and the brain power of a mentally challenged goldfish.

'Come on babe, a good Aryan girl like you should be with us.' He began to drag her towards the corner his friends had just dis red around.

_ _.tepped forward. 'Let go of the young lady,' I said quietly but firmly in my best teacher voice. He ignored me.

'Fuck off dad,' he snarled 'before you get hurt. She's coming with me.'

'Let go of the young lady.' I repeated sounding calmer than I felt. He tried to stare me down and failed as I met his gaze levelly. In my teaching career, I'd occasion to deal with angry, violent teenagers several times. I had studied martial arts; thirty odd years ago at university. I had not been involved in a fight since junior school. As a student, I had had the odd altercation where I had squared up to someone, but that was about display to avoid violence. However, this character was leaving me desperately short of options other than the physical. I grabbed his wrist. 'I…said… let…go!' I left a gap between each word to emphasise them.

'Don't fucking touch me!' he said letting go of Lisa's wrist. He swung his right fist at my head. The punch was slow and telegraphed, or perhaps the adrenalin rushing into my system made it seem so. I snapped my arm up to block the blow, the way I had been taught all those years ago. Then I hit him. All of the anger, frustration and emotion of the past few days went into that punch, it felt marvellous. It drove into his face, catching him on his nose and left cheek. I felt something give way, but I was not sure whether it was his face or my fist. He staggered backwards and fell over the gutter, blood pouring from his nose. I stood shocked by what I had done but rather proud.

'You fucking bastard!' he snarled trying to wipe away the blood gushing out of his ruined nose. Lurching to his feet he pulled a knife out of his pocket. 'I'm gonna cut you good for that. Then we'll 'ave a bit of fun with the babe.' He slashed the knife at me and I jumped back, my heart was pounding fit to burst. As he thrust a second time at my throat, a defence from my karate days flashed through my mind. I was surprised at how the training came back to me. I crossed my wrists and brought them up sharply, catching his wrist and forcing it up away from me. As my hands locked on his wrist, I brought my left elbow over his arm, twisting my body so that his trapped arm was now being levered against his elbow joint. I pulled back on his arm with my right hand, the arm lock forcing his elbow to bend in a direction it was not designed for. I could not afford to take prisoners. Being in my fifties and none too fit, the longer this went on the more likely I was to lose. I yanked the arm viciously. With a sickening snap like a rotten branch, his elbow gave way. The knife fell to the ground from his nerveless fingers and clattered on the pavement. I noticed the tattoo on the inside of his wrist, a runic S looking like a single SS lightning flash, with the numbers 4 and 5 in the two angles of the 'S'. He looked stupidly at the right arm which would no longer obey him. I stepped away to his left side, thinking this was our chance to escape.

'Come on Lisa, we need to get out of here!'

He stood there, 'You wait 'till I get my mates. You're fucking dead!' With his left hand he pulled out a mobile phone - I had to stop him. I did not hesitate. I kicked sideways into the side of his knee, ligaments and cartilage tore as his leg gave way. He collapsed to the ground with a shriek, the mobile slipping from his hand and skidded into the gutter. Lisa at once used her heel to stamp it into a collection of useless components.

'Come on, run!' she yelled. I had no breath to spare for speech as we sprinted down the road. We switched direction at random, twisting and turning to elude any pursuit. As I said, I'm none too fit and was soon red faced and panting; there was a stitch in my side and a burning feeling in my chest. We turned into the main road, twenty yards in front of us a bus was just about to pull away.

'Bus!' I gasped, pointing. We jumped aboard as the bus pulled off carrying us away from the revenge of the thugs. Neither of us was even worried about the its' destination.

'My hero!' Lisa smiled and kissed me on the cheek. 'Thank you, I didn't know you could do that.'

'Nor did I,' I wheezed, still not recovered from my exertion. My hands were shaking as the reaction set in. 'Some hero,' I thought, 'I'm sitting here trembling like a newly born lamb.'

My right hand hurt like hell, it was swollen around the knuckles and my ring finger was stiff and difficult to move. Lisa noticed me wince as I tried to move my finger.

'That looks nasty, you alright?'

'Hurts like the blazes, I don't know whether I've broken a bone or whether it's just badly bruised. I'll be okay when I can get some ice on it and get the swelling down.'

'What do you think that was all about?' she asked. 'It seemed to be orchestrated.'

'Yes, one of them was clearly the leader and the others were taking his orders. Did you see the tattoo on his wrist? I'd bet my pension that was Storm45. If your friend was right about their link to the BNRA, I suspect they were taking advantage of the fact that the rally in Trafalgar Square would probably draw a good number of the police there, giving them a freer hand to wreak havoc. Though I can't see what Sinclair has to gain, he's gone to great lengths to appear respectable.'

The affair had rather ruined our day out. We set off for Hackney. Arriving at Lisa's flat, she went to the freezer and returned with a bag of frozen peas for my hand.

'Sorry,' she said, 'no ice - this is the best I could manage.'

After a few minutes the aching cold of the peas anaesthetised my throbbing hand, leaving it pleasantly numb. We rehashed the events of the afternoon and I must admit that being cast in the role of gallant hero did massage my bruised ego. Lisa switched on the TV, the news was just starting and unsurprisingly, the BNRA rally was the headline item. Conservative estimates put the crowd at fifteen thousand. The rally had been well ordered and peaceful, with BNRA stewards marshalling the participants, leaving the massed ranks of police as little more than spectators. This seemed even more at odds with the actions of Storm45 around Covent Garden, what on earth did Sinclair have to gain?

The man himself appeared on the screen, giving the usual sound bite for the cameras.

'This gathering today, is a gathering of concerned citizens. We see our MPs more concerned with profiting from their position than serving the people who sent them to Parliament. We see alien elements taking over our cities, turning them into places that we no longer recognise as Britain. We see disorder on our streets that a demoralised and underfunded police service can do little to stop. We see our people feeling swamped and threatened by those who have no intention of fitting in with British culture. We see British people feeling disaffected and ignored, whilst the parties of the past pander to and fawn upon newcomers. This can only lead to conflict on our streets. We see British jobs being hijacked by foreign conglomerates, whose aim is to exploit our people and protect their own people. I ask you, is that you want for your children? Is that what you want for your country? No! It is time for us to send a message to those who govern us. We have had enough! The British National Reconstruction Alliance will change this; we will rebuild the Britain that our parents and grandparents knew. We will restore our national pride. We will make our people proud to be British once more.'

'Phew!' said Lisa, 'his rants get more Hitleresque by the day. Why can't people see that? Are they really that gullible?'

'I think we've just seen the reason for today's incident.' I said. 'Sinclair can now pose as the prophet, predicting trouble on the streets and laying the blame on the multicultural society. With his respectable image, no-one will make the connection between Storm45 and him. As you pointed out, he's gone to great lengths to prevent any hint of that leaking out.'

'It makes sense…' Lisa was interrupted by the ringing of the phone. Lisa jumped up. 'That's probably James from Prague.'

She picked up the phone and listened for a few minutes, the call seemed very one sided. When she hung up, she looked puzzled. 'That was my boss. I've been summoned to an urgent meeting at the office tomorrow? I wonder what's going on.'

We parted an hour later and I returned to my hotel. Lisa had promised to call me in the morning, as soon as her meeting was over.

Chapter 7

Lisa phoned at ten the next morning. She sounded upset.

'Can we meet?' she asked. I agreed to meet her in twenty
minutes at the concourse at the Tower of London. I walked along
Tower Hill Terrace, past the ancient fortress on my left. The noisy
traffic was deafening as it poured in towards the centre of the city.
The newly cleaned and restored curtain wall of the Tower was
dazzling in the sunshine. William the Conqueror's White Tower
loomed over the fortress like a brooding presence. I arrived first
and waited for her outside the bunker-like brick structure that
housed a fast food outlet selling fried chicken, a small café and a
few shops selling tourist trinkets. I bought two cappuccinos and
settled at a table outside the café, facing the glass, steel and
concrete high-rise that seemed so out of place in juxtaposition to
the main mediaeval palace of the English kings. Carrying the
cappuccinos was not easy, the knuckles of my right hand were
still badly swollen and my ring finger was painful and had limited
mobility. Lisa appeared, forcing herself through a crowd of
Japanese tourists who seemed intent on photographing everything
in sight, even the litter bins and pigeons. She sat down next to me.
    'It's over,' she said. I could see that her eyes were red from
crying. I could not tell whether she had been upset or was blazing
with anger. My guess was the latter.
    'What's up? Problems?'
    'You could say that. I was summoned by my boss. The
programme has been shelved. Three of us had been working on it
all for nothing. I tried to tell Peter, my boss, about our unique
angle, but he cut me dead. Orders from the top. The top men don't
think it's a suitable subject with an imminent election. They say
no responsible broadcaster would touch it. What a load of
bollocks! This is a major scoop. I could see Peter wasn't too
happy about it, but that's that. I can't understand why it's all been
closed down so quickly. I've been reassigned to a new project

that'll take me to Madrid, if I take it. It feels like it's a sweetener to make me give up like a good little girl. All that work for nothing! I'm really pissed off! I can't understand why.' Her expressive blue eyes flashed with anger. 'It's all so bloody unfair! Sorry Ian it's not fair to rant on at you.'

'Don't worry about it.' I said. 'You said that you thought your friend's story about the BNRA was killed off by some sort of behind the scenes pressure. Do you think this is the same? I can't imagine why, but something doesn't feel right. But look on the bright side, the Madrid job is a pretty choice one. I wish someone would send me out to Madrid, it beats Suffolk.'

'Yeah, I know, but I don't like being pushed around, especially when I don't know why.' She pulled out her mobile phone from her pocket and slid it open. She scrolled through the numbers, selected one and dialled.

'Excuse me a minute, Ian.' She said as she stood up and walked away a few yards. She spoke animatedly into the phone for a few minutes then listened. She returned to the table.

'I've just spoken to my friend Hannah, she's PA to the Managing Director. I thought she might know something. She was a bit cagy, but she did say that she was called into the office yesterday, which is quite unusual on a Sunday. The MD had several calls from Gerald Aylmer, head of Aylmer Enterprises, he's a major league shareholder; then the great man himself appears with a face like thunder and a solicitor in tow and stomped into the MD's office. They were together about fifteen minutes and there were some raised voices, it sounded a pretty fiery meeting. She couldn't hear much, or if she did she's not letting on, but she heard the MD shouting about editorial integrity and my name was mentioned. If the fix has gone in, that's where it came from. The bastard!'

I wasn't sure whether she meant the Managing Director or Aylmer.

'Why should Aylmer want to kill your programme?' I mused. 'Aylmer .....Aylmer, where have I heard that name recently?'

'He's a pretty big noise in industry; he's often on the news. He's sort of like a right-wing Sir Alan Sugar, only with rabies.'

'No, it was some thing closer to home than that.' I racked my brain, but frustratingly I could not make the connection, the harder I tried, the further away the idea went. I gave up, it usually works, stop trying to remember and things come back to you. 'What are you going to do then? Take the Madrid job?'

'I don't know. Part of me is buggered if I want to be pushed around by Gerald bloody Aylmer.'

'You always were stubborn, but I don't see what else you can do....' I tailed off. 'Gerald Aylmer! Got it!' I recalled the last Easter holiday, sitting at the dinner table discussing her dissertation with my daughter Lucy. She was looking at the influence of industry and industrialists on the political process and public policy. She had mentioned Aylmer then, but what had she said? 'I need to phone Lucy.' I told Lisa, 'I think she might know something, though I'm not sure what.' I dialled Lucy's mobile, it went straight to voicemail. 'Shit!' I hung up and tried again, still voicemail. I left a message 'Lucy, this is Dad, can you ring me ASAP.'

I had barely put the phone away when it rang. 'Dad? Is everything okay? Your message sounded so urgent.'

'Sorry love, I didn't mean to scare you. I've been doing some historical research for Lisa Mann,' Lucy knew Lisa, she had been two years below at school. 'We've hit a roadblock in the person of Gerald Aylmer. I remembered you saying he had come up in your research, but I couldn't remember the context.'

'What have you been doing to upset Gerald Aylmer, Dad? I didn't think you moved in those circles.'

'We were looking into something to do with the British Union of Fascists in the 1930's, notably one particular member and his links to events in Nazi Germany.'

'That would do it Dad. Aylmer would not want anyone stirring the shit and drawing attention to British fascist parties, even in the past. According to my Prof, there is a strong suspicion that he is heavily involved in bankrolling the BNRA along with Sinclair, but he keeps it very quiet. Dad, be careful, if you're treading on the toes of the likes of Aylmer and by proxy Sinclair, they're not good people to cross.'

54

'Don't worry, love, I'm a historian, not a political journalist, my interest is purely in the politics of the past.'

'Don't forget what you told me Dad, "Historians are dangerous people, they are capable of upsetting everything." Khrushchev wasn't it?'

I smiled, it was the quotation I had on my office wall at school, along with the one from Santayana, which in the current political climate was perhaps even more apt: "The one who does not remember history is bound to live through it again," a chilling warning I had seen on a plaque at Auschwitz concentration camp. 'Don't worry, I'll be good. Speak to you soon, bye love.' I hung up. 'That's it, Aylmer is closely involved with Sinclair and the BNRA, he could be one of the major backers. Though quite why that would make him want to kill your story, I don't know. What do you want to do?'

'I don't know. I'd like to get to the bottom of it but….what do you think?'

'My gut reaction is to carry on. I don't like being pushed around and told what I can and can't be allowed to find out, it's called academic freedom, but it's easy for me, my job isn't at risk,' I replied.

'If I carried on, would you?'

'Gladly, I told you that this project has been a lifesaver for me, and I mean that literally. But what about your job? What about the project in Madrid?'

'I'm due three weeks holiday; I could take it on the grounds that I could not go to Madrid until James is back from the Czech Republic. The job in Madrid would hold for that long,' she explained.

'Sure?'

'Definitely.'

'Okay, let's give it another shot.'

'One thing though, now the project is officially on ice, the expenses will dry up. I can't cover your hotel bill after today, but…'

'Go on.'

'Well there's the spare room at the flat, if you're prepared to rough it.'

This was tricky, staying over at Lisa's flat for one night because we had been working late was one thing; but doing it for a protracted period was a very different thing. Lisa was a very attractive young woman and I didn't want anyone getting the wrong idea. That applied particularly to James, I had screwed up my own relationship with Jane, I did not want to be responsible for screwing up Lisa's. I thought for a minute.

'Okay, on one condition, if you phone James and explain the circumstances to him and he has no problem, then I'm up for it.'

'Done!' She said. 'I'll ring him now. It should be his lunchtime on Czech time.'

'I'll pop to the loo.' I said nodding to the public toilets in the base of the high rise opposite, to give her the privacy to make the call. I lingered in the toilet as long as I could, without being thought a pervert, then I returned to the café.

'It's fine, he's cool with you staying. He said he appreciated your consideration in asking. I told you he's a real sweetie.' She smiled the smile of a young woman in love. I felt jealous, not of James, but of both of them and what they had and I didn't, not any more.

Lisa winced as she noticed my blackened and swollen hand.

'You ought to get that x-rayed. It looks like you've broken something.'

'Naah, I'll be okay, it's stopped throbbing, it's just a bit stiff and sore,' I stated bravely.

'We should at least get some strapping for it.'

I gave in gracefully. She obviously was not going to let it drop. We stopped at a chemist and bought some self-fixing strapping that she wrapped round my injured hand. It did actually feel better, or maybe it was the psychological effect of seeing that someone cared.

We went to collect my clothes and the Saab from the hotel. Lisa settled the bill and we loaded my case into the car and set off for the flat. As we drove, she looked at her mobile.

'I've got a voicemail, it must have come in whilst we were on the tube. I don't recognise the number.' She listened to her phone. 'I'm having a really great day. That was Mrs. Coleridge from the Grange in Forest Row, it's no deal. "Sorry, it's not our policy to disclose the financial affairs of our patients, even after they have died. We have to be very scrupulous about the Data Protection Act." She sounds a snooty cow. 'Shit, I really hoped we might get a lead there. How do we get round this?' Lisa asked.

I had no answer. 'Let's just take a moment and think it through. There's bound to be another avenue that will present itself. Remember the old management bullshit – every problem is an opportunity.'

'Thanks for that. Very reassuring.' She said dryly.

I grinned, 'I haven't been in teaching for thirty odd years without learning some of the wisdom of management. I've been on all the courses. I even managed to stay awake through some of them.' I said with mock pride.

We arrived in Hackney and I found a parking spot round the corner from Lisa's flat, a difficult feat to achieve. Now I would not dare use the car again, because I'd never find another one. We unloaded my stuff and carried it up to her flat.

'The bed's still made up from Thursday. Make yourself at home.' She called from the kitchen. 'Want a coffee?'

'Yes, thanks,' I replied. We sat in the sitting room and discussed the problems of our research and potential ways we could proceed, but the lack of co-operation from the Gables was a major stumbling block. An idea occurred to me. Its morality was dubious and it was certainly illegal, but it might work. If we were caught, there would be hell to pay. 'Are you still in touch with Matt Nice?' I asked innocently.

'He's a friend on Facebook, so I could get hold of him. Why?'

'Don't you remember when he was nearly thrown out of school for using the school system to hack into some official database or other? It was only my intervention with the Head that saved him. What's more, he knows it - he owes me, big time.' She caught my drift. Every school had its would-be hacker, but ours had been exceptionally talented. He had not done it for any malicious reason, but for the challenge, he wanted to see if he could. He saw it as a competition between himself and the guy who had designed the protective firewalls of the system, and more often than not Matt was the victor.

'I suppose if anyone we know could do it, then it's Matt. We were in the same crowd at school and I knew he always fancied me, but I was too involved with Lee at the time. He got a first from Warwick in I.T. and I heard he has started his own company here in London and is doing quite well for himself. I haven't seen him for eighteen months or so. You're thinking he could hack into the Gables' system to get what we need, if we can persuade him. I'll look him up.' She fetched her laptop and opened her Facebook page. She found him amongst her friends and went to his page, which had his email address on it. She noted it down then called up her own email. She typed:

Hi Matt,

I've been working on a project with Mr West from school and we think you might be able to help us with something. Could you email me or give me a ring on 0775 236784.

See you soon

Lisa x

She sent the email off into the electronic ether. Now all we could do was wait and see if Matt got back to us.

Chapter 8

There was no reply by the following morning. Lisa checked her email as we sat eating cereals at the table.

'No response from Matt yet, where do you think we should go from here?'

'I suggest we start to flesh out William Howard Miller more. At the moment, we have him being born, then appearing as a twenty-four year old in 1933 setting fire to the Reichstag, then getting into trouble with the law and disappearing totally in 1939, never to be seen again, or at least not by his mother. Aylmer does not seem to want us delving too deeply into the Miller family and I should think that it relates more to son than mother. So I say we need to try to find out more on Miller.'

'I agree, he does seem to be the key to all this. But before we start, I have to go into the office and arrange my leave. It should only take an hour or so. What are you going to do?'

I looked up from her laptop. 'It says here that all the court records for Middlesex from 1834 to 1939 are kept in Kew. I'll head there and see what I can find out. You join me when you can.

'Sounds like a plan,' she said. 'I'll catch up with you later.'

'Okay, text me when you get to Kew.'

Forty minutes later I was settled before the Old Bailey court records for August 1939. This time I had enough detail to refine my search, so it was not difficult to find what I wanted. William Howard Miller of 34 Park Gardens, Fulham had been charged with possession of two Mauser C96 machine pistols in contravention of the 1937 Firearms Act. Evidence had been given by the police that Miller had been found in possession of the pistols after a tip off had led to the search of his home. Inspector Evans of the Metropolitan Police had added that Miller had a criminal record, having been found guilty of affray three years earlier. Miller gave evidence to explain that he had only recently returned to Britain after several years in Spain. The pistols had been keepsakes of his time there and as he had not been in the country since 1936, he had no idea that the ownership of such weapons was prohibited, as they had been perfectly legal when he had left the country. He had explained that having only just returned to Britain, he had not had the opportunity to apply for a firearms certificate. He added that he believed the whole trial was politically motivated and he was being persecuted for his political beliefs. In his summing up, the Judge had warned Miller that he faced a maximum prison sentence of two years, if found guilty. Before the jury could begin its deliberations, Miller had jumped bail and fled the country, he was believed to be in France. If he was located, the prosecution stated its intention to have him extradited.

I thought about what I had discovered. With the outbreak of war with Germany just ten days later, I supposed the authorities were too busy to worry about pursuing Miller. I felt my phone vibrate in my pocket; it was a text from Lisa, who was waiting outside. I gathered my notes, returned the records and joined her outside.

'I think they must have felt guilty about axing my research, they've given me a month off with pay, rather than the three weeks I asked for. If I can go to Madrid before then, I get to keep any outstanding leave. Any joy this morning?'

'Oh yes!' I declared and went on to give her the gist of my discovery as we walked the to tube. When I was finished, she looked at me.

'What do you think he was doing in Spain?'

'Well the time is right for the Spanish Civil War. If he'd been a socialist or communist I'd suspect he was fighting with the International Brigade, but that's not likely with his political allegiance. Could you really see him fighting alongside communists and anarchists against the Nationalists/fascists?'

'Could he have been on the other side?'

'I don't honestly know. You usually only hear of those who fought for the International Brigades, people like Eric Blair...' She looked blank. 'You'd know him as George Orwell, you know, the guy who wrote Animal Farm and 1984.' I explained and saw comprehension dawn on her. 'I think the poet Stephen Spender fought with them too. I suppose there must be some Britons who fought on the Nationalist side, but the only foreigners you hear of there are the German Condor Legion and the Italian volunteers sent by Mussolini'

'Could we find out?'

'Find me internet access and I'm sure we could,' I said nodding to the laptop bag hanging on her shoulder.

We abandoned our walk to the tube and located a coffee shop that offered free internet access. We purchased coffee and a Panini each and logged on to the net. It did not take long to discover that there were indeed people who went to Spain to fight for the Franco's Nationalists. According to Wikipedia, there was an entire Irish unit and one of the founders of the National Front, Commander Fountaine had fought for Franco. All interesting information, but not proof of what Miller had been up to.

'Do you think that old lady you spoke to in Forest Row might know any more?' I asked, grasping at straws.

'I'm sure she did, but I didn't even get her name.'

'Great!'

'We could try to find her. Let's go down this afternoon, it's not like we've got loads of other things to do.'

By three that afternoon we were back in Forest Row, having collected the Saab and had a relatively smooth run down. I had an idea that might just work. I led Lisa back to the grave yard and we located Lisl Miller's grave once more. I turned and looked around. When Lisa had met the old lady, she had been laying flowers on her husband's grave. There was only one grave nearby with fresh flowers on it. I walked across to it, beckoning Lisa to follow. The head stone read:

> Arthur Philip George
> 1937 – 2005
> Beloved husband of Rosa
> Much loved father of Ann and David
> Forever in our hearts

We had a name, Rosa George. All we had to do was find her.

'Let's split up again. You go to the post office and see if they can tell you her address. Spin them some sort of yarn about her having dropped something last week that you wanted to return. I'll have a drive around and see if I can find a hotspot, then I could use the internet to try to track her down.' Lisa set off for the Post Office; I opened her laptop and began to search for a wireless signal that was not security enabled. There wasn't one. I drove the car a few hundred yards and tried again. Still nothing. I moved again towards some newer houses away from the main A22. This time there were three signals and one was not secure. I connected the laptop and used the internet to search the electoral roll, again it was a pay site, but it gave me the information I was seeking. Rosa Alice George, 23 Wheelers Lane. I drove back and picked up Lisa.

'I got it,' she said. '23 Wheelers Lane.'

'That's what I got too, let's go.' I typed the address into the satnav and followed the instructions given by the annoyingly correct female voice. We pulled up outside a well-kept 1930s semi-detached house with a bay window and lovingly tended garden bordered by a privet hedge. Lisa opened the green painted gate and walked down the path to the door. She rang the doorbell. The door was opened by the old lady I had seen the previous week. She was in her eighties, small with neatly permed white hair and brown eyes that displayed a lively glint.

'Hello,' Lisa began, 'we met in the graveyard last week and you told me you knew my great aunt Lisl, do you remember?'

'Of course I do dear. What do you want?'

'Well this is my dad, and I was hoping you could tell us a little bit more about great aunt Lisl.'

The old lady smiled and stood back from the door. 'Come in dear, 'she said. 'When you get to my age, a little bit of company is always welcome.'

I smiled and offered her my hand 'How do you do. It's very kind of you, I'm afraid that my daughter has a real bee in her bonnet about her great aunt.' I felt bad lying to such a kind old lady. We followed her in to her sitting room. It was a little gloomy, but homely and clean. There was a small TV in the corner and a three piece suite was arranged around the fireplace. In the corner of the room a budgerigar swung in its cage whistling and squawking merrily. A sideboard sat beneath the bay window with its floral curtains. She invited us to sit and disappeared into the kitchen, Lisa and I sat on the sofa. She returned a few minutes later with a tray on which were three bone china cups and saucers, a teapot, milk jug, a bowl of cubed sugar and a plate of biscuits.

'Please, let me get that.' I stood up and took the tray from her and set it on the low table in the centre of the room. She sat down and poured the tea. Lisa turned down the offer of sugar, I took two lumps.

'Now dear, tell me what you want to know.'

'Well you seemed to know great aunt Lisl, though I think she was really my great, great aunt, but that's a bit of a mouthful. I want to know what she was like. I've never even seen a picture of her.'

'I can solve that , dear.' She went to the mantelpiece and selected one of the many framed photographs that were displayed there. She showed us the photograph. It showed three women, one middle aged that I immediately recognised as a younger Rosa George and two other women who were much older. They were sitting on a bench in a garden. She indicated a frail, white-haired, dignified old lady on the left, who despite her age, was still very upright and was staring into the camera with bright, alert eyes. Wizened she might be, but she still had all her marbles and a certain dignity. 'That was Lisl. The lady on the right was another friend, Marion; she died the year after Lisl.'

'You said she had a son.' Lisa prompted.

'Yes, his name was William, a bit of a black sheep I think. She was always talking about him, even though she had not seen him for years. She always had a picture of him in her room and she treasured the letters she got from him. Apparently he got into some trouble with the law just before the war and ran off to France, she never saw him again.'

'That's terribly sad.' Lisa said. 'I wonder what happened to him.' She was good, I could see her steering the conversation in the direction we needed. 'Did she say what he was like?'

The old lady thought for a minute, then crossed to the sideboard. She opened the second drawer and searched for something. Failing to find it, she rummaged through the bottom drawer. She pulled out an old A4 manila envelope. 'Here,' she said. 'When Lisl died she left everything to Marion, but she died soon after and left her things to me.'

Lisa dipped into the envelope and pulled out a hand coloured photograph and a creased letter. She looked at the photograph then handed it to me. It showed a good-looking blonde man in his late twenties. He was dressed in a military uniform that I didn't recognise. I turned it over, written on the back in faded black ink was "Willi Dec 1938." Lisa was looking at the letter; she frowned and peered at it before handing it to me. It was all in German. It began "*Liebe Mama*". I recognised the writing, it was Miller's.

'It starts "Dear Mum", but that's as far as my Year 9 German will get me. After that I only know the odd word here and there.'

'It beats my German. That only amounts to asking for a glass of beer.' I said.

'You sound like my Arthur, he spent three years in the army in Germany and all he could manage was please and thank you.' The old lady laughed at the memory.

'You keep them, my dear,' she said to Lisa. 'They'll mean more to you than to me.'

Lisa thanked her. We spent another half hour with Rosa before making our excuses and setting off back to London, leaving her Lisa's number in case she thought of something else. It was dark when we got back to Hackney. It took a while to find a parking space, but at last we went up to the flat. We put on the lights and sat down. There was no need to get food; we had stopped off to eat on the way back. We looked closely at the letter, but between us we could only decipher the odd phrase, nowhere near enough to work out its meaning.

'Who do we know who speaks German?' Lisa asked.

'Do you have a scanner?' I asked.

'Yeah, the printer's one of those all-in-one things. Why?'

'Well, if you can scan the document, I'll email it off to Graham Price at school to get him to translate it.'

'God is Pricey still there? I thought he'd retired or died years ago. He was like eighty when I was there.'

'Careful,' I warned, 'He's only a year or two older than me.'

'Oops sorry. It's just that he always looked and acted old. We never thought of you as being the same age. You seemed....' She paused, 'more full of life. You had the same outlook as the younger teachers.'

I was touched.

'Thanks for the compliment. Please feel free to keep going.'

She laughed, 'Do you know that's the first time since we started this that you've sounded like the old Ian?'

She scanned the letter and I emailed a copy of it off to Graham for translation. Lisa checked her email. There was a response from Matt Nice.

Hi Lisa,

Good to hear from you again. Sorry I can't meet up with you until later in the week as I'm currently in the Big Apple. I'll give you a ring as soon as I'm home. Give my regards to Mr West.

Matt.

Lisa sighed, 'That'll slow us up. I was hoping we could get Matt to weave his magic and answer some of our questions.'

I took over the laptop. Whilst Lisa had been reading her email, I had scanned the photograph too. I now called up the digital image and expanded it. It really was a beautifully coloured photograph, whoever had coloured the original black and white image had been an artist. I was now able to zoom in on some of the detail of the uniform. It was well fitting; its style seemed to be better suited to an officer than rank and file. If the colouring was correct, the uniform was a greenish khaki. Three six pointed stars decorated the sleeve of his jacket just above the cuff. The most notable item was the sidecap he wore, which had a tassel hanging from the front. In his hand he held a steel helmet adorned with a gold eagle insignia. I had seen the cap with the tassel before somewhere; it certainly was not standard military garb. Then I remembered a picture I had seen in a textbook of General Franco wearing a similar cap. Half an hour's surfing the internet had confirmed that the uniform was that of a Captain in the Nationalist army. Fascinated, Lisa watched over my shoulder the whole time. When I tired of staring at the screen, she took over and located a picture of the eagle adorning the helmet, the same in every detail, even down to the five arrows clutched in its talons. We could now prove that Miller had gone to Spain to fight. It felt as if we were finally getting nearer to the man himself.

Chapter 9

It was just over an hour before I received a reply from Graham Price. I was surprised by the speed of his reply.

Hi Ian,

Have you got nothing better to do than to give me extra work? It's bad enough trying to keep the little buggers in line at the end of term, especially when we're our best Head of Year missing, without some skiving sod treating us as a free translation service!! Seriously Ian, I was terribly sad to hear about you and Jane. If there is anything I can do, night or day, give me a call.

Graham

Your letter reads as follows, please forgive me if the English is stilted, but I did it in a bit of a rush:

23rd October 1938

Dear Mum,

Here is a picture of me in my uniform, don't I look handsome? I'm sorry for leaving, but I feel I have a duty to do whatever I can to stop the spread of the communist poison. I was not greeted with open arms at first; I don't think they quite knew what to do with me. However, I soon met with some of the officers from the Condor Legion and made some useful contacts. They were very welcoming, especially after Sepp contacted them and vouched for me. There are one or two of the old style Prussian officers who mistrust my Nazi connections, but most have accepted me without a problem.

Thanks to the influence of my German friends, I succeeded in gaining a commission in the Nationalist Army, where I was a liaison officer with the Condor Legion. My job was to help co-ordinate the military action of the two forces.

I have made some good friends amongst the German contingent, one officer; Karl Lander comes from Mellendorff, only a few kilometres from Wedemark. He even knew the road where Granny and Grandpa lived. Karl is a Lieutenant in the Luftwaffe. He flies fighter aircraft and already has a good number of kills to his name.

Luckily I was able to arrange a transfer to more active service. What would be the point of coming all this way and never getting the chance to shoot a Bolshevik? My company did rather well at the Ebro, they resisted the Republican's attacks stoutly. The fight gave me some insight into what Papa must have experienced in the Great War. My men were at the spearhead of the Nationalist advance into Catalonia. The incident at Montegrillo has been much exaggerated, though my dedication to the cause has increased my prestige with many of my brother officers. The work was not pleasant, but anarchists are vermin whose ideas have to be expunged.

I know you will be concerned for me dearest Mama, but I am undergoing the greatest experience of my life. I will be perfectly safe, as my unit has been withdrawn to Burgos and I suspect I may once more find myself in a liaising role, as the number of German speaking officers is quite limited. Whilst I would enjoy the break, I really do not want to spend the rest of the war behind a desk. I realise times are hard for you at home, with me here, so I have arranged for half of my pay to be sent to you at three monthly intervals. Hopefully it will ease your financial hardship.

Your loving son
Willi

Again, as in so much of this story, things were alluded to cryptically, rather than stated clearly.

'Looks like our boy has become something of a war hero. Do you know anything about the history of the period?'

I thought for a second or so. 'I studied the Spanish Civil War a bit at university, as part of modern European history, but I don't remember much beyond the basics of who was fighting who. The Nationalists had rebelled against the Republican government. They consisted of the Army, monarchists, Spanish fascists – the Falange and a ragbag of other right wing and conservative groups. I think they were supported by the Catholic Church too. They had a great deal of help from Fascist Italy and Hitler sent the Condor

Legion, basically a big chunk of the Luftwaffe. The Republic was a coalition of liberal republicans, communists, socialists, anarchists and Basque and Catalan separatists. They received some aid from Russia, though it cost them their entire gold reserves, about 40 metric tonnes. There were also the International Brigades. As for the rest, it started in 1936 and ended in1939. That's your lot.'

'Okay, let's see what we can find online.'

We discovered that the date of the letter coincided with the end of the Battle of the Ebro and that fitted with Miller's account.

'The Ebro seems to have been more like a First World War battle than Second. It was just a series of pointless frontal assaults by both sides that were doomed to failure. It sounds horrible. The casualties must have been terrific,' Lisa said.

'The Republic lost over half of its hundred thousand men,' I said reading on. 'They were so weakened that they ceased to exist as a serious fighting force and were forced to give in to Franco in April the following year. Seems to have been a bit of a watershed.'

'What do you make of the reference to Montegrillo?'

'Not a clue.' I tried googling the name and found nothing beyond the fact it was a village on the border between Catalonia and Aragon, with a population of 516. 'There were a hell of a lot of atrocities on both sides. That could be what he is alluding to.'

'Any way of finding out?'

'We could try text books on the Spanish Civil War. A think there was a hefty one published a few years ago. There was also a mammoth one in the 1960's, Thomas? But I doubt they'll have that sort of detail. You'd probably have to go to the central archive in Madrid or maybe Barcelona.'

'Woop! Road trip.'

'Hang on. We can't go flying off all over Europe without thinking it through. We don't even know if it's Madrid, Barcelona or even Zaragoza that we'd need.'

'Spoilsport!'

'We could ring the Spanish Embassy tomorrow and see if we could get any guidance.'

As it happened, we decided to go to the Spanish Embassy. Checking the internet for the address, we set out for Belgravia. we emerged from the underground at Knightsbridge. Lisa was casting longing looks as we passed Harrods, its line of green canopies jutting out from the elaborate brickwork, like a row of eyelids blinking over the windows of the shop.

'Down girl,' I smiled, 'no retail therapy for you today. Keep your eyes on the prize. You've already got enough footwear to shoe a small army!'

She pouted prettily, 'They'd be a very fashionable army though. You're turning into a real spoilsport Ian. You know Harrods is my favourite shop. Pleeeease! Just for a little while.'

I looked at her in amazement. She couldn't be seriously thinking of shopping? She suddenly burst into peals of laughter. 'Your face, you really thought I was serious. I admit to being a shopaholic, but I'm not that much of a bimbo. As my Nan says, there's a time and place for everything! Come on.'

'Yeah, yeah! You got me there. I was beginning to think I didn't know you as well as I thought.'

'That'll teach you to take me for granted, maybe on the way back though....' She looked at me with her eyes twinkling with amusement.

She crossed the road and strode off down Sloane Street with me in her wake. Ten minutes later we were standing outside of the Spanish Embassy in Chesham Place. The façade of the building must have been undergoing some major renovation, as the entire structure was covered with scaffolding, which was itself swathed in plastic sheeting. The flags of Spain and the European Union hung over the street from the entrance, the only part that was not clad in the industrial version of clingfilm. We walked up the steps and in through the imposing doors. Lisa had to have her bag checked by security before we could gain admission. Inside a pretty, raven-haired young woman at the reception smiled at us, displaying perfect teeth.

'Can I help you?' she asked in flawless, but attractively accented English.

'Yes, I hope so. I've a question about the location of certain historical archives in Spain. Would that be the Cultural Attaché's office?' I asked.

'I think so.' She picked up a telephone, pressed a button and spoke in rapid Spanish. I speak some Spanish, but I could follow little. 'Señor Lorente will be down in just a minute. Would you like to take a seat?' She indicated a row of green leather armchairs.

Lorente appeared within a few minutes, he was a tall handsome man of about thirty, unusually blonde for a Spaniard. He shook hands and introduced himself, his eyes lit up with interest as Lisa introduced herself. He shook her hand, paying particular attention to the naked ring finger on her left hand. Lisa smiled prettily. Why couldn't I have that effect on the opposite sex? He led us up the stairs to a small office, where he offered us seats.

'I believe you have a question about historical archives in Spain.'

'Yes, we're writing a biography of a 1930's chap called William Miller,' I said. 'We've found reference to an incident during your Civil War, in the Catalan village of Montegrillo in late 1938. Our references are very vague, but could be important to our narrative and we wondered if you could advise us where the best archives would be for us to conduct our research. I was unsure whether it would be at the Archivo Nacional in Madrid, or a regional archive in Barcelona.'

He looked at us pensively, stroking his chin. 'It is a strange thing, I come from Lerida, which is the nearest town to Montegrillo. I don't know exactly what happened, but I do know it was... how do you say...unpleasant? I believe any records would be kept in the central archive in Madrid, but I can check for you. I have a cousin who teaches history at the Rey Juan Carlos University. He is something of an authority on the history and politics of Spain in the early twentieth century. I'm sure if he does not know the detail of the event in question, then he will know the best place to look. I will email him.'

We thanked him and Lisa gave him her card. He kissed her hand.

'Señorita, it has been my pleasure to be of assistance to such a beautiful young woman. I will be in contact as soon as Joachim gets back to me.'

We left the Embassy and walked back towards Knightsbridge. It was quite frustrating, we had a number of irons in the fire but we could do nothing but await developments.

'Fancy lunch in Harrods?' I asked. 'But no shoe shopping!'

She pouted once more. 'Meanie!'

We spent the afternoon wandering around the shops in Knightsbridge. We had just reached Hyde Park underground when Lisa's mobile trilled. She flipped it open.

'Hello.......I can't believe you've got back to us already......He knew all about it already?....Yes of course, it's lisa dot mann, all lowercase, dot seneschalproduction at business dot net.... You will, well thank you......No, I'm sorry, I'm very flattered but I'm in a relationship. ....Thank you goodbye'

She had flushed a bright scarlet during the latter part of the conversation.

'Do I get the impression that you made an impact on Señor Lorente?' I asked innocently.

'Lay off Ian,' she snapped.

'Sorry, I was only teasing, I didn't mean to upset you.'

'No, I'm sorry, it's just that it gets a bit tedious at times, when half the guys you meet hit on you. Mind you, he was fit, if it hadn't been for James, I might have accepted his offer of dinner.'

'It's your own fault, you should not look so bloody appealing. Other women must hate you.'

'I thought you didn't notice.'

'I noticed, I am a man. But I hid it well, professional ethics and all that. Besides which I'm nearly three times your age, I'll settle for the relationship we've got. I look on you as a favourite niece.'

She smiled at me, 'I always knew that you were the one I could come to when I was in trouble or had a problem. I like that, Uncle Ian.'

'Okay enough of the sentimental mush, unless you want me to get all misty eyed. What did he say?'

'His cousin knew all about it, he had researched it himself for a thesis on the atrocities of the Spanish Civil War…that must be a cheery read! Anyway, he's emailed us all of the information. Unfortunately. No road trip to Madrid.' She stuck out her bottom lip. 'Come on let's get home.'

Chapter 10

Forty-five minutes later, we had it. Lisa had gone for the laptop even before I had closed the door. She waited impatiently whilst her email loaded. Sure enough there was an email from Senor Lorente at the Spanish embassy. She hurriedly opened the attachment and began to read.

"The Battle of the Ebro and the massacre at Montegrillo.

The Battle of the Ebro began on 24th July 1938, when the Republican Commander-in-Chief, General Rojo ordered an offensive to attack across the River Ebro, aiming to break out and link Catalonia with the rest of the Republic. The Republican Colonel Modesto's troops crossed the Ebro along an eighty kilometre front. Initially successful, the Republican forces crossed 80,000 troops over the river advancing on Gandesa. On 26th July Modesto attacked the strategically important Hill 481 at Gandesa, an area well fortified with trenches, bunkers and barbed wire. The hill was vigorously defended by the Nationalists and the Republicans suffered heavy losses. After six days the Republicans retreated to Hill 666, which they successfully defended from a counter attack from troops of General Yague's Army of Morocco, assisted by falangist and requetes militia."

'Falangist, Requetes?' Lisa queried.
'Fascists and Carlists, another right wing paramilitary.' We read on.

"The Nationalists counterattacked on 1st August and successfully forced the Republicans to withdraw. Massed heavy artillery gave the Nationalists a great advantage; General Queipo de Llano used 500 artillery pieces to fire up to 13,500 rounds per day. The Nationalists also had total air superiority, allowing the Condor Legion to continuously attack Republican positions. The Republicans were unwilling to withdraw and suffered heavy casualties. The Republican International

Brigades were withdrawn in September after an agreement between President Negrin and the League of Nations. By October the Republican forces were being forced to withdraw and when the battle ended on 16th November, all of the Republic's troops had been forced to pull back across the Ebro.

Republican casualties are estimated at 50,000 killed and wounded and nearly 20,000 taken prisoner. Nationalist casualties were lower at 37,000 killed and wounded."

'Bloody hell, this reads like a history text book. It's told us nothing useful,' Lisa snorted. 'This is useless.'

'Hold your horses,' I said. 'It fits with the letter, hinting at World War One type conditions, and we haven't finished yet. Read on.'

"On 20th November, two companies from the 40th Division were ordered to cross the Ebro in a raid into Republican territory. The raid was led by Commandante Sanchez de Vega and consisted of troops who had so gallantly held Hill 481. Commandante Sanchez de Vega was killed during the crossing of the river and Capitan Molinero assumed command. The raiders penetrated 20km into Republican territory, arriving to the village of Montegrillo just after dawn. Montegrillo was an anarchist commune established some fifteen years earlier. As day broke, the company of about 200 men stormed the largely unarmed village. On the orders of Molinero, all the male inhabitants of the village over the age of 10 were shot by firing squad. The women and children were held captive in the school. Molinero encouraged the mass rape and murder of all the captive women over the age of 12. Finally the village was destroyed by explosives and fire.

The children were released, only after the surviving boys had been mutilated to incapacitate them. It is from these survivors that the story of the massacre was pieced together by Republican forces sent to repel the invasion. Despite close pursuit, the raiders succeeded in returning safely to Nationalist territory, without loss. Capitan Molinero was censured for his role in the massacre, but no formal action was taken against him. When the war ended, he disappeared from the record."

Whilst reading this, Lisa's voice had thickened with emotion and her eyes blazed with anger. 'What a bastard!' she exclaimed.

'Civil wars are always nasty, you seem to get far more atrocities than in normal warfare, perhaps because the hatred is stronger in an internecine struggle.'

'That's hardly an excuse for murder, rape and the mutilation of children!'

'Agreed.'

'Do you think Miller was involved in this?'

'It matches with the letter, but that's not real proof.'

'I'd better phone Lorente and thank him for his help, you never know, we might need his help again.' She picked up the phone and dialled. I wandered into the kitchen to make two mugs of tea, then began to leaf through the free newspaper I had been handed outside the tube station. Once again it was full of election-mania and the words of Richard Sinclair, in particular. Despite his party being a small, and in my opinion, extremist group, Sinclair had challenged the Prime Minister to a face to face debate, as if he were the leader of one of the main opposition parties. His speech in Kilburn was quoted. "We have all seen the corruption of the big political parties in parliament, corruption that the government was responsible for failing to prevent. Why? Could it be because their party too had their noses in the trough? I call upon the Prime Minister to meet me in open debate, where he will have the opportunity to reassure the public that his government has their interests in mind. However, it is an offer I doubt he has the courage to take me up on, for that would take a moral courage that he has shown himself to lack." The Prime Minister had declined to even dignify the offer with a reply. I could understand his point, but I was not convinced that ignoring Sinclair was the best way to counter the poisonous threat of the BNRA. A series of vox pop interviews by the paper seemed to bear out my instinct. To the man in the street, Sinclair was beginning to appear to be the heroic man of the people, who was standing up to the arrogance of the unpopular big political parties. The mainstream parties were only serving to make Sinclair more popular by their tactics. I finished reading the article and saw Lisa was putting the phone down, there was a strange look on her face.

'What's wrong?'

'Senor Lorente told me something that makes this all the more relevant to our research.'

'Oh. What?'

'Molinero, it's the Spanish for Miller!'

Chapter 11

The next day my world came crashing down around my ears. I was awoken by the ringing of my mobile phone. I blearily peered at the caller ID displayed on the screen - Jane. I slid open the phone.

'Hello.'

'Ian, is that you? Where are you, I've been to the house several times, but you're never there.'

'I decided to get away for a few days, to lick my wounds as it were.'

'I need to see you, we've things to discuss.'

'I'm not going to be back for a couple of weeks. What do you want to discuss?'

Her voice softened, 'I really didn't want to do this over the phone.' A pause. 'Look Ian, I really don't want to hurt you. I still care about you. I love you; it's just that I'm not in love with you. I've been thinking; I want to get on with getting my life back. I don't want to wait two years for a divorce. I want to get this over as soon as we can.'

'I thought you had to have grounds for a quicker divorce, adultery, unreasonable behaviour or something. I don't really want to wash our dirty linen in public. You do know that it all has to be put in writing to the court. Isn't it easier just to live apart for two years and get the divorce that way?'

'I'm sorry Ian, but I want my life back now, not in two years.'

'What's the hurry?' I paused, not wanting to go on, but unable to stop. 'Is there someone else?'

'No...yes...sort of. There's a potential someone else. We've met a few times, I'm seeing him at the weekend; we've not slept together, if that's what you're worried about. But if it takes me committing adultery to get the divorce, then…..' She left the sentence hanging.

'Who is it...? No, don't tell me, that would be worse.' The thought of Jane with another man made my stomach turn to ice, I felt physically sick. That Jane could move on so easily didn't just hurt, it tore me apart.

'How can you move on so quickly, does the last thirty years mean so little?' I asked.

'I've done my grieving Ian, the last five years of our marriage. I'm ready to move on. I'm not being callous; it's just the way I feel. I want my life back.'

I understood what she meant, but that did not stop me feeling like a worn out old shoe that had been cast aside. It did nothing for my feelings of self worth, in the past days my ego had taken a battering. That Jane could replace me so quickly devastated me. She had not committed adultery, but she already had another man with whom she felt she might establish a relationship. How could she toss me and the years we had spent together aside so easily?

'I don't think I can do this at the moment. You need to get legal advice and so do I.'

'Okay Ian, I'm sorry if you're upset, you know I wouldn't deliberately hurt you, but having made the decision to end our marriage, I need to get on with my life. I can't remain in limbo for the next two years. Will you think about it?' I agreed and we said our goodbyes.

I collapsed on the bed and cried. I had shed tears before this, but this time I cried as if my heart was breaking, which it was. I lay there for ten minutes, the tears soaking into my pillow. There was a gentle tap on the door and Lisa poked her head tentatively round the door. I was mortified that she should see me in such a state.

'Ian, what ever's the matter?'

'Jane phoned, she wants a divorce now, she's got a potential man in her life,' I said sobbed haltingly. 'I've been replaced already. It's a shock to find out I'm so easily...... disposable. I don't think I have anything left to lose.' She took my hand in hers.

'Ian, I'm so sorry. Is there anything I can do?' I shook my head, mopping my eyes with my sleeve. I fished out a handkerchief and blew my nose.

'Any chance of a cup of coffee? I'm in danger of getting dehydrated with all this undignified weeping. I'll try to pull myself together while you get it.' I went to the bathroom and washed my face in cold water to try to make my eyes less red and puffy. When I went into the sitting room, she was sitting there with two mugs of coffee.

'I'm sorry about that,' I said. 'I didn't mean to make an exhibition of myself and embarrass you.'

'Don't be so bloody stupid!' she snapped angrily. 'Give yourself a break, you're going through some serious shit, you're only human, you're not bloody Superman. If you weren't affected by something like this, you'd have to be Mr Spock from Star Trek, you know, no emotions. I can't believe your wife could treat you like this after so long, what a bitch!'

'No, she's not; she's just had enough and can't take any more. She doesn't mean to hurt me, but she needs to move on. It's just that I'm not ready to let her go.' I sipped the coffee. 'Can we just get on with our work? If I don't find something to occupy my mind I'm going to make a bloody fool of myself again.'

She gave me a glare. 'Ian I don't want to hear any more of that crap. Stop being so hard on yourself.'

I was saved the rest of her lecture by the ringing of the telephone. Lisa picked up the receiver.

'Hello.' Pause. 'Oh it's nice to hear from you again, I didn't think it would be so soon.' Pause. 'Yes, I would.' Pause and she scribbled on a pad beside the phone. 'That's marvellous!' Pause. 'That's really useful; it was so kind of you to let me know. Bye.'

I raised my eyebrows enquiringly.

'That was Mrs George. We set her thinking yesterday. She had a root around in some other papers she inherited and found a Red Cross postcard. It was sent by William to his mother in August 1940. He told her he'd been interned by the Germans and was being held at St. Denis.'

80

'Sounds interesting. Fancy a trip to France? If I dash back home to pick up my passport, we could catch a Eurotunnel shuttle this afternoon.' I jumped at the chance to escape the mess my life had become.

'Hold on Ian, we can't get carried away. I know why you're eager to be gone, but you taught me better than that. We're can't just head off to France at random hoping that we might find something. I don't even know where St Denis is. Let's do a bit of research first and see if it's worth going to France.'

'Yeah, you're right of course. I do know where St Denis is though, it's a suburb just north of Paris. It's where the Stade de France is, where they played the 1998 World Cup final.'

'Helpful!' She said sarcastically.

The internet is a marvellous thing; within a few minutes we'd discovered that St Denis was an internment camp run by the Germans. It had held over a thousand British, Commonwealth and American men in a former army barracks. What was better still, it had been preserved as a museum, with its own displays and small archive.

'Looks like you get you road trip Ian after all Ian. The shopping won't be as good as Madrid or Barcelona, though,' she teased.

I left her to book our passage on the channel tunnel and somewhere to stay, whilst I headed to Suffolk to pick up my passport and a few clean clothes. In just over three hours I was back, having driven like a bat out of hell; the speeding tickets would probably catch up with me later. We arrived at the terminal in Folkestone just ten minutes before check-in closed. We were directed over the bridge and down to where the shuttle awaited. I pulled the car into the carriages and drove down the interior. We travelled a considerable distance through the inside of the train.

'Are we driving to France, or what?' Lisa asked.

'Not been through the tunnel before?'

'No, I don't really like the idea of tunnels underwater; the Blackwell Tunnel freaks me out enough.'

'Half an hour and we'll be through.' I said pulling the car to a halt. 'You can get out and stretch your legs, if you want to.'

'Thanks, but I think I'll stay here.'

With a gentle lurch the train moved off and in a couple of minutes, the daylight outside disappeared. The crossing took just half an hour. As we drove out of the carriage into the afternoon sun, Lisa tapped our destination into the satnav and guided by the bass timbre of the mechanical voice (I had turned off the annoying female voice), we set off into France. An hour later we were driving through Picardy, past the former battlefields of the Somme and on round Amiens. Another ninety minutes and we reached the outer fringes of Paris; we stopped to pay our toll at the Péage after a surprisingly good journey. At the bottom of the A16 things changed, the traffic began to increase and our rate of progress slowed to a frustrating crawl as we were caught up in the frantic Parisian rush hour. At long last we pulled in to our suite hotel in the shadow of the futuristic bowl of the Stade de France. We parked the Saab and carried our bags into the six storey modern concrete and glass structure. The reception area was striking, with light wood modern furniture contrasting with the black flooring. We were greeted by a young female receptionist, who rapidly changed to speaking English after being subjected to my Franglais. After checking, in we went to our impressively appointed neighbouring rooms, complete with TV, microwave and sitting/dining area.

We bought food from the refrigerators in the gourmet bar and carried the packs of soup, pesto pasta and fresh bread upstairs and heated it in the microwave in our room. We sat at the table eating and discussing our plans for the following day. I put on the TV, typically French, the news channels were all in French and so rapid that I found it difficult to follow. Then the news cut to something we recognised, with pictures of rioting Asian youths in London and several other cities, the commentary said: *'Les émeutes suivant des attaques aux communités asiatiques....'* - The riots followed attacks on the Asian communities. This is what we saw the start of on Sunday, and now the reaction was setting in. The TV then cut to a familiar figure, Sinclair. We could not follow his speech as it was dubbed into French, but it did not take a genius to work out what he would be saying, 'The problems in society caused by incomers who did not consider themselves to be British or accept a British way of life... then he would go on about the values of our forefathers which had made Britain great.' I could hear the measured, reasonable tones of his educated voice, even though it was drowned out by the French commentary.

'I can't believe that we've come all the way to France, only for that bloody man to dog our footsteps,' Lisa exclaimed.

'You can see his strategy; use Storm45 to stir up trouble in the Asian communities, then when they respond to the provocation, he uses it to blacken non-British residents.'

'He'll get away with it too, as long as people don't make the link between the BNRA and Storm45, and the troublemakers don't get caught.'

'It's worse than that, once riots like that start, they develop a life of their own and will go on without the initial provocation, making the ethnic communities look bad and the government ineffective. You've got to give him credit, he's a clever bastard. What's worse is, it'll work and people will turn to him as the man to keep law and order.'

The news was too depressing, so we bought in an American movie and watched it in companionable silence before Lisa retired to her own room for the night.

Chapter 12

Breakfast was croissants and coffee in Lisa's room at 8.00 the next morning. A quick internet search gave us the address of the St Denis internment camp; again I drove as Lisa punched our destination into the satnav. The sun reflected off the windscreens of the Parisian traffic, as we fought our way through the mayhem that was the rush hour. I swore as I swerved to avoid a manic French motorist in a Citroen.

'Shit, what the hell does that fuckwit think he's doing? I'm bloody glad we're not trying to get any closer to the centre, that'd be deeply scary.'

Lisa laughed at my indignation.

'Fine for you, it's not your car these lunatics are trying to wreck; it's like a destruction derby.'

We eventually pulled into the car park of the camp museum. We got out and surveyed the camp. Two-storey wooden huts surrounded a central square, the whole camp being encompassed by rusting barbed wire and the odd guard tower. We followed the gravel path in through the gate.

'At least it doesn't have *Arbeit macht frei* over that gate.' I commented.

Lisa looked at me quizzically.

'It's what was over the gates of the concentration camps, the old lie – 'work sets you free.''

We walked around the museum, looking at exhibits and photographs that chronicled the lives of the inmates. Compared to Prisoner of War camps and the concentration camps and death camps, the inmates her, were lucky. With extra rations from the Red Cross, the internees had a reasonable diet and had sports facilities and other luxuries, though having a thousand men confined to this camp would have been friendly to say the least. After an hour, we had exhausted the museum and looked for someone who would help us with our enquiries.

A young man was crossing the central yard; he had dark hair, an aquiline nose and wore black framed spectacles. I approached him and began to explain in halting French what we required.

'Perhaps it would be better if we spoke in English.' He told me with only the slightest hint of an accent. Lisa giggled as I coloured. 'Can I 'elp you Monsieur and Mademoiselle?' He noticed Lisa and acknowledged her with a smile.

She seized the opening. 'Actually, we've heard that you have records here that relate to the British internees that were imprisoned here. I'm Lisa Mann and this is my associate, Ian West'

'That is true Mademoiselle. The Nazis were nothing, if not efficient and left behind detailed records relating to all the internees. When the camp was liberated, all these archives came into our possession. I am Guy Lefebre, the curator of this museum.'

'We're trying to find out about one internee, in particular. His name was William Howard Miller; he would have been about 31 years old,' I said.

'Do you 'ave 'is prisoner number?'

'I'm sorry we don't, is that a big problem?' Lisa fluttered her eyelashes at him. I tried not to laugh at the effect it had on the young man.

'No, it would just be easier as the Nazis catalogued all the inmates by camp number. It is still possible to find one man, but it is a little more difficult. If you would follow me, I'll take you up to the archive.

The archive was stored in boxes arranged on shelves along the side of a long room that must have been a dormitory. Alongside the shelving, there were a number of filing cabinets containing overall lists along with files and photographs recording each inmate; with over a thousand records to search, this was going to take some time.

'As you do not 'ave the number of this internee, may I suggest you start with the admissions lists, that will give you 'is number, then it will be easier to locate his file,' Guy advised.

'That sounds a good idea, where do we start?' I asked.

'With these files,' Guy said, indicating a series of box files. 'I am afraid they are listed in arrival order, so it could take you a while. I will return in an hour to see 'ow you are doing.'

I took down the first box file and passed half of its contents to Lisa'. There was a table at the other end of the room and we settled there to our task. The records were in German, but it was not difficult to work out the column headings. Name, camp number, nationality, date of entry into the Ilag and a column, usually empty, indicating date of release or transfer.

'I read somewhere that this is where John Amery tried to get recruits for the Legion of St George, or the British Freikorps, effectively a British division of the SS,' Lisa told me, trying to impress me with her knowledge.

I came across a Miller, but he was Philip, not our William Howard. We had been scanning the lists for three quarters of an hour, when Lisa exclaimed, 'I've got it!'

'Come on then, what does it say?'

'Number 436558, Miller, William Howard, British, arrived 25th July 1940 but it says released 19th September 1940. He was only here for two months. Where the fuck did he go then?'

'Perhaps we'll find out when we see his file.'

Guy arrived ten minutes later to see how we were going. When we gave him Miller's number, he crossed to the third filing cabinet and opened a drawer. He perused the files for a moment and then withdrew a thin brown manila folder. He handed it to me. The first thing that caught my eye was a black and white photograph that was instantly recognisable. It was our Miller. The rest if the slim file consisted of two sheets of typed paper. I looked at them, they were all in German.

'Could you translate these please,' I asked Guy. 'My German is not up to it.'

He read through the two sheets silently.

'To summarise, William 'Oward Miller was interned here for two months in 1940. It appears 'e was released in September 1940.'

'How could he be released?' Lisa asked. 'Surely the Germans were not going to allow a British national to wander about occupied France unsupervised.'

'The first page is the standard admission form, listing details, height, description, occupation. The second page is an order for his release into the custody of Gruppenführer Sepp Dietrich of the SS Leibstandarte Adolf 'Itler. It is a little strange, it says 'ere that Wilhelm Miller was a Hauptsturmführer of the Allgemeine SS. It is signed by Reinhard Heydrich, 'ead of the RHSA.'

'RHSA?' Lisa enquired.

'Reich Main Security Office, he was head of the SD, Gestapo, the criminal police and the foreign intelligence service.' I said, ever the teacher.

'It appears that your Monsieur Miller 'ad some very powerful friends.'

'Do you know how we could find out more about Miller's role in the SS?' Lisa asked Guy.

'I would think that, if you are to find anything, it would be in the Berlin Document Centre in Germany, but if you do not read German, it would be very difficult for you.'

We thanked Guy and set off back to our hotel to get lunch and decide what to do next. Over a lunch of fresh orange juice, French bread and cheese, we reviewed our options.

'We could head off to Berlin; we could be there the day after tomorrow, if we drove. But what could we achieve there if we can't read German? The records will mean nothing to us,' I offered.

'It's a problem. There is a freelance I know, we sometimes use him, but he doesn't come cheap. We could either get him to do the research for us, or we go to Berlin and use his help as a translator. What do you think?'

'What's this guy going to cost us?'

'I could give him a ring and see.' Lisa pulled out her mobile and began to scroll through names. 'Here we are, Franz Wolfe.' She paused then, 'Hello Franz, it's Lisa, Lisa Mann…..Yes….I need someone to help me research one particular SS man in the Document Centre in Berlin…….Yes, how much would you need to take this commission on......shouldn't take more than a day or two...can't we get that down a little, we don't have a big budget for this....Okay, I'll ring you back.' She turned to me and said, 'Whether we go or not, he would want £250 a day. I could raise enough for one day, could you cover the other?'

'Yeah, I think so, Jane and I still have a joint account, so whatever I spend, it's less she'll be able to take from me. She's taken everything else, my life, my home and my self respect, so yeah, let's go for it.'

'Do we go to Berlin or head back to London and wait for Franz to check in?'

'We'd just be wasting money if we went. Let's be honest, we don't have a lot to offer.'

'Okay, I'll ring him back, you never know, he might have something for us by the time we get home. It's too late to get to the tunnel today, so the earliest we cold get home is tomorrow.'

'Don't forget to warn him about Miller's trick of translating his name, like he did in Spain.'

She phoned Franz back and made the arrangements. He would go over to the Centre in Lichterfelde that afternoon and begin the search. We decided to check out of the hotel and make our way towards Calais, in order to catch the first shuttle the next day. At Amiens we stopped to eat, finding a pleasant little creperie on the bank of the River Somme itself, close to the cathedral. I took a detour to show Lisa the memorial at Thiepval to the missing from the Battle of the Somme. We walked around the memorial, built of brick and 45 metres in height; it had the names of over 73,000 British and South African dead who had no known grave. Lisa looked at the long lists of names, her blue eyes filling with tears. As she read one inscription, Mann, D.A. Private London Regiment, I saw a tear trickle down her cheek.

'That's my brother's name,' she sniffed.

I showed her the book that carried the details of all the names on the memorial. When she found that Private Mann, was, indeed, a Daniel Alexander and like her brother was twenty-one, she just stood there with her head bowed, until she regained some composure.

'You know how to show a girl a good time, Ian,' she said, dabbing her eyes with a tissue.

'Yeah,' I said bitterly, 'that's obviously what Jane thinks.' To my surprise I realised that I was no longer simply upset, but I was angry at what Jane had done to me. I did not hate her, but I hated what she had done, she had robbed me of my self-respect. I realised for the first time that my marriage really was over. By seeing another man, Jane had done the one thing that I could not forgive. Despite being tempted at times, I had always been faithful to Jane and I realised that I put a high value on that fidelity. It dawned on me that the gnawing pain inside me had eased, to be replaced by a vacuum. I was not sure whether that was better or worse.

'Ian.....Ian!' I snapped out of the depth of my thoughts. 'Are you okay, you've got that thousand yard stare again.'

'I'm okay, I've just made a decision, I'm going to get on with my life. Jane has crossed a line, there's no going back. I have to move on, I'm just not sure where to.'

'Good for you, Ian, you can't let her ruin your life.'

'I told you, I'm moving on, but I still don't know what sort of life I have left to me. I'll just have to play it by ear, one day at a time. It's a bit like being an alcoholic, only without the alcohol. The real problem is, I still can't think about the future, I can't see beyond tomorrow.'

We set off once more and found a cheap motel outside Calais and at just before eight the following morning we were on the shuttle back to England.

Chapter 13

Back in the Hackney flat, Lisa checked her email, but there was nothing yet from Franz. There was, however, a message from Matt.

Hi Lisa

I'm back from the US, though a bit jetlagged. Give me a ring 077653986870

Matt

She showed me the text of the email and then pulled out her mobile and dialled. She paused for a minute and I heard a distant voice answer.

'Hello, Matt? Hi it's Lisa, how are you? It's been ages...When did you get back?...Good flight?...Yeah, he's here with me...Yeah I'll tell him...Actually, we want a favour...Where?...Okay, in an hour. See you then, bye.'

'Well?'

'He sends his regards...'

'And?'

'He'll meet us in a coffee bar in Camden, in an hour. Let's get going.'

'Hey, slow down, I'm nearer fifty-five, than twenty-five.'

'You've always done that, put yourself down and claimed you're old. Ian, you're anything but. I know some thirty year olds who are older in outlook and behaviour than you. You underestimate yourself.'

'Okay, you've caught me,' I laughed. 'Let's go.'

The coffee bar was a small, dingy, Italian owned café off Camden High Street. Inside was better than the outside, with clean tables along the wall and two booths at the back. There was the delicious aroma of roasting coffee. Matt was waiting for us, seated in one of the booths. He stood to greet us. He looked exactly as I remembered him. At five feet eight, he was shorter than me and much slimmer. He was wearing an expensive suit and an open-necked white shirt. He sported a surprisingly healthy tan for a self-confessed computer nerd. I looked at his face and saw the signs of fatigue that was probably the result of jetlag. His long face broke into a smile and his eyes twinkled as he looked Lisa up and down. I noticed that despite his youth, the curly blonde hair was thinning on top.

'How are you both, it's good to see you.'

'Hi Matt, it's been a long tim,' I said shaking his hand.

'Yeah, far too long. Lisa!!' He swept Lisa up in a huge hug that threatened to envelop her completely. 'This place doesn't look much, but it serves the best coffee in London and there's free internet access.' He called out to the barista 'Francesca, tre cappuccini, per favore.'

The barista, a plain dark haired girl of about seventeen, broke into a smile. 'Si, Signor Matt.' She turned away and began to fiddle with the complex machine that proceeded to gurgle and hiss.

'Okay,' Matt said, 'let's cut to the chase. You wanted a favour.'

'You've become more direct and to the point than I remember from school.' I pointed out.

'Something I learned in business, time is money, you can't waste one if you want to make the other.'

'Well Matt,' Lisa began 'we're investigating an interesting historical problem.'

He pulled a face: Matt had always hated history, despite my best efforts to inspire him. If it did not involve computers or maths, Matt hadn't wanted to know.

'Well,' she went on, 'we've hit a problem. There's this nursing home in Sussex. We wanted to know who had been paying an old woman's bills up to when she died twenty years ago, but they won't play ball with us. We've been meeting a lot of obstruction throughout this project and we don't know why.'

'And how do I come into this?'

'All the nursing home records are held on their computer..' I paused.

'And you want to know if I can...locate...information for you. I try to avoid the term hack these days, now I've gone respectable.'

'Basically, yes.'

'I gave up that sort of thing a long time ago, it causes too much trouble.' He looked at me with steely blue eyes. 'But I haven't forgotten how much I owe you; I'd have been kicked out and never got to uni and got all this, if it hadn't been for you.' He waved a hand indicating his suit and Rolex watch. He paused as Francesca arrived with the coffee. Once she had retreated he went on. 'I suppose I could do it, it's almost worth it to see Lisa again. I had such a thing for you at school, you know.' Lisa looked uncomfortable and opened her mouth to say something. 'It's okay, don't worry I'm long over it,' he said. 'I'm getting married next month, to Charlotte Peters, you remember her.' Lisa nodded. I looked blank.

'You wouldn't know her.' he said to me, 'She didn't attend our school, but went to one on the other side of town, but she ran with our crowd. You'll both have to come to the wedding.'

'Look Matt,' I said, 'I don't want to screw your life up by asking you to do something illegal. My life is screwed enough, without me wanting to screw up someone else's.' Out of the corner of my eye I saw Lisa mouth 'wife,' and make a gesture over her shoulder with her thumb.

'Hey, I'm really sorry, Sir, that's harsh.'

'I'll get over it...eventually. And it's Ian, you left school a long time ago.'

'Okay Ian, I can do it easily. I doubt there's much risk; I can't see a nursing home having too much in the way of internet security. I'll be in and out without leaving a trace. Who and where are they and what's the name of the old lady?'

Lisa handed over the details she had written out on a sheet of paper.

'I've got meetings all day tomorrow, I've just opened an office here in London and things are a bit crazy, but I'll try to have a look at it the day after, that okay?'

'If you're sure, anytime over the next few days would be fine. Thanks a lot Matt, it's very good of you.' Lisa told him.

'No worries, just don't be a stranger, keep in touch. And I meant what I said, I'd like you to come to the wedding, I'll email you invitations.'

We finished our coffee, Matt was right, it really was very good. Matt, however, had to get back to work, so we parted with his promise to be in touch soon. Once back in Hackney, we checked again to see if there was any response from Franz. There was. The email read:

Hi Lisa,

Initial findings. I have located a file that I believe is your man. You were right. He went by the name of Muller. I'm fairly certain that he is your man, not many Germans have the middle name of Howard! I have copies of the whole file and I will translate it tonight and send you the English version tomorrow morning. What I have so far is his rank, Hauptsturmführer, dating from 1933. There does not seem to be anything then until 1940. After that it goes on to list his postings during the war and his promotion to Sturmbannführer, what you would call Major in 1942 and Obersturmbannführer or Lieutenant Colonel in 1944.

I will be in contact tomorrow.

Franz.

Lisa looked excited. 'Now we are getting somewhere. I can't wait for the full brief tomorrow. What a bastard Miller must have been, an Englishman in the SS.'

'He was half German remember, divided loyalties and all that. He wasn't the only one anyway. Ever hear of the British Freecorps, or the Legion of St George?'

Lisa nodded. 'They were a Waffen SS unit recruited from British and Commonwealth prisoners of war.'

'That's right, I don't think there were many, fifty or so, but that shows that friend Miller was not on his own.'

There was nothing to do until Franz delivered, so Lisa settled down in front of the TV and I began to read the free newspaper I had been handed on the tube. The front page was full of Sinclair making the most of the situation. The main story covered a speech he had given in Blackburn, attacking the insular communities who were causing such disorder on the streets. He went on to question the insularity of those groups, suggesting that if they did not want to assimilate and be part of British society, then perhaps they should find another place where they could accept the culture. He had gone on to praise the French for their insistence that all of their citizens conformed to French values and used the French language for all official purposes. He reiterated the attack of the French President on the wearing of the Burka as a symbol of unacceptable subjugation of Moslem women.

'That's bloody rich!' I exploded. 'As if he gives a rat's arse about the equality of Moslem women!'

Lisa looked up enquiringly.

'Sorry,' I said, 'it's that smarmy bastard Sinclair going off on one again. There's something about that man that brings out the worst in me.' I showed her the article.

'See what you mean,' she said 'I wouldn't bet on British women having equality if he has his way, never mind Moslem women. You're right, I just can't see why people don't see through him.'

'You can thank the right-wing press, they're always willing to publicise his views and polish his image. It's not that surprising; the Daily Mail supported Moseley's Blackshirts for a time in the Thirties. This is the same. It's a pity that no-one can pull back the curtain of his image and let people see what lies beneath.'

The next morning, we both woke early, excited by the prospect of Franz's juicy email. Due to the time difference, it was already waiting in Lisa's inbox.

Hi Lisa,

I spent all last night translating Herr Miller's record. You owe me, and more than just the fee we agreed!

Miller became a member of the Allgemeine SS in February 1933. I cannot account for why, but he joined with the immediate rank of Hauptsturmführer, which is very unusual. So was his membership form, which was signed by Reinhard Heydrich, the Deputy Head of the SS. Despite his auspicious start, he seems to disappear until September 1940, when he is listed as a member of the Liebstandarte SS Adolf Hitler, where he is recorded as an aide to Obergruppenführer Sepp Dietrich. He served in the Greek campaign, before being transferred to Berlin in June 1941 to become adjutant to Reinhard Heydrich at the RHSA. When Heydrich was appointed Reichsprotektor of Bohemia and Moravia in September 1941, Miller, or Muller as he is recorded, went with him to Prague. As Heydrich's adjutant, he helped plan and direct much of the purge that followed the Night and Fog Decree. Over six thousand political opponents and resistance helpers simply disappeared in the occupied territories. Many were executed or died in concentration camps. Muller next appears in January 1942, when Heydrich chaired the Wannsee Conference, at the same time he was promoted to Sturmbannführer. In April 1942, he was sent by Heydrich to oversee work at the concentration camp at Birkenau. He was still there, when Heydrich was wounded by assassins in May 1942. He seems to have returned to Prague and was with Heydrich when he died of his wounds in June. Muller was one of the officers in command of the reprisals at Lidice later that month. He then returned to Birkenau, where he spent the next two years as an 'advisor' to Rudolf Höss, the Commandant. In August 1944 in the wake of the July Bomb Plot, he was recalled by Kaltenbrunner to the RHSA office in Berlin. It was at this time that he was promoted to Obersturmbannführer. He remained in Berlin until February 1945; he travelled to Munich in March where he is listed as missing. The Allies searched for Muller in the aftermath of the war, he was actively pursued by the Nuremberg investigators, but no trace of him was ever found. I hope this helps your research, I will email you my invoice later.

Franz

'There's a lot here that goes right past me,' Lisa declared. She scanned the email. 'What was the Wannsee Conference?'

'The conference Heydrich chaired where they decided on the Final Solution to the Jewish question. It's the place where the Nazis decided to murder all the Jews in Europe. If I remember rightly they produced a list of each country in Europe and how many Jews lived there, a sort of wish list, or maybe death list would be closer.'

'Nice. So Miller was one of the creators of the Holocaust. The next bit I don't know about is Lidice. And don't look at me like that, the course you taught me ended in 1939!'

'Okay, okay, fair comment. Lidice was a village in Czechoslovakia. When Heydrich died after an attack by the Czech resistance, one of the assassins was traced to the village. All of the men were shot, the women and children sent to concentration camps and the village was destroyed. Only a few of the women and children survived to return after the war. It's one of the most famous war crimes.'

'Shit, was there a war crime this guy wasn't involved in?'

'I'm afraid it's even worse. You do realise what was meant by him spending time at Birkenau?' Lisa shook her head. 'It's what most people refer to as Auschwitz, the big extermination camp with the gas chambers and crematoria. Up to 1,500,000 people were murdered there.'

'What do you think happened to him, when he disappeared?'

'My guess is that either he was killed in the fighting or he could have just lost himself amongst the British prisoners who were being released from P.O.W. camps. The Allied war crimes investigators were looking for a German called Muller, not an Englishman called Miller, even if he didn't adopt a completely different name.'

'You mean he could have got away with it and returned to Britain?'

'I don't know, but it's quite possible.'

'How can we find out?'

'I don't think there's any way. Better investigators than you and me couldn't find him at the time, with all the resources at their disposal. It's even possible that Odessa could have helped him disappear.'

'Odessa?'

'A supposed organisation of former SS officers, formed just before the end of the war to help SS officers escape prosecution for war crimes. They're the ones that supposedly helped Mengele, the Auschwitz doctor of death, to escape.'

'So it's a dead end?'

'Looks like it. We could find out more about his time at Birkenau, there's a big archive at Krakow in Poland, the nearest city to Auschwitz. But as to his fate, yes, it's a dead end.'

Chapter 14

We spent two hours fruitlessly debating whether it was feasible to continue with our investigation, when we were interrupted by the ringing of my mobile. I looked at it; Jane's picture appeared on the screen. I was tempted not to answer, but I slid open the phone.

'Hello Jane.'

'Ian, thank God I've got you at last. I tried yesterday, but all I got was voicemail. Didn't you check your messages?'

'No, sorry. I'm in London, I was probably on the underground when you called yesterday.'

'It's not important. The house has been broken into, they've left the place in a terrible mess. The police have been in, but they're not a lot of help.'

'Do you need me to come home?'

'It would be helpful. Where are you anyway?'

'I didn't think that mattered to you any more.' I was not going to admit that I was staying with Lisa. Jane would get the wrong impression - she had always been suspicious of my relationship with Lisa and I was not going to give her any more ammunition than I had to.

'There's no need to be like that, Ian!'

'Sorry love, things are still a bit raw. Give me a couple of hours and I'll be with you.' I hung up.

'Problems?' Lisa asked.

'You could say that. My house has been broke into in my absence. That was Jane on the phone. I think I'll have to go home for a day or so to sort things out.'

'Of course you must, I'll see if there's any more to be done about Miller. I'll get you a key, so you can get in if I'm out. The code to disarm the alarm is 1212.' She went into her room and returned with a key. 'Go on, you get off, I'll see you when things are sorted out.'

Two hours later I pulled on to the drive of my four bed roomed detached home. It was a typical 1970s house with a clapboard fascia and integral garage. It was home, the place where my children had grown up. The place I would soon lose. Getting out of the Saab, I unlocked the front door and went in. It was a mess. Drawers had been pulled open and emptied all over the floor in the hall.

'Ian, is that you?' Jane's voice came from the living room.

'Yeah, it's me.'

I went into the room. Jane was kneeling on the floor, I looked down at the woman I still loved. Jane was three years younger than me, but she did not look a day over forty, she was still a very attractive woman. Her hair was still black, though I knew that dye played its part in that. She had olive skin and was slightly overweight, not unlike me. She looked up at me with her dark brown eyes brimming with tears.

'Oh Ian, they've made such a mess. I can't see that there's much missing, but everything's been ransacked. Every drawer and cupboard has been emptied out; it's almost as if someone was searching for something.'

I lifted her up from the floor and hugged her. At first she accepted the comfort, then pulled away, holding her hands up.

'No. We're not together any more, you mustn't.'

I felt choked. It was my natural reaction to seeing her distressed; I had not meant anything by the gesture. 'I'm sorry, getting used to new ground rules after all these years is difficult. I reacted without thinking.'

'It's alright. What are we going to do?'

'Start clearing up. Make a list of anything missing or damaged for the insurance.'

We worked all afternoon and into the evening, putting things back into drawers and refilling cupboards. There seemed to be nothing missing, which was strange. Although there was a mess, it could have been far worse.

'Look on the bright side,' I said. 'We had to clear things out if we were to sell up and move out. It could have been far worse, you read of cases like this where they crapped all over the floor, at least we haven't got to clear that up.'

'It's not like you to be optimistic.'

I realised I was happy just to be with her again. I could not do this. I would be back to square one again if I allowed myself to be drawn in.

'Look,' I said, 'it's getting dark, you get off to your place.' She had rented a place of her own when she had left me. 'I'll finish up here tonight and tomorrow morning, before I go back to London.'

'What's the fascination with London all of a sudden?'

'I've just been involved in doing some historical research for a friend. It stops me from dwelling on other things.'

'Okay, I'll be off then. I'll see you.' She gave me a peck on the cheek and left. My heart sank as I heard her close the front door. It was still difficult to contemplate life without her and I was deluding myself if I thought I was getting over the break up. I busied myself, clearing up and tidying away. I phoned Lisa to tell her what had happened and warn her I would be back the following afternoon. It was nearly two o'clock in the morning before I finished. I fell into what had once been our bed, but was just mine now. I was asleep almost before the light was off.

The following morning I slept late and was woken by the phone ringing. It was Jane.

'Hi Ian, I just phoned to thank you for coming back so quickly. I know we have our differences, but I know that I can always rely on you if I'm in trouble too. How is the place?'

'It's tidy enough, as far as I can see there's nothing missing or even damaged. It's a real conundrum.'

She rang off and I went to the kitchen to make some coffee. As I was drinking the coffee, I heard the letterbox rattle and the post fell onto the hall carpet. I picked up the trio of envelopes. Two were brown enveloped bills; the third was an expensive cream vellum envelope. On the reverse was printed in an ornate but tasteful font: Ainsworth and Cummings, Solicitors, 117A Leadenhall Street, London EC3A 7AQ.

A solicitor's letter? It could only be Jane serving me with divorce papers, how could she do that to me? She could have said something to me when she saw me yesterday, or even when she called just now. Perhaps Lisa was right and she was a cold-hearted bitch. The woman I had known and loved for over thirty years would never have done that to me. My eyes started to fill with tears as all the dread of the future without Jane swamped my mind once more. I thrust the letter into the inside pocket of my jacket. If that was her attitude, she could bloody wait until I felt like reading it.

I packed a few clean clothes in a holdall and telephoned Lisa to warn her I was on my way back. Locking the house, I climbed into the Saab and headed back to London. Once back in Hackney, I told Lisa about the break-in and the solicitor's letter.

'That letter's a bit harsh Ian; she might have given you some warning. That's a bit dirty, if you ask me.'

'Yeah, well it can wait until I'm ready to deal with it,' I said, pulling the letter out of my pocket and throwing it on the table.

'This break-in sounds strange, Ian, why should anyone search your house like that? Because that's what it sounds like, if nothing was taken.' Lisa said changing the subject to a less emotive one.

'Beats me.'

'You don't think it could be to do with our investigation?'

'Why should it be?'

'I don't know, but look at the way the story was killed by Gerald Aylmer. There seem to be some powerful people who are unusually sensitive about this story and remember what Lucy told you about the Aylmer-Sinclair connection.'

'It's all a bit conspiracy theory isn't it?'

'Suit yourself, but there's definitely something fishy about all this.'

'Even if someone is trying to put me off, I've already told you, it's a matter of academic freedom, I won't be dictated to. Besides, if it was due to our research, it would make far more sense to break in here than my place. I know you've got an alarm and all, but all the same…'

Lisa fell silent for a few seconds, as if struggling to remember something. She looked up at me with her big dark blue eyes wide.

'I know why.'

'Why what?'

'Why no-one has broken in here, even though we've been away. No-one knows I live here. I only moved in here with James three months ago. I've just realised that I never got round to telling them at work that I had a new address. They always use my mobile or email to contact me, so they would not have known and therefore Aylmer would not be able to find out from Seneschal.'

'It's possible, but not likely. I doubt Aylmer has nothing better to do than to burgle us.'

'Okay, have it your own way; so what do we do now then?'

'We could go to Krakow and see if we can find more about Miller's time at Auschwitz.'

'Won't that be a bit expensive?'

'No, when I used to take sixth form visits to Auschwitz, the flights from Luton, with a low-cost airline were quite cheap. Fifty or sixty quid each way, and the hotel we stayed in was clean, comfortable and inexpensive. Give me your laptop.'

A few minutes on the computer revealed that I was right about the cost of flights and the hotel was only about the same cost per night. With Lisa's agreement, I booked flights for the next day and three nights in the hotel; this was about as far as our budget would stretch.

'What are you going to do about that solicitor's letter, Ian?'

'It can wait until we get back, Ainsworth and Cummings will still be there.'

Lisa frowned, 'I know that name from somewhere, but I can't quite recall where. Never mind, it'll come back to me.'

The rest of the afternoon involved packing and finding somewhere that could supply us with Polish zloty at short notice. Mid-morning the next day saw our arrival at Luton Airport. With both of us having no more than a small holdall, which could be carried as hand luggage, check-in was a quick and perfunctory affair. We passed through security and passport control without undue difficulty. The garish orange aircraft took off on time and just over two hours later we disembarked at Krakow airport. With no need to wait for suitcases to be unloaded, we were rapidly processed through passport and customs checks and found ourselves outside the terminal.

'That was a lot easier than the first time I came,' I commented. 'That was in 2001, not too long after the fall of communism. It was all stern faced officialdom and lack of facilities then.'

'Sounds like fun. Thank God for the EU. How do we get into town? Bus or taxi?'

We opted for a taxi, which twenty minutes later dropped us outside our hotel. The hotel stood at the foot of the Wawel hill, with the huge castle that was the home of sixteenth century Polish kings. The steep hill was topped with massive ramparts, over which the three ornate towers of the Wawel cathedral peeked. Opposite the hill was our hotel, the Royal, a three story Art Nouveau building, with an impressive frontage complete with Romanesque columns and pediment. We checked in and went up to our rooms. After a quick wash, we went out in search of a meal. We wandered through the grid pattern streets to the main square, a huge plaza fronted by impressive eighteenth century buildings, surrounding the Sukiennice, the cloth hall in the centre. The evening sun gave the brightly coloured buildings a magical quality. Lisa was entranced.

'This place is awesome,' Lisa exclaimed.

'Yeah, it's sort of like York meets Bavaria or Austria.'

We ate in one of the restaurants in the Sukiennice, sitting outside at a table in the still warm sunshine. It was expensive but worth it.

'Can we explore a bit?' Lisa asked.

'You don't have to ask me, I'm not your father. If you want to explore go ahead.'

Lisa whooped with delight as she discovered the stalls lining the inside of the Sukiennice. She flitted from stall to stall, looking at the inexpensive amber jewellery, the crystal and the collection of tourist trinkets. It was then I realised how young she really was. We had been working side by side as equals and in terms of the support she had given me, she was an adult, but here I saw that the girl that I knew from school was still there. I trekked indulgently behind her as she bought matching silver and amber earrings and necklace for herself and presents for James, her parents and siblings. At last she was all shopped out and we made our way down the hill, past the baroque cathedral to our hotel. I was weary from the travelling, but the shopping expedition had reinvigorated Lisa.

'Come on, let's go into the bar for a drink.' She led the way into the long room that was reminiscent of a German bierkeller, with drinking mottoes painted on the vaulted walls. Lisa ordered a beer and despite the medication, I joined her. Lisa wiped the foam off her top lip with her fingertip and daintily licked it off, 'Where is the archive?'

'It's appropriately enough in Kazimierz, the other side of that main road. It was the Jewish Quarter before the war. A guide pointed it out to me on one of my school trips here. We'll head down there tomorrow morning.'

'Cool.'

We finished off our drinks and retired for the night.

Chapter 15

I slept deeply, helped by the beer until five in the morning, when the first tram rumbled along the main road under my window like a mobile earthquake. After that I dozed, woken intermittently by the passing trams. I cursed myself for forgetting the trams and not requesting a room on the town side of the hotel, away from the noise. At seven, I gave up trying to sleep and showered, shaved and dressed. At eight, I rang Lisa's room.

'Hiya,' she greeted me enthusiastically. 'You ready for breakfast? I've been awake for ages. I don't know why, but I woke up quite early this morning.'

'It's the bloody trams,' I grumbled, 'they start at five. It's like trying to sleep through an earthquake after that.' Lisa laughed.

'Now you sound like my Dad, he's always grumpy if he doesn't get a full night's sleep.'

'Gee thanks!'

She laughed again. 'Come on, let's get breakfast.'

I met her in the corridor outside our rooms and we made our way down to the bar we had drunk in the previous night, that doubled as a dining room. Breakfast was an all-you-can-eat buffet and we both wolfed our food down hungrily. Leaving the hotel, we crossed the main road and walked the half mile into Kazimierz, passing through the central square with its ritual bath house and two synagogues.

'How big was the Jewish population?' Lisa asked. 'This place is huge.'

'At the start of the war, there were around 70,000 Jews in Krakow'

'How many survived?'

'At the end of the war, about 10,000 returned here. It's reckoned that there are only about one hundred Jews here today and most of those aren't practising.'

'Auschwitz?'

'No, most died at an extermination camp just outside town called Plaszow, just across the river. Haven't you seen Schindler's List?'

'The film? That was here?'

'Yes, Schindler's factory is about a mile away, it's a museum now.'

Following the map, we crossed into a side street and followed the road past yet another synagogue to the Holocaust Archive. The heavy wooden door was firmly locked, it was closed. I peered at the sign on the wall outside and consulted my phrasebook.

'I think it says closed. It seems to be open four days a week; today isn't one of them. If I've got it right they're open at 9.00 tomorrow morning. It looks like we've got the day off. What would you like to do?'

'Well....It doesn't feel right to be this near to Auschwitz and not to visit it, to sort of pay our respects. I know you've been loads of times, but would you take me?'

'No problem, if you're sure, it's a pretty grim place. I can't think of anywhere that is more upsetting,' I said, adding to myself, 'Unless you count my home.'

'I'd really like to go and it's where Miller was based for two years, so it is relevant....sort of.'

'Come on then.'

We made our way back to the hotel where a helpful receptionist arranged for us to join a coach party setting off for Oswiecim. We sat together on the coach, watching the Polish countryside pass by.

'It's amazing how many of these houses look Austrian.'

'Yeah, presumably this part of Poland was once part of the Austrian Empire.'

The rural air to the countryside was marred by occasional coal mines that stood out like black scars on the landscape. Forty minutes later we disembarked outside the former concentration camp. We joined a party with an English speaking guide and passed beneath the famous iron gateway with the motto 'Arbeit macht frei' picked out in metal letters above it. We entered the camp, past the double rows of rusty barbed wire suspended from

106

electrical insulators on the concrete posts. The camp itself consisted of a series of brick built two storey barracks on each side of a wide tree-lined boulevard. The guide ushered us into one of the buildings that housed a museum containing the evidence of the holocaust. She recounted how the Jews were transported to Birkenau and selected for slave labour or immediate extermination in the gas chambers. When confronted with the glass container, the size of a water cooler bottle that contained the ashes, which were all that remained of over one million people, Lisa just stood there in stunned silence. She was simply lost in her own thoughts. We made our way through gruesome exhibits, one after another; large display cases of artificial limbs from the victims, shoes, hair brushes and suitcases. We followed the guide up to the first floor and my stomach gave a sickening lurch as I remembered that this was the place where they had on display part of the seven thousand kilos of hair cut from the victims. As we reached the landing outside, Lisa looked into the room and gave a sob; tears filled her eyes and began to trickle down her cheeks. I put my arm round her to comfort her. She made a second attempt to enter the room, but try as she might, she could not get herself across the threshold.

'How could they do that?' she sobbed.

'It's worse, you can't see the cloth they made from the hair from here, that's got to be one of the most obscene things I've ever seen.'

'How do you manage to come back here every year with the Sixth form?'

'Because there's no better way to teach the Holocaust: you can understand it intellectually in the classroom, but when you come here, you understand it emotionally, you feel it. You start to see the Holocaust in terms of individuals rather than simply numbers. You're not the first person I've seen have problems with that room.'

We followed the guide into a room displaying children's' clothes, this was my Achilles heel. I looked at the display case, covered with rose petals left by visitors. Inside I could see the clothes of a baby. It got to me every time, the small shoes. I could see Lucy and Rob when they wore small shoes like that and tears welled up in my eyes. What pathetic excuse for a human being could throw a small child into a gas chamber? I knew the answer, William Howard Miller. Fortunately, Lisa was watching and listening to the guide and I was able to retreat to a corner and mop my eyes before she noticed my moment of weakness. We carried on, exhibit after exhibit, testimony to how low humanity could sink; until we were both emotionally numb by the time we reached the first gas chamber where Russian prisoners were gassed with Zyklon B gas as an experiment to find a more efficient way of mass murder. Lisa had once more sought the comfort of my arm and hugged me close, as if my presence could protect her from the horrors she was seeing.

'I never realised how bad this place was Ian. I'm sorry, I shouldn't have asked you to bring me here after all the emotional turmoil you've been through. I saw your reaction earlier; it was unfair of me to get you to come here.'

'I hoped you hadn't noticed, but don't worry, just for once my unmanliness had nothing to do with my marriage; the kids' clothing always hits me. It's a parent thing. Not your fault.'

At the end of the tour, the guide gave us a few minutes to look in the bookshop before we headed off for Birkenau, some five to ten minutes away. She approached us.

'Your daughter is very affected by what she has seen here.' I did not disabuse her of her assumption.

'It's a very emotive place. How do you do this every day? I find it difficult bringing a group here annually, I can't imagine what it must be like to come to work here every day. How do you manage it?'

'It gets easier with time, but no-one can come here and not be affected. Why do I do it? Because someone has to, someone must tell people what happened here.'

I understood, but I still didn't think I could do it. We boarded the coach once more and took the short journey to Auschwitz II, Birkenau. The guide got us off the coach and led us along the railway track, through the famous gatehouse. We followed the track to the disembarkation platform, where sixty five years earlier, the SS selected who was to live and who was to die. The guide was going through a description of the selection process, when a board with pictures of the camp from 1943 caught our attention. There were pictures of the selection, the lines of prisoners making their way into the women's camp or the men's camp, or worse still for a 'shower'. Another picture caught Lisa's attention.

'Look!' she hissed. I looked; it was a picture of four SS officers standing in the camp, smoking.

'What?'

'Look closely'

I scrutinised the photograph. The text said underneath ' *Left to right: Dr. Josef Mengele, Commandant Rudolf Höss, Josef Kramer, Commandant of Bergen-Belsen, and an unidentified officer.*'

'Don't you see? The unidentified officer is Miller.' I looked closely. She was right - concrete proof that Miller had been here. I focused my camera and took a photograph of the picture to have a record of our discovery.

The guide had already moved off and we hurried to catch her up. She had led the group into the women's camp, with its brick-built barracks. We entered one of the buildings and saw the three levels of brick shelves that served as bunks for at least nine people. Even in summer, the wind blew across the plain and cut like a knife. The barracks was dark and draughty, Lisa shivered in the gloom and I put my arm round her again.

'If it's like this in summer, what was it like in winter, wearing only those thin striped uniforms?' she asked.

'Bloody cold! The kids I brought here came in February and March and I was freezing, despite wearing a thick army parka.'

We followed the guide out of the barracks, feeling like a child in a crocodile line on a primary school visit. The next building was a toilet block with limited washing facilities and a long concrete topped bench with back-to-back lines of round holes running along it.

'The inmates were tattooed with a number on their right arms, Auschwitz was unique in that. Once done, it was a breach of discipline to use someone's name; only people had names, the inmates were subhuman, animals. Emptying these latrines, the

109

Scheissekommando, was considered to be a prized job, because the guards did not come in here because of the smell and fear of disease. The work party could work without supervision and be people, rather than animals.'

'Scheissekommando?' Lisa asked. 'Doesn't that mean.....'

I nodded.

'Shit squad. The only time in this vile place you could be a human being was when you were up to your thighs, shovelling shit.'

The guide shepherded the group out of the building and back to the railway line. We followed behind the group.

'Why the tattoos and all of this hassle?' Lisa asked.

'The process dehumanised the inmates, breaking them mentally, just as the poor diet and low calorific intake, allied to hard manual labour broke them physically. They were less likely to cause trouble or resist.'

'And Miller was involved in all of this. What a heartless bastard!'

'Not sure exactly what his role was, that's why we're here isn't it? There were jobs that didn't involve any contact with the inmates, administration and so on.'

'He was still part of the system, either way. I'm getting to hate him. The more we find out about him, the more loathsome he seems to become.'

The guide was pointing out the area where the store rooms containing the possessions of the murdered Jews had been. These had been known to the inmates as Kanada, the land of plenty. Then it was down to the ruins of the gas chambers and the crematoria. Ahead of us, a party of uniformed Israeli soldiers stood clustered round a rabbi outside the crematorium, heads hung in mourning.

'It's strange,' Lisa whispered, 'I feel as if I want to apologise to them for what happened here. I wasn't born and it wasn't my country that did it, but I still want to tell them I'm sorry.'

'Our fathers' generation, or grandfathers' in your case, have much to answer for; they knew what was happening here and did nothing to stop it. Burke got it right, all that is necessary for evil to triumph, is that good men do nothing.'

We stood along the side of a rectangular pool of muddy water next to the gas chamber and crematorium ruins, as the guide recited how even the ashes from the crematoria were disposed of in these pools and flushed into the river. Lisa hung her head, then caught sight of the white flecked earth underfoot.

'Is that chalk in the soil?'

'I'm afraid not, that's burned bone from the crematorium.' Lisa stepped back hurriedly, her pretty face drained of its colour.

'Can we get away from here?'

I put my arm round her, as she led us over the cobblestones towards the monument that stood at the back of the camp. There, twenty grey granite slabs, inscribed in every major European language, were placed in the ground. We walked along until we found the one in English. In a low voice Lisa read the inscription aloud.

'For ever let this place be a cry of despair and a warning to humanity, where the Nazis murdered about one and a half million men, women, and children, mainly Jews from various countries of Europe. Auschwitz-Birkenau 1940 - 1945'

For a few minutes we stood in silence with our heads bowed, then turned and began to make our way back along the railway track towards the gatehouse. Ahead of us our party had separated into small groups, walking in silence, heads bowed, isolated in their own thoughts. Lisa and I walked together; I felt her hand slip into mine, looking for some human contact and reassurance, as she struggled to come to terms with what she had seen. Once through the gateway, we boarded the coach that set off for Krakow. Lisa turned in her seat to face me.

'That was the worst place I have ever been.'

'I did warn you, it's a monstrous place. You can't go there and remain unaffected, not if you've got any humanity.'

'It's strange; I found the first camp worse than the second, despite the horrible things that happened there.'

'Yes, I know, I think it's because by the time you get to Auschwitz II, you're emotionally bankrupt, there's nothing left, you just feel numb. It sinks in later. The first time I went there, I was so emotionally traumatised that it took a week for everything to sink in, and then it hit me like a train. It's better that you get upset while you are there, it sort of gets it out of your system.'

'I think I'll be having nightmares for weeks.'

'You won't be the first. Remember Miss Best? She had nightmares when we returned from the excursion last year.'

'Let's hope I don't have them then.'

She leaned her head against my shoulder and remained there for the duration of the journey. It was then I realised how much Lisa had come to mean to me. If it hadn't been so sad, I could have easily fallen in love with her, but a man in his fifties, with a young woman in her twenties reeked of desperation. Lisa already had a man in her life; she had no need of me. Nevertheless, I knew that I would give my life to protect her, just as I would for my own children.

Chapter 16

We disembarked from the coach at the mediaeval barbican and walked into the town. After returning to the Royal for a quick shower, I led Lisa once more into the former Jewish town of Kazimierz.

'Where are we going?' she asked.

'Wait and see; somewhere appropriate after today.'

I took her down into the old town to the square with an open green area in the middle, surrounded by an iron fence in the shape of menorahs, the seven branched candelabra that was symbolic of Judaism. At the head of the square was a three-storey building built of old brick, buttressed by blocks of white stone. As I led her in through the doorway to the restaurant within, the sounds of accordion and fiddle music drifted from inside, that mixture of the joyous and the soulfully plaintive that epitomised Jewish folk music. I took her into the dimly lit restaurant, where we were led to a table lit by candles. The trio of players, an accordionist, violinist and double bassist made conversation difficult and unnecessary. I ordered for us both and in the gaps between the music, we talked about what we had seen that day. The Jewish cuisine, whilst not kosher, was still good and traditional. Lisa ate hungrily, I picked at my food; I never felt like eating after Auschwitz. Nevertheless the Polish beer that accompanied the meal went down well and after a visit to Auschwitz, I felt I had earned it.

At the end of the meal, we left the restaurant and walked through the darkened streets. A light rain was falling and Lisa huddled beside, me sheltering under my jacket. The streets were mostly deserted as we made our way back to the hotel. Damp but happy, I led the way into the vaulted bar and we ordered another beer as a nightcap. Ascending the stairs, we stopped in the dimly lit corridor outside Lisa's room.

'The archive tomorrow, then?' she asked

'Yes, it'll be open if we get there at ten. Can I borrow your laptop tomorrow?'

'Sure, what do you want it for?'

'I thought I'd upload the photograph I took that had Miller/Muller in it. It's possible the archivist might be able to tell us where it came from.'

'Good idea.' She lingered outside her room with the key in the lock, reluctant to leave me. 'Ian, thanks for today, I won't say it was fun, but I wouldn't have missed it for the world. It'll be something I'll always remember.'

She turned and hugged me. I wrapped my arms around her, never wanting to let her go, but I knew that if I was not careful, I would do something stupid that could change our relationship for ever. I kissed her on the top of her head and let her go.

'You're welcome, kid, have a good night, don't have nightmares.' I unlocked my door and went into my room, closing the door behind me without a backwards glance.

Part of me was kicking myself for not taking the chance Lisa had appeared to offer, but the rational part of my mind told me that even if she had responded, it would have been a mistake that we would both come to regret. Even so, as I climbed into bed and turned out the lights, I could not help feeling if only...

The 5.00 a.m. tram shook me back to consciousness after what felt like only a few minutes sleep. I swore foully and turned over, burying my head beneath the pillow. It had no effect; the next tram rumbling by roused me from the light doze I had managed. By 7.00 I had given up and went for a shower. Looking in the mirror, I noticed that I was looking rather hollow-eyed - early mornings did not agree with me. Being with Lisa might make me feel young again, but my body did not fully agree.

At 7.45 I called Lisa's room. She answered brightly.

'Hiya, Ian, you ready for breakfast?'

'Sure am. Can I come round and upload that photograph first?'

'You're welcome. I'll fire up the laptop now.'

I gathered the camera and a USB card reader and knocked at her door.

'It's open, come in.'

Lisa was sat on her bed, a picture in blue jeans with the legs rolled up to her shapely calves and a light blue strappy top that showed off her figure to its best. Her hair hung damply round her shoulders and she looked good, despite the minimal make-up. She waved a hand towards the laptop in the table beside her.

'It's all yours.' I removed the flash card from my Nikon SLR and inserted it into the reader, plugging it into the port at the side. A moment later we were able to view the photograph blown up to fill the screen. The photograph was in black and white as one might expect from the 1940s, nevertheless, it was possible to zoom in and examine every detail of the image of the man we knew as William Miller. The blonde hair was still there, but closely cropped beneath the cap with its deaths-head badge. His face appeared a little more gaunt than in the Spanish photograph, which gave his nose a more aquiline appearance than I remembered. He looked stockier than he had earlier. His uniform carried the SS collar badge showing four small rectangular pips, matching Miller's known rank of Sturmbannführer - I recognised the rank badge from our previous research. On his left breast pocket was a silver badge showing a German helmet with a swastika over crossed swords and a star on which there seemed to be some sort of white cross, but the detail was blurred.

'What's the importance of those badges there?' Lisa asked, pointing to his left breast pocket.

'I'm not sure, but if you look closely, the other officers don't have it. It's beneath his medal ribbons, so it doesn't appear to be that kind of award. It's a pity there's no internet access here. We'll just have to come back to it later.'

We left the room and descended the stairs to the dining room. In the reception area I noticed a pay-as-you-surf internet machine. As soon as we had eaten, I sat at the machine and pushed in the relevant zloty coins. The machine activated and I used google to research Nazi military badges. There was no sign of the star, but on the third screen of images I saw the silver badge with the helmet. Clicking on the image I was taken to a militaria collectables web site.

'Well?'

'It seems to be a wound badge.'

'Miller had been wounded?'

'Apparently.'

Returning to her room, we examined the image on Lisa's laptop again. Zooming in more closely, we examined the picture of Miller. Starting from his head, we worked down the picture, looking for more detail.

'Look!' Lisa was pointing to Millers left hand that was holding a cigarette.

'What?'

'His hand, he's missing his little finger. I'm sure that finger was not missing in the Spanish photograph. Move over!' She took my place at the keyboard. 'I scanned the Spanish picture into the laptop while you were back in Suffolk. Here!'

She called up the original image and we leant over the screen. It was not easy to make out as the image pixilated as we zoomed in, but we could see enough to be sure that he had a full complement of digits on his left hand.

'It's a good bet that's what he got his wound badge for. I'd have thought it unusual; most missing fingers would have come from frostbite on the Russian Front, but he was never there. An explosion would have removed more fingers, unless he was just very lucky. Von Stauffenberg, you'd know him as Tom Cruise, lost a complete hand and two fingers.'

'You're treating me as blonde again! I remember what you taught us about Stauffenberg and the July bomb plot. I always thought how unlucky it was not to kill Hitler. He had the luck of the devil, a bit like Miller in some ways.'

'Come on, we'll be late if we hang about here and we might need a complete day in the archives. We have tickets to fly home tomorrow, remember.'

We walked down to Kazimierz once more, a pleasant stroll in the morning sunshine that had replaced the light rain of the night before. This time the wooden doors of the Holocaust Archive were open. We entered into the gloomy exterior. A slender young woman of about Lisa's age, with dark hair and olive skin came up to us.

'Czy mogę ci pomóc?'

'I'm sorry, we don't speak Polish. Do you speak English?' I asked hopefully. The guide books said most young Poles spoke English; it would be just my luck to find the one who did not.

'I do speak some English,' she said in accented English, 'but I am afraid not very well.'

'Your English is much better than our Polish,' I smiled. The young woman smiled in acknowledgement.

'How may I help you?'

'We're researching an SS officer who...er... served in Auschwitz from 1942 to 1944 as an advisor to the Commandant. We were hoping that that you might have information here in your archive.'

'I do not think the word served is the correct term for anyone who committed the atrocities at Auschwitz,' she said stiffly.

'You're right, I could not think of the right word. I did not mean any offence.'

'I understand, I am sorry if I was a little abrupt, but I am sure you can understand that anything to do with Auschwitz is a sore point with anyone of Jewish heritage.' That explained the Mediterranean appearance of the young woman. 'I am afraid that we do get the occasional Holocaust denier here, trying to spread their poison.'

'I can understand that, I've never been able to comprehend how those idiots have the nerve to call themselves historians.' She smiled at this and held out her hand.

'I am Ania.' I shook her hand.

'I am Ian, this is my student Lisa.'

'You teach history?'

'Yes.'

'Our archive is considerable and it does take time to go through the papers.'

Lisa's face fell. 'We only have today; we have to return to England tomorrow.'

'Luckily for you, in the years since the end of Communism, we have scanned many of the documents into our computer to allow more rapid research. If you would come this way, we will see what we can find.' She led us deep into the building and up a flight of stairs to a windowless room in which there were eight computer terminals. She indicated a computer terminal.

'Would you like to work here? There is a database of known names of SS men that you can search and each name you find is linked to the scanned documents we have about that person. Do you read German or Russian, or would you like me to remain and help you?'

'That would be very kind,' Lisa replied. 'I'm afraid we are reasonable historians, but poor linguists, like most English people. We would appreciate your help, if you are free.'

'It is a very quiet day, we have no-one booked in, so unless we get more people arrive unannounced, then I am at your disposal. What was the name and rank of this officer?'

'Wilhelm Muller, Sturmbannführer when he came, he arrived at Auschwitz sometime after May 1942 and was posted back to Berlin in August 1944,' I said.

She gave a sharp intake of breath. 'That is one man I know is in our records. He was a well-known war criminal, who was never brought to justice.' She tapped away at the keyboard.

'There.' She pointed to the screen on which Muller's name appeared with a list of attached links. 'What do you want to know?'

'Everything you can tell us. If possible we would like copies of the relevant documents.'

'I can do that, but there will be a charge of five zloty for each copy.'

'That's no problem. What documents do you have?'

'This is his service record from Auschwitz. This is a report from Konrad Morgen of the ReichsKriminalPolizeiAmt into corruption at the camp. These are testimony from surviving witnesses. This relates to the Russian investigation into Muller as a war criminal. And these are photographs that relate to Muller.'

'Could we start with the photographs?' Lisa asked. 'We have one photograph we think is him that we found displayed in Birkenau.' She pulled out her laptop and woke it. 'There, we're almost sure that this is Muller.'

'Let us see.' She called up a jpeg on the screen, examining the caption underneath. 'This is Muller,' She said, pointing to one of two men in the picture with a number of young women.

'That's definitely him,' Lisa stated. 'Can you print it?'

'Certainly.' Ania pressed a key. 'There, it is done.'

We went on to print five other photographs and then Ania called up and translated Muller's service record for us.

'Muller, arrived Auschwitz on March 24th 1942. He had been sent by Heydrich, it does not appear that he was too welcome, as he was seen as a spy, reporting back to the SD on the lack of progress in converting Birkenau to a death camp. It was Muller who encouraged Commandant Höss to begin using the White House outside the camp as an ad hoc gas chamber. Having overseen the beginning of the extermination, he left here on June 1st for Prague, returning on July 17th. It seems that he had been wounded when he returned, there are attached medical records that show a hand injury caused in action in Czechoslovakia sometime in June, for which he received the silver wound badge. On his return to Birkenau, Muller was the officer responsible for the exploitation of Jewish belongings. He arranged for the finding, cataloguing and collection of Jewish valuables. He was responsible for the storage and "repatriation" of the contents of Kanada. In October 1943 he was one of the officers investigated by Obersturmbannführer Konrad Morgen of the financial crimes section of the RKPA. There is a whole separate document on that. There does not appear to have been enough evidence against Muller, so he remained in his position until 10th August 1944, when he was transferred back to Berlin and the SD on the orders of Obergruppenführer Kaltenbrunner. The file ends there.'

'That's really useful, thanks Ania,' I said. 'What about the report by Morgen into corruption? I saw something about that in a television programme, but that's about as much as I know.'

'And that's a lot more than me!' added Lisa.

'There was great corruption amongst the SS at Birkenau. It came to light when a package containing two kilos of dental gold was intercepted by customs. It had been sent by an officer in Birkenau. There had long been suspicions that there were fewer valuables than expected coming out of Birkenau. There were stories of lockers containing piles of currency from all countries as well as gold, diamonds and pearls. There were also allegations of fraternisation between the SS guards and some of the more attractive female inmates. This led to Morgen's investigation.'

'What does Morgen have to say about Muller?' Lisa asked. Ania called up another document.

'He went to Auschwitz in August 1943, as part of an investigative commission with three other SS officers, Reimers, Bartsch and Dr. Fischer. Along with Commandant Hoess, he made a through tour of the facility, including the gas chambers and crematoria. He describes how he met SS guards in Birkenau and was surprised to find them dozing and staring glassy-eyed. The exception was Sturmbannführer Muller, who seemed to be alert and in control. The practice of having attractive oriental Jewesses cooking and feeding these men, with suspicions that the relationship was more intimate, scandalised Morgen. The excuse was given by Muller that the men had a hard night's work ahead as several transport trains were due for processing. Morgen describes how a locker search found cash and valuables secreted by the men. He estimates that there was a discrepancy of somewhere in excess of fifteen million Reichsmarks, which would be about five million dollars. He names three SS officers he believed to be implicated, Gerhard Palitzsch, Hans Aumeier and Wilhelm Muller. There was enough evidence to court marshal Aumeier and Palitzsch, but the evidence against Muller was destroyed, when the barracks where it was deposited burned down on 7th December 1943. It seems that Muller had powerful political connections and the case against him was then dropped. The missing money, in the form of foreign currency, gold and jewellery was never recovered.'

I whistled, 'Five million dollars in 1943, that's the equivalent of over fifty million dollars today!'

'Convenient that a fire came to Muller's rescue, after his earlier activities,' Lisa commented dryly.

'That's probably what gave him the idea; it also served to remind the powers that be of their debt to him.' I turned to Ania. 'What were the Russian War Crimes charges against him?'

Ania called up the relevant document. 'My Russian is rusty, but I believe this says he was accused of organising and carrying out mass murder, theft and crimes against humanity. However, he was never caught. Russian investigators scoured their occupied zone and alerted American and British investigators, but he was never apprehended.'

This had taken us about four hours, but we now had a fairly comprehensive account of Miller/Muller's activities in Poland. We collected and paid for the documents that Ania had printed for us. Then thanking her for her help, we left the Holocaust Archive and walked out into the afternoon sun.

'Do you think Miller escaped with all of those missing valuables, Ian?'

'I don't know. Even if he escaped with a third share, that's still over fifteen million dollars in today's money. If he had that, he would certainly have had the wherewithal to organise his disappearance in 1945. That's more than enough to create a new identity and re-invent himself after the war. Our problem is that we'll never be able to track him. If the Nuremburg investigators could not trace him in 1945, we haven't much chance after all these years.'

'We've got one advantage; we know that he was really a Brit called Miller. If he survived I'd bet that he swapped being a German for being British, joining the winning side so to speak.'

We found a café in which to have a late lunch and we spent the afternoon typing up our discoveries on Lisa's laptop. The following day saw an uneventful return flight to Luton and a rather more stressful drive through the rush hour traffic to Hackney. We both felt that we had now reached a cul de sac. If Miller had disappeared so successfully in 1945, it was unlikely that we would find any trace of him now.

Chapter 17

Once back in London, both Lisa and I felt rather flat. It was clear that we had reached the end of the line and our time together was coming to an end. Switching on the television to see that Sinclair and the BNRA had increased their standing in the polls in our absence due to the rioting in Bradford, Southall and Leicester, only served to increase our feeling of gloom. Lisa got up to switch off the television - to see Sinclair's smug yet earnest face disappear before we were subjected to yet another of his diatribes at least gave us some satisfaction. Lisa picked up the solicitor's letter from the table where I had left it three days earlier.

'What are you going to do about this, Ian?' she asked. 'You can't go on ignoring it indefinitely. Didn't you always tell me that problems had to be faced up to, not run away from?'

'That applied to adolescent girls, not self-deluding middle aged men.'

'Come on Ian, you've got to deal with it sooner or later. What doesn't kill you makes you stronger.'

'Where did you get that? A motto in a Christmas cracker or a fortune cookie?'

She laughed and tossed the letter over to me. I took a deep breath and with my hands shaking, tore it open, I dreaded what I was about to read, the legal jargon that would end thirty years of marriage and change my life forever. I extracted an expensive sheet of paper. The letter was from Ainsworth and Cummings, solicitors of Leadenhall Street in the City. It simply read:

Dear Mr West,

I would be grateful if you would contact me at the above address, where you may hear something to your advantage.

It was signed with a flourish by David L. Cummings, Managing Partner.

I was shocked; this was not at all what I had expected. I offered Jane a silent apology for my earlier assumptions. I frowned in disbelief, this was the type of letter one might receive when one was about to receive an unexpected inheritance, but I knew for a fact that I had no relatives, or even acquaintances, who could use such a firm of solicitors.

'Well, is it bad?' Lisa asked.

I refolded the letter and slid it across the table to her. She read it and smiled at me.

'Looks like your luck is changing. Maybe Bill Gates has decided to leave all his money to you.'

'Funny. They must have the wrong Ian West. I don't move in the circles that use expensive solicitors like that. I don't know why it didn't occur to me earlier that Jane would not use an upmarket outfit like that. I'm not thinking clearly when it comes to my impending divorce.'

'What are you going to do?'

'I'll give Ainsworth and Cummings a ring tomorrow and find out what this is all about. It'll come to nothing, though.'

She frowned. 'There's still something about that name, Ainsworth and Cummings, but I just can't remember what it is. It's really pissing me off.'

'Stop thinking about it and it'll come back to you. It always works for me.'

We watched some mindless television and retired to our separate rooms for the night. Whilst I was curious about what Ainsworth and Cummings might want, I was more concerned that my time with Lisa was coming to an end and I would no longer be able to avoid the problems that awaited me at home. I was not sure I was ready to face them yet. Could I cope, or would I go back to being the neurotic wreck that had been rescued by Lisa and the mystery of William Howard Miller?

I slept badly, my dread of facing the future, or lack thereof, invading my dreams and making me wake in a cold sweat. I lay awake for hours, my mind going round in circles. I seemed to have just fallen asleep when Lisa knocked on the door and entered with a cup of tea.

'Come on lazybones, it's 9.30.' She looked at me more closely. 'Are you alright? You look a bit rough. If I didn't know better, I would think you were hammered last night and had a hangover.'

'Bad night. I spent the night fretting about the future. Since I've been with you I've been able to put it out of my mind, but occasionally things catch up with me. It's not easy when you have nothing to live for, I've lost everything, there's nothing left to lose.'

'Stop that Ian; you're feeling sorry for yourself again. You haven't lost everything, you've still got a lot to live for, Lucy and Rob for a start and...'

'And what?'

'Me, you've come to mean a lot to me over the past couple of weeks. You are a good friend and I wouldn't want to see anything happen to you. I'd do anything I can to help you and get you through this.'

My eyes misted over with tears. 'Thanks, I've become very fond of you too and I've really appreciated the help and support you've given me.'

'Our adventure's not over yet, we might still get something useful from Matt and you never know, maybe Ainsworth and Cummings are going to tell you that you've inherited a fortune from a distant relative.'

'Yeah, I'll marry a thirty year old slim blonde, just to piss off Jane.'

Lisa laughed. 'Go for it! That's more like the old you, what was it you told me during one of my rucks with Lee, don't get upset, get even!'

'Okay, you're right, I'll stop feeling so sorry for myself and phone Mr Cummings and see what he wants.'

As it turned out, it was not that easy. I could not get beyond Cummings' secretary, who could squeeze me in for an appointment at 4.45 that afternoon. I would have to wait until then.

At 4.30 I found myself walking down Leadenhall Street, partly annoyed by the delay and equally curious about what Cummings wanted with me. Ainsworth and Cummings occupied a Georgian style building with arched windows and doorway. I walked up the steps through a dark oak-panelled door into the air-conditioned luxury within. The receptionist was seated behind a stylish yet functional desk and ushered me down a thickly carpeted corridor to another impressive room. There Mr Cummings' briskly efficient and attractive PA spoke into the telephone, then offered me a comfortable leather padded seat until he was ready for me. She offered me tea, but I declined. I was not to be kept waiting long. A few minutes later, the impressive double doors opened and a balding middle aged man with a round fleshy face and horn-rimmed glasses came into the waiting room. He was taller than me, but stooped, so that he didn't appear to be. He was wearing a very expensive suit and a club tie. He offered me his hand.

'Mr West, I'm David Cummings, it's good of you to come here. Please come in.'

The handshake was firm but clammy. He stepped back and waved me into his office. I stepped in to a different world. Cummings walked behind an antique desk the size of a swimming pool. The room was tastefully decorated in pastel shades, with impressionist paintings, that I assumed to be originals, decorating the walls. The pile on the carpet was so deep that you could have lost a small child in it. He beckoned me to sit in another leather padded armchair.

'Right, let us come to the point shall we, time is money, particularly in this business.'

'Yes,' I thought, 'about £250 an hour.'

'I understand that you have been undertaking some historical research.'

'Yes,' I answered warily.

'Your recent work with Miss Mann has come to the notice of my client, who has been impressed with your tenacity and skill. He wishes to offer you a commission. There is a delicate historical matter that he wishes you to clarify for him. It would certainly involve foreign travel. I presume you have a passport?'

I nodded.

'Good. My client estimates it should take you five or six weeks to fulfil his commission, for which he is prepared to pay you a fee of £10,000 plus expenses.' My eyes widened with surprise. 'Of course, my client would expect to have your exclusive services, I'm afraid you would have to cease your current research.'

'And you client is...?'

'I'm afraid that must remain confidential, all matters pertaining to research must be dealt with through me.'

'Okay. Can you tell me what the research is about?'

'I do not wish to be difficult, but that too must remain confidential until we have your agreement to undertake this commission. All I can tell you is that it is relevant to your area of expertise.'

'So, you want me to undertake an unknown assignment for an anonymous person, for which you will pay me £10,000. If it was not for your surroundings Mr Cummings, I'd suspect you were having a joke.'

'I do not joke, Mr West. My client is very keen for you to undertake this commission and I have been authorised to make an offer of £20,000 if necessary.'

Twenty grand for five weeks work! That was almost footballer's wages. Opportunities like this do not fall into your lap every day, at least not into my lap, but I could not help feeling there was a hidden catch. If I accepted, it would mean letting Lisa down, but we had already reached the end of our trail and I was sure she would understand.

'You've certainly piqued my curiosity Mr Cummings, but I'm not comfortable with all the mystery. It's also a fact that you could get a far better qualified historian than me for the sum you are paying.'

'That is very modest of you, Mr West, but my client is adamant that he wants you. He has been very impressed with what he has heard about you. He is quite happy for you to employ

Miss Mann as your assistant, if that is what you wish, but she would also have to sign a confidentiality agreement.'

'How has your client heard of our research?'

'I am sorry, Mr West, I am afraid that I simply do not know. All I can tell you is my client is a man who is very well connected and well informed about such matters.'

'As I said, Mr Cummings, this is all very mysterious and unexpected. If you don't mind, I would like a day or two to mull over your proposal.'

'That would be no problem, Mr West, but my client is very anxious that you begin work as soon as possible, as you have a limited amount of time to complete your assignment. He would have to have an answer by the day after tomorrow.'

'That's fine; I'll consider your proposal and give you my answer within 48 hours.'

'That is marvellous. I look forward to hearing from you. Thank you for coming. Louise, my assistant, will show you out.'

He stood up and offered me the clammy handshake once more. The efficient PA was waiting for me at the office door and led me to reception area, once again thanking me for coming. I stepped outside with my mind in a whirl. Twenty grand; that was half a year's wages! All for five weeks work. How had the mysterious client found out about our research into Miller? That was the big question, along with who was he and what did he want me to do? I was still thinking things through when I opened the door to Lisa's flat.

'Well? What did he want? Have you inherited a fortune?'

'No, I've been offered £20,000 to undertake some undisclosed historical research for an anonymous man. I can even employ you as my assistant. It would mean that we'd have to give up the Miller thing though.'

'Don't you think this smells a bit fishy, Ian? Why should you be offered such a job? I don't want to appear rude, but there are far better qualified professional historians out there.'

'That's what I told Cummings, but apparently our mysterious benefactor knows of our Miller research and is impressed.'

'How could anyone know about what we've been doing, except for my bosses, who are aware of some of it at least.... But Gerald Aylmer knew, he killed the programme. Hang on, Hannah mentioned a solicitor with Aylmer...'

'Come on how many solicitors do you think there are in London?'

She ignored me and pulled her mobile phone out of her handbag and scrolled through her contacts.

'Hi Hannah, just a question, when I phoned the other day, you mentioned that Sir Gerald Aylmer had a solicitor with him when he called the other weekend. Do you know who it was?....No? Can you describe him?....Yes, thanks....No I'll tell you all about it when I'm back in the office. Byeee.'

She turned to me with a triumphant smile.

'How did you describe Cummings?'

'Tall, stooped, balding...'

'With a round chubby face and horned-rimmed glasses. Bingo, we have a winner. Aylmer's solicitor is Cummings!'

'A coincidence, I'm sure that a company like A & C have a plethora of big clients.'

'Coincidence, huh! Coincidence is the word we use when we cannot see the levers and pulleys - Emma Bull.... I always loved Bone Dance.'

'I didn't see you as a sci-fi reader.'

'I have layers, that's my mystery. Don't change the subject; it's too much of a coincidence.' She opened her laptop. 'Ainsworth & Cummings....' She muttered as she typed, 'I don't know why I didn't think to Google them before.' There was a lengthy pause.

'Yesss!' She punched the air. 'I'm good! Look.'

She turned the computer round so I could see the screen. It was an article from the Evening Standard dated a year ago. I scanned the article; then I saw what she had already seen. "At the Tower Point planning appeal today, Mr David Cummings of Ainsworth and Cummings, representing Aylmer Enterprises introduced a petition signed by 2000 local residents in support of the project..."

'So if it is Aylmer, he killed off my story off and now he's trying to buy you off. Pay you a huge amount to divert you away from the Miller story. The question is, why?'

'I think you're right. Aylmer knew about the Miller story and stopped it. Now this, you must be right. Why else would someone offer such an obscene amount of money for a mysterious non-project.'

'So what are you going to do? Take the money and run? I wouldn't blame you.'

'No way! I'm not Aylmer's stooge, I don't like being manipulated.'

'So what next then? We've hit a brick wall with Miller.'

'I'm not sure, maybe we should find out a bit more about the opposition. I know a few basics about Aylmer, but it's time we found out more about him. If he's behind all of this, then the more we know the better.'

Chapter 18

It was too late to engage in much research other than the internet. A quick search found a potted biography for Sir Gerald Aylmer.

Gerald Aylmer had been born in Cookham, Berkshire on 3rd August 1953, the son of Dr James and Lillian (nee Stevens) Aylmer. He had been educated at Charterhouse and Keeble College Oxford, where he graduated with a degree in engineering. He started a masters there, but his father died before he completed it and he dropped out. He began work for Phillips, who employed him until 1976, when he branched out to form his own company, Aylmer Enterprises. Raising finance from friends, he got in early on the computer boom, Aylmer made a fortune before diversifying into property development, the media and financial services in the 1980s. But in 1981 he took a year out to complete his masters at Brasenose College Oxford. He married Emily Baston in 1977, having three children, sons Joseph and Charles, born 1979 and 1982 and a daughter Emily, born 1984. He was knighted for services to industry in 1993. A generous backer of the Conservative party, he became disillusioned after the fall of Margaret Thatcher. In the years that followed he spoke out for anti-immigration and anti-European policies, supporting a number of ultra conservative minority parties in the 1990s. Renowned for his business acumen, Aylmer also had a reputation for ruthlessness and getting his own way. Some of the less reliable websites, who traded in conspiracy theories linked Aylmer to the finance of both the BNRA and Storm45. Unfortunately, they also accused him of conspiring in the death of Princess Diana and the murder of Alexander Litvinenko, as he was allegedly connected to both the masons and Russian Mafia. There were as many rumours about Aylmer as he had pounds in the bank.

Having got as far as we could that night, we gave up for the evening, intent on delving into the history of Aylmer in greater depth the following day.

The next morning I was awoken by the rain beating on the window in a blustery spray. I rolled out of bed and pulled back the curtains. It was of those grim days of an English summer, grey, wet and windy.

'Bloody marvellous!' I declared. 'Too wet to be without a coat, and too windy for an umbrella.'

A head popped round the door.

'Talking to yourself? You cracking up on me again?'

Lisa smiled at me to take the sting out of her words.

'Just moaning about the weather. I omitted to bring a coat, I mistakenly believed it was summer...shit I must be getting old, I'm starting to talk about the weather'.

Lisa's laugh echoed round the room.

'I've told you before Ian, you're not old. Just back-dated!' she added playfully.

'Thanks a bundle,' I grumped. 'You're in a good mood today.'

'Yes, James phoned me late last night, he's coming home next week. It'll be really cool to see him again; I've missed him so much.' My face fell. 'Oh, sorry Ian, I don't mean that I haven't enjoyed our time together, I told you, you have come to mean a lot to me. It's just that James is....'

'Special?'

'Yes, I hate it when we're apart.'

'I used to feel like that with Jane, I never felt quite complete until she was home again.'

The thought that Jane and I would never be together again suddenly overwhelmed me as, again, the threat of an empty future loomed before me. She had crossed the line going off with her new man, I knew that there was no going back. I would never be able to forgive her, but I missed her. For more than thirty years, ever since University, there had never been another woman in my life, now there was a void in my life where she used to be. I was deluding myself if I thought this young, beautiful woman could

131

fill that void. She had a life and hopes of her own, which did not include me as a major protagonist. Lisa looked at me with sympathy in her eyes.

'You will meet someone else Ian, Dad did, you remember he got remarried when I was in Year 12 and he's really happy.'

'I don't think so. I can't see me going back to dating at my age. The very idea terrifies me. In fact, if I ever tell you I'm getting married again, hit me, with something heavy – like a chair!'

She laughed again.

'You'll heal Ian, you are a strong man, stronger than you realise. You'll get through this.'

'What doesn't kill us makes us stronger eh?'

'Something like that, only less trite.'

'You're right, I was veering towards self-pity again; I tend to do that now and again. Sorry.'

'No, it's my fault going on about James coming home like a love-sick schoolgirl.' I took her hand and looked into her eyes.

'Lisa, I don't begrudge you your relationship, I envy you. Make the most of it kid; I hope you'll both be happy. If James makes you that happy, there must be something in your relationship, so go for it. But take a word of advice from one who knows, keep working at your relationship, never take it for granted, I did and look at the fix I'm in. When's he coming home?'

'Friday of next week.'

'Okay, that gives us a time limit to get this Miller thing put to bed, so I can clear out and leave you lovebirds to it.'

'You don't have to…'

'Yes I do. You don't need me hanging around like an antiquated version of Banquo's ghost, when your man is coming home. I've got things in Suffolk that I have to face up to anyway. I can't put them off for ever: solicitors, divorce papers and all that crap. Now let's change the subject. How do you propose looking into Aylmer and his links to Sinclair? This is more your territory than mine.'

'Well I thought we could go to Companies House and check up on the Aylmer Empire, it might reveal something.'

'Sounds like a plan. Where is Companies House?'

'Off the Tottenham Court Road, not far from the British Museum.'

'Okay, let me get washed and dressed and we'll head out.'

In under an hour we were on our way. The rain had stopped for the moment, but it was still windy and chilly for the time of year, the low leaden clouds scudded across the sky like a pall of grey smoke. We took the underground to Tottenham Court Road, where Lisa took the lead and we shouldered our way through the throng of shoppers, nearly being killed crossing the busy road by a small woman who had tried to jump the traffic lights in a huge four-wheel-drive tank.

We walked down Great Russell Street, lined as it was with impressive Georgian style buildings, and then turned into Bloomsbury Street with its four-storey brick terraced buildings. At Companies House Lisa led the way in.

'Go on,' I said, 'this is your area of expertise not mine, you're the one with a business management degree. I'm well outside my comfort zone. You lead and I'll follow.'

'Okay, let's get on with it.'

Two hours later, Lisa had navigated our way through the labyrinth of red tape and incomprehensible financial and business documentation. As we left, she had in her attaché case copies of everything we could find to do with Sir Gerald Aylmer. We could now go back to the flat and go scrutinise them in detail. We sat around Lisa's table with a stack of photocopies.

'This financial stuff means nothing to me, I'm afraid you'll have to make sense of it.'

'These are the current financial returns filed by Aylmer Enterprises that should tell us about his assets. These are the original articles of incorporation from when Aylmer Enterprises was founded in 1970. That lot over there relate to subsidiaries that Aylmer has a stake in. If we search through, we should find out who, besides Aylmer, has shares in the company and who the other directors of his companies are or were.'

133

'Okay, it's all a bit foreign to me, but I'll start with this lot.' I picked up the papers relating to Aylmer's subsidiaries as Lisa started to go through Aylmer's declared assets. We scoured through the documentation, a never-ending record of legal and accounting gobbledegook. It seemed to make sense to Lisa and I wondered how a girl with her qualifications ended up as a television programmer researcher. I decided not to break her concentration by asking, but filed the question away for later.

I carried on wading through the details of Aylmer's subsidiaries; his tentacles seemed to have spread far and wide. I started to write out a list of his companies, it ran to three pages, ranging from Alpha Property Development, Carlisle Investments through the Lambton Medical Group and Towton Computer Management to Xenon Engineering. I pointed out to Lisa the considerable stake he held in Seneschal, her employers. Lisa had begun to comb through the records. Two hours had passed yet we still had a mass of information to process.

'This is a mammoth and monotonous task,' I said. 'Why don't we call it a day and start again tomorrow?'

'You might be right; all the masses of figure are starting to swim in front of my eyes. One thing that's certain is that Aylmer is a sharp operator. The number of hostile takeovers here is unbelievable.'

'Lucy said he was an unpleasant character and not one to cross.'

'We still don't know why Aylmer is so intent on blocking our research into Miller though....Hey, you don't think the break-in at your place is related do you? You said it looked as if the place had been ransacked, but there was nothing missing. Who else would have been interested?'

'That's rather a leap in logic. The police thought it was kids.'

'They would, it's a soft option, but kids would either have done more damage or have stolen stuff, especially easily transportable and disposable things like stereos and televisions. Do you think Aylmer could be behind all of this?' Lisa asked.

'I wouldn't have thought he would want to dirty his hands with violence. The inducements offered to you seem to be more his style. With the exception of the wilder theories, there are no hints of violence.'

'What if he was using the BNRA or Storm45? My friend Claire said he was rumoured to have been funding them, maybe he's been calling in favours.'

'It's an interesting hypothesis, but you've no evidence beyond a hunch. Certainly not something we could go to the police with.'

'It still doesn't mean it didn't happen. I think we need to take extra care from now on. What was it that Lucy told you? He's clearly not a good person to cross and it seems that somehow we've been treading on his toes.'

'Yeah, you might have something, we should probably try to be more stealthy and try to stay beneath their radar until we find out exactly what is going on and why William Miller is so important to him. I don't think Lucy's explanation about rocking the boat by dredging up scandals from past fascist parties is enough. There's something we're missing.'

'What are you going to do about Cummings' offer?'

'That's a quick change of tack. I'll turn it down, of course.'

'But what about the money, you're not in the position where you can turn down £20,000.'

'That's true enough, but I'm damned if I'm going to be bought by a sleazy bastard like Aylmer. I'll manage without his tainted money.'

'I had an idea. A friend of James' is a journalist with one of the Sunday heavyweights. They're always printing these historical type articles, if we were to write this all up, about Miller I mean, not Aylmer, we might to be able to sell the story as freelancers. I can see the headlines now, "Hitler's British Accomplice". It won't be £20,000, but it could get us a reasonable fee.'

'Won't it piss Seneschal off if you sell the story elsewhere?'

'My contract with them isn't exclusive and they had their chance and blew it. Besides, it's not the only job in the world. I sort of fell into it almost by accident. I'd really like to get into business, that's what I'm qualified to do, after all. It's a bit competitive at the moment though.'

'That's settled then, I'll phone Cummings tomorrow and tell him thanks but no thanks.'

Chapter 19

'Hello, I'd like to speak to Mr Cummings please.'

'I'm sorry, Sir, Mr Cummings is not available at the moment; I can take a message, if you would care to leave one.'

'Thank you, this is Ian West.'

'Mr West?' she interrupted. 'I'll put you straight through, Mr Cummings left strict instructions to interrupt him, should you call. Please hold for a moment.'

There was a short delay then Cummings answered.

'Good morning Mr West, kind of you to contact me so promptly. You have made a decision?'

'Yes, I regret that I must decline your offer. In my current circumstances, I'm afraid that I cannot commit myself to this enterprise.'

'Are you quite sure, my client will be most disappointed. He is not a man who gives up easily.'

'I'm sorry, my mind is made up, but I'm both flattered and grateful to your client for the opportunity.'

'I would beg you to reconsider; my client may even be prepared to improve the financial inducements. He does not take rejection kindly and will be most displeased.'

'I'm sorry, Mr Cummings, I've made my decision. Goodbye.' I hung up.

'Well, what did he say?' Lisa asked.

'I think I've just been very subtly and politely threatened.' I went on to recount the conversation.

'I see what you mean. It does sound rather ominous and in keeping with the offer coming from Aylmer. We really need to watch our step from now on. Aylmer could turn nasty, if we tread on his toes.'

'Yeah, we'll need to be careful and try to leave less of a trail, if you're sure you want us to continue. It's getting a bit heavy; no-one would blame you.'

'We've started and I'm determined to see it through as far as we can, regardless of Aylmer.'

At that point, Lisa's mobile rang.

'Hello.....Hi Matt..........The same place?........What time?.....Okay, see you in an hour.'

'I gather Matt wants to meet us again. Did he get anything?'

'He didn't say, just said he needs to see us. He didn't sound happy.'

'Okay let's go then.'

Three quarters of an hour later, we entered the Italian coffee shop in Camden. Francesca was once more behind the counter and greeted us with a smile.

'Signor Matt is waiting for you,' she said gesturing to the booth in the back of the shop.

Matt was sitting at his customary table. He looked his usual laidback self, but on closer examination of his face I could discern worry lines around his eyes. He looked up at us with concern and beckoned us to sit.

'What have you two got me into?'

'What do you mean, Matt,' I asked.

'Well, your nursing home has some heavy duty security and firewalls for a care home. I mean, it's not the Pentagon, but it's up to industrial standard. Far more than you would expect. Then I as I was trying to...er...gain access, I got this.' He flung a sheet of paper onto the table. I picked it up and read:

Dear Hacker,

If you continue your activities, you will meet with severe repercussions, both legal and otherwise. We are actively tracing your IP address and would advise you to cease and desist now. To continue may prove costly.

'What the hell is going on?' he asked, in a low voice. 'I've never received cryptic threats like that before.'

'We don't know Matt. This whole investigation is turning nasty, we should have warned you,' Lisa said. 'Can they trace you like that?'

'No way.' He smiled 'I used an anonymising service and did it from my car in the street where there was an unsecured Wi-Fi. There's no way it can come back to me.'

'Did you find anything?'

'Sure, the Home is owned by the Lambton Medical Group. I never managed to get near the accounts because of the security.'

'Well, thanks for your help, we appreciate it. Drop it now Matt, you don't want to get involved with this,' Lisa said.

'It would appear that I'm already involved, besides, I don't like being threatened, and then there's the challenge of it.' He smiled

'No Matt,' I told him. 'You've got too much to lose. You need to drop this now. I'm sorry we got you involved.'

'I'm not at school now and I can make my own decisions. There's no way this can be traced to me, so I'm totally safe. Besides, there's a small matter of professional pride. I don't like being beaten, that's why I've been so successful. Anyway, I think I've found a way in, there's a backdoor to the system.'

'What do you mean backdoor?'

'A way into the system built by the people who designed it; so that they could access and update it if necessary.'

'And you've found this backdoor?'

'I think so. I'm going to have a crack at it tonight.'

'Be careful Matt, this whole affair is becoming a bit sinister, there have been no casualties so far; I don't want you to be the first. Take every precaution.'

'Will do. Now get out of here, I can't afford to be seen with disreputable people like you two.'

Lisa and I left the coffee shop. We said nothing until we were walking alone through Victoria Park. I could see that she was shaken.

'What's going on Ian? What was a piece of historical research is turning into a Matthew Vaughan movie.'

'I'm not really sure myself, but maybe we ought to pack it in before it goes any further.'

'I didn't say that. I'm just a bit freaked out by the threats. And why should a nursing home have such computer security?'

'Because there's something they don't want to be made public?'

'What would that be?'

'Maybe Matt will tell us.'

We entered the flat and Lisa offered to make tea. Whist she was in the kitchen, I settled to read the Evening Standard I had picked up on the way back. I scanned the front page.

'Hey,' I called, 'listen to this.' I began to read. 'In a speech today Richard Sinclair, leader of the BNRA, set out his terms for his party to join a coalition government after the next election. Speaking in Fulham he said; "If the true British electorate decide not to give a mandate to any one party and have enough faith in our party to hand us the position of holding the balance of power, then I should accept the will of the British people. The BNRA is prepared to work with other parties in government, provided that our core values are heeded. In order for that to happen, the BNRA leadership would want to have a great input into the domestic policies of this great nation, to ensure that the interests of the British public are upheld and we can create a society that puts Britons first. We would have to ensure that the immigration and law and order policies are acceptable to our voters. In these circumstances we would be prepared to join a coalition." This was the first time that the BNRA had suggested that it was prepared to enter a coalition, but any union with Labour remains an unlikely marriage. Spokesmen for both the Conservative and Labour parties reiterated their confidence that they would be able to win enough seats to form a majority government. However, polls released today suggest differently, with the Conservatives on 34%, Labour on 30%, The Liberal Democrats 15% and the BNRA on 22%.'

'Jeez, the arrogance! How can people tolerate him?' Lisa said.

'It's more than arrogance, he's effectively demanding for the Home Office as his price for joining a coalition.'

'Sinclair, Home Secretary? The world's gone mad.'

'The world might have, but Sinclair hasn't. He would control immigration policy, the police and even appoint the

Commissioner of the Metropolitan Police. He would control policing nationwide and that would give his members control of the streets. It's straight from Hitler's playbook. When he became Chancellor in 1933, there were only two other Nazis in the government, Frick the Interior Minister and Goering, Interior Minister for Prussia. That effectively gave the Nazis control of the streets. Sinclair is trying to do the same. And it looks as if he's going to get away with it, if the election goes as predicted.' I said.

'That's a deeply scary thought. I wouldn't want to live in a society where the policing and security was under the control of someone like Sinclair.'

'Me neither, but that's what we're going to get unless the electorate wakes up to the danger of the man and his detestable ideas.'

'What about our problem? How do we make sure that Aylmer doesn't stop out investigation?' Lisa asked.

'I'd say we need to be less obvious about our lines of enquiry and see if we can throw him off our track by going in a direction he would not expect.'

'Which is?'

'I haven't got that far yet,' I demurred.

'Marvellous.'

'How about we spend another hour on the Companies House documentation and then go out for a drink?' I enquired.

'Deal!'

Before we could start, we were disturbed by the ringing of Lisa's mobile. She flipped it open and answered it.

'Hello?.....Oh hi Hannah….yeeesss…how did he know?...that sounds great, of course I'd be interested, but what about Madrid?.....Why didn't he phone himself?....Okay, tell him I want to think it over and I'll get back to him tomorrow. Bye Hannah.'

She closed the phone. I looked at her and raised my eyebrows.

'That was Hannah.'

'Yeah I got that far on my own.'

She stuck her tongue out at me.

141

'It's as you predicted, you've not sold out, so they're trying me. Hannah called to offer me a six week assignment in Dresden, researching a programme on the bombing in 1945. Apparently Dresden is only 60 miles or so from Prague, so I'd be able to see James regularly. How convenient, the same day as you turned down their assignment, along comes a plum job for me, right in the neighbourhood of where my boyfriend is working.'

'What are you going to do?'

'I'm not going to be bought off any more than you were.'

'Not even tempted?' I asked.

'Of course I am, they've done their homework and tailored an offer specially to tempt me. You said they'd try to manipulate me if they failed with you and you were right. But they underestimate me, I've got my teeth into the Miller story and I'm not letting go now. I'll phone the MD tomorrow and tell him I'd prefer the Madrid job, that'll buy some time.'

'You sure? You'd be able to see James almost every day, I thought you missed him.'

'I do, but I'm not going to let you down, enough people have done that recently.'

'Hey, don't lay it all on me. I fully understand if you want to take up the offer,' I said.

'No. I told you, my mind is made up. End of conversation.'

We returned to the pile of papers on the desk. Many still did not make much sense to me. Lisa continued to scrutinise the sheets pertaining to Aylmer's financial affairs. I idly looked through the list I had made the pervious day.

'What was the name of the company that Matt said owned The Gables Nursing Home?' She referred to her notes.

'Erm...Lambton Medical Group, yes that's it.' I ringed a name on my paper and passed it to her. She read it.

'The Gables is owned by Lambton Medical and Aylmer owns Lambton. He owned the nursing home where Lisl Miller finished her days. The first time we've had a direct link between our Miller story and Aylmer.'

'Coincidence does happen, that's why we have a word for it.'

'Do me a favour! There are just too many coincidences here for it to be mere coincidence.'

'You could be right. Once is happenstance. Twice is coincidence. Three times is enemy action. – Ian Fleming. I can quote authors too!'

Satisfied with our discovery, we adjourned to the pub. At 10.00 pm we strolled back down Victoria Park Road arm in arm in the warm night air. When we got back to the flat, there was a voicemail on Lisa's mobile phone. It was Matt.

'I got the information you wanted. I'll call you back tomorrow morning, I'm going out with Charlotte and her parents; I'll get back to you tomorrow.'

'It's too late to phone him now,' I said.

'And we wouldn't want to upset his in-laws!' Lisa laughed.

'Speaking of in-laws, how do you get on with James' parents?' Lisa coloured.

'His Dad's sweet…'

'The cleavage?' I suggested.

'No, that'd be gross. I think he does have a weakness for a pretty face though.'

'And his mother?'

'Bit of a different case, I'm not sure she thinks I'm good enough for her little boy.'

'Nothing new there then, most mothers feel that. Jane has the same reservations about Rob's girlfriend.'

It was the first time I had thought of Jane that day and I was suddenly overwhelmed by the sense of loss. Lisa must have been able to read it on my face.

'Still hurts to talk about her?'

'Am I that obvious?'

'I'm just getting used to reading the signs, that's all.'

'Sorry to be such a wet blanket, it must be a drag when I keep getting maudlin.'

'Don't be stupid, Ian. You've been going through a life changing experience; of course you're going to take a while to get used to it. Dad said it's like bereavement and it takes at least two years to get through it.'

'Maybe I should have a drink with your dad when I get back to Suffolk. Perhaps he can give me some tips on how you survive divorce.'

'Dad's more than survived, he and Nicola, my step mum are really happy. I'm sure in time you can get there too. You've got too much to offer for some woman not to sweep you up.'

'No way. I'm never going to put myself through this again. I think my trust in women has been fatally damaged. Present company excepted.'

'You'll see, some woman will see you and won't give you a choice.'

'Huh, not in this life. Christ, I really am starting to sound cynical and bitter.'

'You always were cynical. It comes from being a teacher for all those years.'

'Yeah, you're right, it's an occupational hazard.'

'Come on let's call it a day. Goodnight.' She reached up and kissed me on the cheek.

I climbed into bed and tried to sleep, but images of Jane and a future without her swam before my eyes and invaded my dreams when I eventually managed to fall asleep.'

Chapter 20

The next day dawned bright and sunny, which was more than I felt. In the words of my old mother, I felt like a piece of chewed string. An unsavoury description, but in this circumstance, an accurate one. I looked at myself in the bathroom mirror; I looked bleary-eyed and more haggard than ever. I was losing weight, partly because my appetite was suppressed by my emotional state and partly all the exercise I had been getting, trying to keep up with an active twenty something. Still, I had been carrying an extra stone and a half, so I was probably more healthy than I had been. Every cloud has a silver lining, though it was not an adage I subscribed to.

Having showered and shaved, I entered the sitting room, feeling more human than I had earlier. Lisa was sitting at the table with toast and orange juice before her.

'Want some?'

'It's okay, I'll get it myself; you eat your breakfast.'

I was just eating my second piece of toast, when Lisa's phone rang; it was Matt, wanting to meet us at the usual coffee shop in an hour. Lisa thought he sounded worried. At the coffee house, Francesca once more waved us into a corner booth in the back of the shop. Matt was sitting there waiting anxiously. He appeared to be jumpy and stressed.

'I've got the information you want, but you need to be very careful what you do with it,' he stated without any preamble.

'Are you okay, Matt?' Lisa enquired.

'I will be as soon as I can pass this on and get back to normality. The bill you asked about, Lisl Miller was paid by a private : Chabot UK Investments Ltd, whoever they are. But that's not why I'm so worried. After I got that message, I took more care. I changed my internet access to a new address and hence a new IP address. I got in through the backdoor I found and out again with the information, without leaving any trace of my being there, or so I thought. On my way to work this morning, I passed along the road where I pirated the original internet access. As I passed the place where I parked, remember most Wi-Fi systems have a maximum range of 300 feet, there was a car, a Ford Focus, parked at the side of the road that had been absolutely trashed. The police were there and the owners were looking distraught. I think it's the costly repercussions the message warned me about. I think I might be responsible for the damage that was done, simply because I pirated their internet access.'

'Are you sure it was the same place?'

'Absolutely, I know where I parked and it must have been close to the router because the signal was so strong. The wrecked car was just a few metres from where I had parked. What have you two got yourselves into?'

'We think that Sir Gerald Aylmer is behind the obstacles that have been put in the way of our research,' I told him.

'Aylmer? I've had some dealings with his companies, he's a hard-nosed bastard, but I wouldn't think this was his style. He sails close to the edge of the law, but always within it. I don't see gratuitous violence as his style, he would use his financial weight against you; if you pissed him off, he would lean on your employers to get you fired, have you blacklisted, or transferred to Milton Keynes, he wouldn't have your car wrecked. He's not the Godfather for god's sake! No, you've pissed off someone entirely different, someone far more dangerous.'

'He seems to have links to some seriously nasty characters. Thanks for all your efforts, Matt, but you must now go back to your life and forget everything you've done for us. You'll be okay if you do.'

'What about you two?'

'I suspect we're in too deep to get out from under this now, our only choices are to give it all up, which might still be risky, or get to the bottom of what's really going on and use it against our unknown enemy.'

'Then I wish you luck. I'm off back to the States tomorrow; I'll be there for a few weeks, that should keep me out of harm's way. The invitation still stands, to the wedding I mean, if you survive that long. Please, take care. I've already paid Francesca for your coffees, so stay and enjoy them. I'll be seeing you.' With that he got up and left the café. Lisa and I sat drinking the cappuccinos that Francesca delivered to our table.

'Do you really think he's right, or is he exaggerating?' Lisa asked.

'One too many coincidences for my liking. We're getting into something murky here. Do we shut it all down, or go on?'

'Which do you think is safer?'

'I really don't know. My instinct is to covertly get to the bottom of all this and use it as a lever against whoever it is to get him to leave us alone.'

'Sounds good to me.'

'You sure?'

'If you are, I got you into this; I'm not ratting out on you now.'

'Okay, we need to find out about Chabot UK Investments, who paid for Lisl and why they were so secretive about it.'

'Okay, give me a minute.' She pulled out her laptop and began to search the internet. 'There's not much here. It did exist until 1982, when it closed down.'

'Got an address?'

'Not much of one, Marlow, Bucks, is all I can find…. No hang on, here it is. 24C, Spittal Street, Marlow.'

'Shut up shop in 1982?'

'Right.'

'Shortly after Lisl Miller died. This company could have been set up precisely to hide who was paying her bills.'

'It could be. But how do we find out who owned a defunct company from 1982?' she mused.

'I hope that was a rhetorical question, because that's your area, not mine, I don't have a clue.'

'Look, let's go back to the flat, we've still got several hours' worth of company documents to sift through.'

At the flat, we sat at the table examining the photocopies. After half an hour, my disturbed night's sleep began to catch up with me. It became more and more difficult to keep my eyes open and my concentration was gone.

'Do you mind if I leave you to it for a while? I had a crap night's sleep and I can barely keep my eyes open, I could do with a nap.'

'No problem, be my guest. It'll be easier to concentrate on the papers without you fidgeting because you're so bored.'

'Sorry.'

'Don't be; go have your sleep and come back refreshed and more focused.'

I lay on the bed and closed my eyes. The next thing I knew, Lisa was standing over me, shaking my shoulder.

'Ian...Ian, are you awake?'

'Uh...I am now. How long have I been asleep?'

'About an hour; sorry to wake you, but I've found something.'

'What?'

'I was going through the Articles of Incorporation for Aylmer Enterprises and guess who was the parent company? Chabot UK Investments!'

'The same people who paid Lisl's care bills?'

'The very same.'

'So it looks like Aylmer was paying for the home?

'It's a working hypothesis, but we'd have to find out who the hell Chabot UK Investments were.'

'That's a good question, and not one that I can answer at the moment.'

Our speculation was interrupted by the ringing of my mobile phone. I was tempted to ignore it when I saw Jane's image appear on the screen showing the caller. At the last minute I repented and took the call.

'Hello Jane, what can I do for you?'

'Ian, I went to the house today and we've been broken into again.' I ignored the 'we', there was no 'we' where Jane and I were concerned anymore. 'The place has been ...wrecked, absolutely trashed.' She was close to tears. 'This wouldn't be happening if you were at home.'

'So you don't want to be married to me, but I'm supposed to just stay at home like some caretaker?'

'There's no need for you to be like that.'

'Okay…I'm on my way home. What do the police say?'

'They think it's vandals, probably the same ones that broke in before.'

'Mmmm, they would do. I'll be with you in a couple of hours. Meet me at the house.'

'Trouble?' Lisa enquired.

'You could say that, I've been burgled again and this time they've gone out of their way to cause as much damage as possible. I've got to go home, at least for a while. If you're right, it looks as if Storm45 have been active again.'

'I'll come with you; I can stay at Dad's.'

'Good idea. I didn't like the idea of you being alone here, if I was away overnight.'

'You think this is the same as the car Matt saw?'

'Don't you? I turn down the assignment that would have kept me out of the way; lo and behold my home is broken into again.'

'I think I'll take all our research with us, just in case the same happens here.'

'Good idea. You might want to leave the lights on so it looks as if someone is in.'

Once more I found myself driving at speed up the M11 towards home; a home that had been violated, for the second time this month. I dropped Lisa off at her father's, she had wanted to accompany me and help, but I dissuaded her - her presence would only have made my dealing with Jane more difficult. Jane was waiting in her car on the drive.

'Ian, what's going on? This is rural Suffolk, not inner-city Manchester. I can't believe it that we've been broken into again.'

'How bad is it?'

'Go see for yourself.'

I opened the front door. In the hall the drawers had been emptied out and the chest overturned. I went into the lounge. It was worse. The sofa had been slashed and the stuffing pulled out, the stereo lay smashed on the floor and the entire television

149

console had been overturned. Lamps had been broken and the pieces ground into the carpet. The surfaces were covered with a grey powder, where the police had been searching for fingerprints. My heart sank, this was the death of my home; I had been expecting it later rather than sooner and certainly not in this way. I looked at Jane, who was watching from the doorway.

'Is the rest of the house like this?' She nodded. 'You want me to stay and help clear up?'

'No. the police need to take photographs and the insurance company need to inspect the damage. They'll also send in a contractor to clear up. Ian, why are you away so much? This would not have happened if you had been home.'

'Nor if you had been.'

'Stop it! You can't blame me, I'm not the one gallivanting about in London with that Mann girl. You've always had a thing about her and now you're shacked up with a girl young enough to be your daughter.'

'Let me guess, you've been talking to Lucy.'

She nodded.

'Well it's not really your business any more, you left me remember. But for your information, my relationship with Lisa is a professional one. I've been acting as an historical advisor for a documentary she's been researching and that's all, end of story.'

'I'm sorry,' she said. 'I'm upset at what's happened to the home we built.'

'You walked out on it.'

'Ian, don't be like that, please. I had to do what I did; our marriage was killing me slowly. I told you, I still love you, but I'm not in love with you. If anyone tried to hurt you, I'd kill them.'

'Except you're the one who hurt me most.'

'I know and I'm sorry, if there had been another way to do it, one that didn't hurt you, I'd have taken it.... honestly.'

'I know, Jane. I know that you wouldn't hurt me needlessly. It just doesn't make it any easier.'

'Let's not get involved in recriminations; I do want our split to be amicable.'

'What do you need me to do?'

'Sign these forms for the insurance claim and I can get things underway.' I pulled out a pen and signed in the appropriate places.

'That it?'

'Yes, for now. I'll take them and get them in the post.'

'Do you need me to stay around?'

'No, not really, you can't stay here, the police want to keep the place closed up.'

'Okay, I'll just pick up some clean clothes and I'll go. You head off, I'll lock up, for what it's worth.'

'Okay, goodbye Ian.' She turned to leave, then seemed to change her mind and turned back. 'Ian, I really hope that you'll find someone else. I don't want you to be alone.'

My eyes filled with tears and I turned away, not wanting her to see.

'Maybe, one day. See you.'

'Goodbye Ian.' This time she did leave, again.

I made my way upstairs, stepping carefully over the debris scattered liberally over the treads. If anything, the mess in the bedroom was worse than downstairs. I retrieved some clean shirts and underwear that the intruders had omitted to throw around and sadly walked downstairs. I picked up the telephone from where it had been cast on the floor. On a whim, I dialled 1571 to pick up my voice messages.

'You have one new message,' the mechanical voice intoned. 'Message one. Thursday 24th July, 01.07 hours.' There was a slight pause, then a cultured male voice said:

'You should have taken the job offered. Don't be stubborn, Mr West, please reconsider your decision, or at least abandon your current enterprise.'

The mechanical voice cut in once more:

'To repeat the message press one, to...' I hung up, cutting off the rest. Now I had the proof, the destruction of my home was retaliation for my having rejected the offer of Cummings' client, who I was now convinced was Aylmer.

Chapter 21

I phoned Lisa at her father's house on the other side of town.

'How bad is it?'

'Bad. What was worse was Jane was there. Every time I see her it all gets so difficult again.'

'What are you going to do now?'

'I don't really know; I can't stay in the house because it's a crime scene apparently. What are your plans?'

'Actually I don't have one. I forgot that Dad and my step-Mum had gone off on a cruise. There's no-one here except for Dan.' Dan was her younger brother. I remembered him from school, a Jack-the-lad character, for whom school work was anathema, but who was very popular with the girls. Lisa and her little brother had a love hate relationship. They were actually quite close, but neither would ever admit it.

'Are you staying there tonight?'

'There's no reason to. Dan's off out clubbing with his mates, so I'd be here alone. You could stay over here, Dad wouldn't mind in the circumstances.'

'No, I wouldn't feel comfortable and it would give Dan a heart attack to meet his old Head of Year over breakfast.'

'Fat chance of him making it to breakfast after he's got hammered tonight! Let's head back to London, if you're alright to drive.'

'I'm fine, when do you want me to pick you up?'

'As soon as you can?'

'I'm on my way.'

I picked Lisa up from outside her father's rather large home in a nice area of town. She threw her bag on to the back seat and climbed into the Saab.

'Was it too bad at your place?'

'There's a bit that's salvageable, but not very much. Furniture damaged and mess everywhere, I don't have to worry about losing my home now, it's effectively gone, all that's left is the

152

house and that'll soon be up for sale. I've said it before, but now it's truer than ever, I've nothing left to lose.'

'I'm sorry Ian; do you think it's related to our work?'

'I bloody know it is. The bastard that did it left me a message on my answer phone, telling me I had made a mistake in turning down Cummings' offer and continuing with our project. If I could get my hands on the shit, I'd...'

'Probably get yourself hurt. These are not nice people and they seem to resort to violence and vandalism quite easily. You might be my hero after you defended me so nobly in Spitalfields, but I think you're in a different league here.'

'Yeah, you're probably right,' I said ruefully. 'I'm pretty well outclassed here. All the same, I'm really pissed off now; I'll see this through just to spite the bastard.'

'Ian, I'm really sorry I got you into this. I feel responsible for what's happened.'

'Forget it kid, you weren't to know and once it started to get iffy, I was as guilty as you, I went into this with my eyes open. It's you I'm worried about, this is getting physical, I'd hate to see you get hurt. I don't really care about what happens to me, but I want you to be safe. Why don't you fly out and see James now?'

'Don't you dare treat me like that,' she flared up at me, her eyes flashing with anger. 'I've been in this from the beginning and I'm not going to be excluded, just because I'm a girl! You sexist...'

She stopped short, cut off by my laughter. She looked at me in angry confusion.

'What's so bloody funny?'

'You are; that's the firebrand I remember from school. There was no way you'd let anyone put you down or upset your friends. You were a real little terrier. I'm glad to see you haven't lost it. Or have you just been keeping it in check because I'm so delicate?'

She began to laugh too.

'Naah, I've learned to keep it in check, it upsets too many people at work, so I save it for when I'm really pissed off. James says I'm scary when I go off on one.'

'Well, all I can say is that I'm glad you're on my side. You're worth a small army of yobs. To paraphrase Wellington, I don't know what you do to the enemy, but by God you terrify me!'

She smiled, somewhat abashed.

'I called in at the office while I was at Dad's and told the MD that I'd prefer the Madrid job. He wasn't pleased, especially as I hadn't phoned yesterday- I think he's being heavily leant on. I told him I had to go home, a family emergency. He accepted my decision though, so that's sorted.'

We continued down the M11, I reached forward to turn on the radio to break the silence. Radio Four came on and Lisa groaned.

'Hey it's better than you having to listen to the music on my iPod!'

'Okay, I give in, Radio Four it is.'

I turned up the sound; interviews with all four political leaders were being broadcast, starting with Richard Sinclair. I was tempted to turn it off or over, even Radio One would be better than listening to him. I reached out to change the station, but Lisa restrained me.

'Wait. It's about time we started to take this guy seriously. Ignoring him doesn't seem to make him go away. People need to listen to what he says, that's the only way the voters will stop him. Most people just listen to the sound bite and don't follow the rest of the poison that he spews out.'

'Know thine enemy, eh?'

Sinclair's educated tones came through the speakers:

'My father fought for this country, I'm just glad he did not live to see the way that our national way of life has been watered down by un-British values and governments that have pandered to minorities at the expense of the true British people.'

'Your father fought in the Second World War?' Kenneth Randall, the interviewer, asked.

'Not only did he fight, he spent four years as a prisoner of war, in a German stalag. And for what? To see our cities become wastelands of crime and decay? To see our way of life and our values constantly undermined? To see British people disadvantaged to the advantage of illegal immigrants and economic migrants?'

'What is this guy like?' I asked. 'He doesn't talk in sentences, he talks in sound bites.'

'Shhhh!'

'Yes, that's all well and good, Mr Sinclair, but our listeners want to know about the man, not simply the politics.'

'My life's an open book, Kenneth. I was born in Marlow, where I still live. I attended Eton and Brasenose College, Oxford, where I read Philosophy, Politics and Economics. I met my wife at Oxford and we have a son, William, who is a student at Cambridge. That should show you how broadminded I am, despite the allegations of my political opponents.' He laughed. 'I took over managing the family business, when my father died, and I've worked there ever since.'

'That's rather a privileged background. Doesn't it mean that you have little in common with ordinary people?'

'Far from it, Kenneth; I have a thousand years of shared heritage, ancestors who have forged this country and most of all I share true British values with them.'

'Like tolerance?'

'That was a low blow, Kenneth and quite unworthy of you'' Sinclair answered, unperturbed. 'I'm talking about values like fair play, justice and service before self.'

'How does that fit with some of your beliefs?'

'That's an easy question to answer. I mean justice for British people, fair play for Britons and I'm willing to serve the state to make these things happen.'

'It's been said that you foster race hatred, by encouraging a policy of affirmative action to discriminate in favour of white Britons.'

'Yes, I've heard that too, but I have no concerns about a man's colour, I care only that he subscribes to British values and beliefs. If his family has been paying taxes to this country for generations and he considers himself British, then I have no problem with that. I do have a problem with the tidal wave of economic migrants who swamp this country, whilst continuing to hold to the values of their home countries. Many of them never even learn to speak English, for heaven's sake! They want to benefit from our welfare state, whilst remaining isolated from, and in many cases hostile to, the society that created it and funds it. Is that fair play or justice? Yet over the past thirty years, these people have been encouraged by multiculturalism to remain apart from the indigenous culture of these islands and remain outposts of alien cultures within OUR society. When I see demonstrations wanting Sharia law in this country, it makes my blood boil, as it should any true Briton, if these people want to live under Sharia law rather than British law, they should relocate to places that have Sharia law! I want to create a Britain, where Britons come first and only people who want to share our values have full citizenship.'

'There are people who say your recent setting of conditions for joining a coalition amount to a demand for the Home Office as your price. Do you have any comment to make?'

'No, Kenneth. My words are a matter of public record. All I did was to state that we would expect the right to fulfil our promises to the electorate, if we were to become part of the Government of the United Kingdom.'

'Well, I'm afraid that's all we have time for, thank you Mr Sinclair.'

'Thank you, Kenneth.'

'Bloody hell, what he has just said amounts to a virtual declaration of war against every ethnic community in Britain,' I snorted.

'Yet, he has the knack of making it seem so reasonable.'

'That's what makes him so dangerous. People have been hostile to areas that are like a little Pakistan or Bangladesh. Especially since the advent of Muslim extremism and terrorist activity, they want to paint whole communities with the same brush, and that's what Sinclair is encouraging them to do.'

'It's taken from the Hitler playbook again, tell your audience what they want to hear. It's almost like Goebbels has been reborn.'

Our debate on the danger of Sinclair continued all the way back to London. I found a parking space and pulled in. Lisa led the way up to her flat and I followed behind.

'I think I'll carry on with the financial papers we got on Aylmer. I've got to get to the bottom of them sooner or later.'

As we approached the front door, it opened and a tall young man with sandy coloured hair sporting a huge purple bruise on his cheek rushed out to meet us.

'Lisa, thank god you're safe!'

'What do you mean Ben? Ian this is Ben, he's our neighbour from downstairs.'

'Look, Lisa I'm sorry, it's all my fault.'

'What is Ben? You're making no sense. Start at the beginning.'

'Well, about six this morning the buzzer on the main door went. When I answered they said it was an urgent delivery for you, but they couldn't seem to wake you, so could I buzz them in? Well, normally I wouldn't dream of it, but it was early and I'd been working late last night and I didn't think, I just let them in. The next thing I heard was a huge crash from upstairs. I looked out, thinking they'd dropped something only to see five men in ski masks. They'd kicked your door in and gone into your flat. Before I could react they came barrelling down the stairs. One of them pinned me against the wall and demanded to know where you were. When I said I didn't know he did this.' He indicated the bruise on his cheek. 'I thought he was going to hit me again, but one of the others called him off, telling him not to waste time. They said they'd pick you up another time, you couldn't be lucky forever. I called the police, they've secured your flat and want to speak to you to find out what's going on. What is going on?'

'I'm not really sure, Ben. Did you get a good look at them?'

'No, not really, it was all rather fast. The only thing I can recall is the guy who hit me had some sort of tat on the inside of his wrist.'

'I'm really sorry you were caught up in this, Ben. We'll contact the police soon, but we need to get into the flat.'

'That's okay, they left a key for you and said to ring this number.' He handed over a padlock key and a business card.

'Thanks, Ben. I'm really sorry about this. I'll sort it out.'

Ben returned to his flat and Lisa and I hurried up to her apartment. The door had been secured with a hasp and padlock above where the door frame had been splintered around the lock. Lisa unlocked the door. Nothing seemed to have been damaged, but the two bedroom doors seemed to have been barged open.

'This isn't good,' Lisa declared. 'I'd bet everything I have that the tattoo Ben saw was a Storm45 one.'

'That's an understatement. You know what this means? First I turned down their blandishments, now you have and Aylmer has taken the game to a new level. We're in serious danger here.'

'What do we do?'

'I don't think this is something we can run away from now. We've no choice, we've got to get to the bottom of this story and find out who's behind this and how they're linked to Miller, then get the whole lot out into the public domain. We might have a chance then. But for now, it's not safe here, we need to pack our stuff and get out as soon as possible. Check into some anonymous hotel and keep moving until it's sorted.'

'Okay, I'll pack some stuff, but we don't need a hotel, my friend Amy has a flat in Bow on the other side of Victoria Park. She left me the keys so I could water her plants. We could go there, it'd be ideal.'

'I don't know; if it's just on the other side of the park, it's a bit close. But we'll check it out and see.'

We quickly packed the belongings we needed and relocked the door, we loaded the bags into the Saab and drove off.

'Keep watching behind us Lisa, I want to make sure we're not being followed. If they know where we live, they could well know my car.'

With Lisa swivelled in her seat, we headed down the road. I had not asked the address we were going to yet and I was not going to until I was sure we were not being followed. I drove, taking random turnings, sometimes doubling back on myself. Lisa could see no vehicle following us.

'Okay, where are we going?'

'I thought you'd never ask. Take Grove Road across the park, then left as soon as you leave the park into Old Ford Road.'

She directed me through a maze of side streets until she told me to pull into a car park outside of an anonymous, but well-kept tower block.

'The flat's up there on the twelfth floor. Even if they found the building, they'd find it difficult to get the right flat.'

'It's ideal. Lead on.'

We unloaded our bags and took the lift up to the twelfth floor. The apartment overlooked the park; it was clean and furnished in a modern style. Lisa showed me round the flat. The kitchen was small but well laid out and there were two reasonable bedrooms.

'Which room do you want?' she asked.

'You choose.'

'Okay, I'll take Amy's room, you take the spare room. You probably don't want to take Amy and John's room when you don't even know them.'

'Amy's married, then?'

'Didn't I say? They're both in the Met and they're on a month's secondment to the West Midlands Police.'

'Pity they're not here, we could do with a police bodyguard.'

The flat was stifling; it had been closed up and benefited from the heat rising from the floors below. I opened the windows as far as the safety latches allowed, which helped a little, but not a lot. We unpacked our research and set about linking Lisa's laptop to the router we found in the lounge.

'We've got no food or milk, there's a shop at the corner of the road, I'll pop down and get some supplies,' Lisa said.

'I'll come with you, just in case.'

'It'd be better if you didn't. It's the two of us together that are being looked for, I'll be less noticeable on my own, if they're about. Whoever they are.'

'You're right, but I don't like it.'

Whilst Lisa was gone I idly began to google Richard Sinclair. Until now, I had treated him with the contempt I thought he deserved, but perhaps that was everyone's mistake and we all should be looking more closely at the man and his policies.

Half an hour on the internet and I was not much the wiser. Information on Sinclair was not hard to come by, but it was the same information wherever I looked, it was almost as if it had been sanitised - the official version of his life.

Richard Alfred Sinclair was born on 12th February 1963 at Marlow, Buckinghamshire. He was the son of Peter and Alice (nee Morrison) Sinclair. Educated at and Brasenose College, Oxford, where he gained a First in Politics, Philosophy and Economics. He married Heather Stewart-Smith in 1986. When his father died in 1988, he gave up his playboy lifestyle to manage the family investment trust. He has one son, William, born 1987. He became involved in right wing politics whist at University and was believed to have helped fund a number of conservative groups, particularly anti-European Union groups, becoming heavily involved in the campaign against the Maastricht Treaty in 1992. He founded the British National Regeneration Alliance in 2003, fighting the 2004 European Elections on an anti-federalist platform. He failed to win any seats, but still fought by-elections in Sussex and Wolverhampton. Benefiting from a surge in popularity after the revelations of MPs sleaze in 2009, he became famous for his charismatic and frequent television appearances and the slogan 'Putting Britons first'.

Lisa had returned safely and had now finished scouring her documents.

'Right, Chabot UK Investments seem to be Aylmer's shell company, they seem to have helped to finance Aylmer Enterprises initially and remained major shareholders until 1982, when Aylmer became sole owner in his own name.'

'Did he buy them out or something?'

'That bit's unclear, all I know is that Chabot UK are listed as shareholders in April 1982, but by the returns for April '83 they're gone and Aylmer is in sole control.'

'Another mystery, then.'

'I'm afraid so. You'd have to get a complete set of Aylmer's financial records to be able to tell. There's no way we can do that.'

'No convenient friends in the Inland Revenue?'

'They're called Her Majesty's Revenue and Customs these days. They stopped being the Inland Revenue in 1985.'

'I still don't like them; they take money from my pitiful wages.'

'Anyway, I don't have any contacts there.'

'In that case, you rise even higher in my estimation. But we're still buggered.'

'I did find some interesting links. Aylmer has a surprising amount in common with our friend Sinclair and his father before him. There are a number of companies where both have considerable interests. There are four or five companies, where both are directors or finance them from the background.'

It was then that an idea occurred to me. I picked up the laptop and called up a map of the Thames between Windsor and Reading.

'There's a geographical connection, too. Aylmer comes from Cookham and according to the records, still lives nearby in Temple. Sinclair still occupies the family estate he inherited from his father near Marlow, Bucks and that's where Chabot were based. A different county but it's only three or four miles away as the crow flies, too close to be coincidence, considering all the other connections...' I paused for a second as the import of my research hit me. 'Aylmer was finishing his masters at Brasenose at the same time that Sinclair was there taking his degree. It's not that big a college, they must have known each other.'

'But why would he be giving us such grief about William Miller?'

Chapter 22

Lisa was going early the following morning to meet James' friend Jack, an old friend from his university days. She had already phoned him to enquire about our chances of selling the story.

'I was thinking,' Lisa said 'if we could get the story published, it might take the heat off us. If everything we knew was in the public domain there would be no point in Aylmer coming after us.'

'Except for revenge.'

'You're such a comfort!'

'Nevertheless, the idea's a good one. Any fee involved might help offset what we've spent these past few weeks.'

'Jack wants me to brief him on the story over lunch. If he thinks it'll fly, he'll take it to his editor.'

'I don't suppose Sir Gerald bloody Aylmer has interests in this newspaper?'

'No, I checked.'

'Okay then, you'd better get off, it'll take a while to get to over to Wapping.'

'He's not in Wapping, but you're right I need to go.'

'I'll see what else I can find out about Aylmer. Maybe I can spot the link with Miller.'

I spent the next two hours on the internet, researching everything I could find about Gerald Aylmer. I checked on his father and mother, to see if they could have some sort of link to Miller. As far as I could ascertain, his father Dr James Aylmer was a renowned surgeon, who had served with the Royal Army Medical Corps during World War Two. Everything about him seemed to be a matter of public record, even his support for the Liberal Party, so there were no convenient links to the far right politically. Next I went to work on his mother. Lillian Stevens was more difficult to trace. A member of the landed gentry, her background was unremarkable and from the limited facts I could find, there was little chance of a link to Miller, unless she once dated him.

Lisa phoned to say she was on her way back and I updated her on my lack of progress.

'What about his wife? Maybe his secret shame was Miller was his father-in-law and he's trying to avoid the social embarrassment.'

'Unlikely, but I'll give it a go.'

I searched the internet for Emily Baston. I found little besides the fact she appeared to have met Aylmer at Oxford.

I got myself lunch and read yesterday's paper. Lisa phoned and she was full of it.

'Jack loved the idea; he's going to speak to the features editor this afternoon. He thinks they'll be very interested; apparently they often buy this sort of story from freelancers. He even offered to meet with us and help us write it, he seemed to think that a good journalistic story is written differently from history.'

'I don't know if it'll be enough to take the heat off us. I have a sneaking suspicion that Aylmer doesn't know we've no link between him and Miller. We need to find it before he finds us.'

'You're right, but where do we go next?'

'We could continue with his wife.'

'Okay. What about her parentage?'

'I don't know. We're not going to find it on the internet. Even if information exists there, it'd be quicker to go to Kew. '

'Look, I'm not too far away, I'm in Richmond. I could go over and see what I can find, but it will leave you stuck in the flat on your own.'

'I'm sure I'll survive. Go see what you can find.'

Hanging around the flat without Lisa was tedious in the extreme. To alleviate the boredom I started to look through the business material Lisa had checked yesterday, not that I expected to find anything she missed and I didn't. Next I tried the internet for information on Chabot UK Investments. There were 18,000 hits. I worked through the first twenty pages without any luck. Then I decided to engage my brain rather than the computer.

Chabot UK Investments existed in 1982 and presumably before, if it was paying Lisl Miller's care bills and then they disappeared around 1983. Maybe the Financial Times for those years might help. I tried the British National Library website, as I would not have time to get there and back and complete my research before Lisa returned. I tried the newspaper search function, but found nothing. Next I tried the address in a search engine: there was nothing related to 1982, but I found out that 24 Spittal Street Marlow was now occupied by a glassware shop. That was no help, but another fifteen minutes' research showed that 24c was another part of the same building, presumably above the shop and was occupied by an insurance brokers. I idly clicked on their website. Anderson's Insurance Brokers of Marlow established 1983. It looked as if Anderson's had set up shop as Chabot UK had vacated the premises.

Lisa returned in the early afternoon.

'I think I might have something. I looked up Aylmer's marriage certificate, there was no father's name recorded for Emily. I thought he would simply be deceased, so I checked up on her birth certificate.' She paused dramatically. 'There was no father's name there either.'

'So?'

'Well if Miller returned to the UK after the war under an alias, he could have had a daughter. He was paying his wife's grandmother's care home fees through Chabot Investments.'

'It's a bit thin. All you can prove is she was most likely illegitimate, a cause for social embarrassment, but not much more.'

'But it would all fit. If Miller was Aylmer's father-in-law, he'd not want people digging into him and he's been using his influence with Storm45 to stop us. It's the only possible link we've found.'

'It's still not much use to us; we'd never be able to use it to prove a link between Aylmer and Miller. If we're to publish anything about this to stop Alymer, we would need concrete proof.'

'You're right, I suppose. It's a pity, I'd love to be able to publicise a link and show up Aylmer after what he's been doing to us.'

'Yeah, me too, but I can't see it happening through this avenue. Everything's too circumstantial.'

Lisa looked disappointed.

'I have had an idea about how we might trace Chabot UK, which could help link to Aylmer.'

'Go on.'

'Well, the building is now occupied by an insurance broker, who seems to have set up business there as Chabot left.'

'So we go to Marlow?'

'Yes, if we leave now, we've got time to do it today.'

'Okay, let's go.'

Chapter 23

Tracking through London took a while, but once we were on the M4 we made up some time. We approached Marlow from the South, a picturesque approach across the suspension bridge over the Thames and past the tall steepled church, nestling in its churchyard beside the river. The river itself shimmered in the hot afternoon sunshine. We parked next to a riverside sports centre and walked along the river watching the ducks and swans until we reached the road. The High Street rose up the gentle incline and was lined with expensive shops, travel agents and mobile phone shops. Lisa was fascinated.

'This place is lovely. Look at all these shops. There must be a lot of money here.'

'There is, but I doubt you could afford to frequent these shops. Look at that!' I pointed to a dress in a shop window, priced at £550.

'It's Dior and it's gorgeous. I'd love to own a dress like that.'

'I'd settle for just being able to afford it. Now control yourself. I think Spittal Street is this way. I led her up to the roundabout at the top of the High Street and left into Spittal Street, a road that ran for just 200 yards between the High Street and a second roundabout. The street was lined with an interesting mixture of Victorian and Tudor buildings, most of them shops. Number twenty four was selling glassware from a shop in a timber-framed seventeenth century building. Next to the shop was a door with a sign "24C Anderson's Insurance Brokers, First Floor." The oak staircase curved up to the first floor, where a bored young woman sat at a reception desk. She was about seventeen, long dark hair and far too much make-up. She raised her eyes from the magazine she was reading.

'Can I help?'

'Yes,' I replied, 'My name is David Fawcett, this is my associate, Amy Stevens. We're from the Marlow Society and we're currently researching the history of the older buildings of Spittal Street.'

'Did you know it's called Spittal Street because there used to be a hospital hereabouts?' Lisa interrupted my geek impression.

'Yes, we're trying to list the owners and occupiers of the buildings back to the time they were built.' The girl looked more bored than ever.

'Yeah, well I can't help you. I don't know anything about that.'

'That's why we'd like to speak to Mr Anderson, if he's in. We wondered if he could tell us who was here before he moved in.'

'I don't think he'll be able to help, he only took over from his father last year.'

'Is there any way we could speak to Mr Anderson Senior?'

'He normally drops in about 3.30, you could come back then.'

I looked at my watch, it was 3.00. We went to a nearby café and drank bitter coffee until 3.30 eventually crawled round. On re-entering the office, we saw a stout man of about sixty, with a round red face and salt-and-pepper hair.

'These are the people I told you about, Mr Anderson.' the receptionist said.

The man looked us up and down, appraising us as prospective clients.

'The Marlow Society? How can I help you?' He shook my hand in a firm grip, then turned to Lisa, his eyes wandering to her chest.

'Yes, we were wondering if you could help us to find out who occupied these premises before you. We're trying to chart a history of the occupants of some of the older properties in this street,' she said.

'Well, I don't rightly know. When I took over the lease, all the arrangements went through the freeholder's solicitor, we had no direct dealings with our predecessors. To the best of my knowledge they were an investment company, Sabot?... No Chabot, Chabot Investments.'

'So, you don't know who they were?'

'I didn't say that young lady; I said I had no direct dealings with them.'

'So you can help us?' I intervened.

'I might be able to, if you could help me out a bit.'

'Help you out?'

'Yes, business is slack in the current economic climate; I wondered if you would take a few of our cards and pass them out amongst some of your members.'

'I'd be glad to.' I took the small pile of business cards he handed me.

'Well, although I never saw or spoke to the previous tenant, Chabot UK Investments, I did have to forward their some of their mail.'

'Did you have a name as well as an address?'

'No, I'm afraid not, all the mail was addressed to Chabot. I could probably find the address, if you want.'

'That would be helpful.'

'Come into my office.' He led the way through the left hand door into a well-appointed office beyond. He crossed to a filing cabinet and began rifling through the second drawer. 'I could have sworn I kept it.....Ah here it is. Frieth House, Mondaydean Lane, Marlow.'

'That's very helpful,' said Lisa, writing down the address. 'Thank you for your help.'

'It's my pleasure,' he beamed at Lisa. 'You won't forget to give out those cards, will you?'

'Of course we won't, thanks again for your help.'

As we left the building, I pushed the cards into my pocket, feeling a little guilty that Anderson would not get the extra trade he had hoped for.

'Shall we take a trip up to Mondaydean Lane?'

'Okay, I'll need to use the satnav; I haven't a clue where it is.'

We got back into the Saab, the heat inside was tremendous; fortunately the air-conditioning soon cooled the car to a bearable temperature. We navigated our way through Marlow and made our way sedately up the gentle incline of Mondaydean Lane out of the town. The road twisted uphill past fields and woodlands. A mile out of town, we came upon a large Georgian house on our left, surrounded by a high wall that was topped by broken glass and pierced by two high, ornate gates. A tasteful sign declared it to be Frieth House. I pulled the car over and got out. Approaching the locked gates I saw a second smaller sign on the gates themselves, "Frieth House, Private Property, Strictly No Admission Without Prior Appointment." I returned to Lisa in the Saab.

'Well?'

'Whoever lives there, they clearly value their privacy. The gates are automatic; you have to go through a speakerphone. There's also no way in without prior appointment.'

'So we're not getting in there soon, then?'

'Nope, we'll have to find out who it belongs, or belonged to.'

'The internet?'

'Looks like it.'

We toured the main roads of Marlow, without finding an internet café.

'I suppose Marlow's a bit too upmarket and conservative to have such an establishment,' I said.

'Okay then, home James, and don't spare the horses!'

'Er, not just yet, I think we've picked up a tail. That red Ford has been behind us for a while. Let's see.' I signalled left and turned at the next junction. The red Ford followed suit a minute later. I took the next right and again the red Ford followed, hanging back, trying to be inconspicuous and failing miserably.

'Yep, we're being followed.'

'What do we do now?'

'Let's slow down and you look to see how many of them are in the car.'

As the gap between the cars narrowed, Lisa turned around as if looking for something on the back seat. From behind her hair she peered intently at our pursuer.

'Just one of them, but he's using his phone, probably to call in assistance. How did he find us?'

'Random bad luck, I suspect. We know this area is frequented by Aylmer and co. It looks as if we've just been unlucky in coming across one of *them*.'

I turned right again, then left, back on to the main road. The big question was how to shake the tail before his support arrived. I'm not a trained spy, I've never been taught defensive driving; I just had to hope that what I had picked up from films and books would work. I kept to the main road at an even speed, whilst my brain worked overtime. We pulled on to the motorway and I put my foot down. Fifty yards behind me the Ford kept pace. The motorway was quite busy and there were solid streams of traffic in the inside and middle lanes. An idea struck me and I turned on the satnav. It took a couple of minutes to locate satellites before it gave me my position. I could see that there was a turn off in a mile and a half. All I needed now was a bit of luck and the traffic to cooperate. I eased off the accelerator so that the distance between the cars narrowed. I could now see the marker warning me that it was three hundred yards to the slip road. Ahead, there was a slight gap in the traffic in the middle lane. I floored the accelerator and, without signalling, swung the Saab into the gap, then braked sharply, seriously upsetting the driver behind. The red Ford overshot us and as he did so, I cut across the traffic in the inside lane and to the sound of screeching tyres and protesting horns I pulled onto the slip road and off the motorway. For a minute, I sat at the roundabout, pale and shaking as the adrenaline rush subsided.

'Shit, that was bloody close,' I declared.

'I thought you were going to hit that car in the inside lane.'

'So did he,' I grinned, 'it was only his emergency braking that gave us the space to get off on to the slip road. But we've lost our tail; he can't get off the motorway for ten miles. As long as we steer clear of the more obvious routes into London, we should be okay. We'll just have to take a roundabout route.'

Getting back to Bow through the rush hour traffic was a nightmare. Two hours later and we were still crawling through tailbacks of traffic. I was feeling tired after the earlier stress and became very frustrated at the delays caused by road works and drivers who had selfishly held up the traffic by having an accident. My mood must have shown, for Lisa was keeping a low profile, plugged into her iPod, whilst I cursed the traffic in a torrent of vitriol. By the time we eventually pulled into the car park beside the tower block, it was late evening and the sun was already setting. Both of us were tired and hungry and had no heart for further research that night. After eating a quick meal, we both retired to bed.

I had no difficulty falling asleep, but within two hours I was wide awake. The room was hot and stuffy, despite the open window. I realised there was no way I was going to get back to sleep again any time soon. My mind was buzzing; I rolled out of bed and went into the sitting room. With nothing else to do, I decided to start tracking down the occupant of Frieth House. Picking up Lisa's laptop I began a search. Googling the address I found only one entry, a site listing property values and prices. I clicked on the link and the site opened. Frieth House was last sold in 1947 for £24,000; its current value was about £8,000,000. Whoever owned Frieth House had serious money. Still frustrated by my inability to track down the mysterious owner, I turned back to the computer. Then I came across Peoplesearch.com, which used telephone directories and electoral rolls to track addresses for names and vice versa. I typed in the address and the page came up. There were no businesses listed at that address. I clicked on the person tab and up came a list of inhabitants of Mondaydean Lane. I scrolled down. Suddenly I saw it, time stood still as I sat staring at the screen. The answer to so many of our questions leapt out at me. How could we have got it so wrong?

I jumped from the sofa and burst into Lisa's room.

'Lisa, Lisa, wake up. I've found the link. I've found out who lives at Frieth House. Now it's all beginning to make sense

171

at......' I tailed off as Lisa sat up in bed and I realised that she slept in very little on a hot summer's night. I quickly, if unwillingly, averted my eyes. 'Err...sorry...I'll see you in the sitting room.'

A few minutes later, she came into the sitting room swathed in a fluffy pink dressing gown. My cheeks still burned with embarrassment.

'I'm sorry for bursting in like that.....I didn't mean...think...er...I was just so excited by what I had found...er.. no that sounds even worse...' Lisa burst into fits of giggles at my discomfort and embarrassment.

'No worries. It was no more than you'd see on a beach in Spain or Greece. It's nothing, you're so proper.'

'Yes...well...er...I've never been on a beach with you and it was rather a shock.

'You're such a gentleman, so delightfully old fashioned. Now never mind my boobs, what have you found?'

Chapter 24

'Well come on then, what have you found that was worth waking me up for?'

'I couldn't sleep, so I decided to put the time to good use and see if I could track down Chabot UK.'

'Cut to the chase, the suspense is killing me!'

'Okay, Frieth House, Mondaydean Lane, Marlow, is occupied, according to the electoral roll, by Richard, Heather and William Sinclair!'

'Fucking hell, are you sure?' I turned the computer towards her.

'See for yourself.'

'Fucking hell,' she said again. 'That would explain a lot.'

'Yeah, but it poses even more questions.'

'Sinclair could have been paying Lisl's care bills, for Aylmer. Why?'

'Not our Richard Sinclair, but his father. Frieth House was last sold in 1947, before Richard Sinclair was born and the family investment trust was run by Peter Sinclair until his death in 1988.'

'So it was Peter who was paying Lisl's bills.'

'Looks like it, but it still begs the question why? Why would he be paying the bills for Aylmer? But it does tie Aylmer in with Sinclair, the BNRA and Storm45.'

'So now we need to know more about Sinclair senior, rather than junior.'

'The only things we know is his wife was Alice Morrison and Sinclair said in that interview that his father had been a prisoner of war; and that's it. We'll need to find out more.'

'Yes, we will, in the morning. It's 3.30 a.m., I'm going back to bed and so are you. Goodnight!'

She got up, kissed me on the cheek and returned to her room, leaving me no alternative but to copy her and return to my own bed. Despite my excitement and the image of Lisa's state of undress that was burned on my mind, I fell asleep easily. The next thing I was aware of was the light coming in through the curtains. I peered at my watch, it was after nine. Bleary-eyed, I pulled on jeans and a tee-shirt and went into the sitting room, where a bright and breezy Lisa was already surfing the net.

'You look like crap again,' she said.

'Thanks for the compliment. I'm well over twice your age and need my beauty sleep.' She laughed.

'Well, you certainly need it this morning.'

I grunted in reply. 'What you checking on?'

'I'm trying to track down Sinclair senior and see if there's a link to Miller, maybe they met in the war or something.'

'And?'

'I'm not having too much luck. I've found the record of his birth, then...nothing.'

I looked at her in confusion.

'What do you mean nothing?'

'Look, I managed to track him from 1945 onwards. Here's the register entry for his marriage to Alice Morrison on 24th June 1948. His age is listed as 36, that means he was born about 1912. Father's name Robert Garibaldi Sinclair, deceased, occupation, Architect. I managed to track down his place of birth, Coventry. So I traced his birth certificate, here's a copy; Peter Sinclair, born 15th September 1912, Radford Coventry, mother Emma (nee Rogers). I can trace no baptism or confirmation records, nor any other trace of him.'

'You probably won't. Coventry was comprehensively flattened by German bombing in 1940. I suppose many of the records were lost in the bombing.'

'There should be some record somewhere.'

'When did his father die?'

'According to the index of death certificates, in November 1940.'

'Possibly during the bombing then. So another dead end.'

'But there must be something.'

'I don't know where, all the census records are sealed for a hundred years, so there's no chance of tracing him that way.'

174

'So…?'

'I've not a clue at the moment.'

'Want some breakfast?'

'Please'

'Cereals, OJ and coffee?

'Please.'

Whilst Lisa was in the kitchen, I picked up the laptop and idly started a search. There was no way to access any records relating to the period after the Second World War, with the exception of births, deaths and marriages. We already had marriage and birth certificates and the death certificate would contain nothing useful about Peter Sinclair that we did not already know. I dug on. His death itself might be useful, what about an obituary? By the time Lisa had returned with breakfast, I had found what I wanted from the weekly local paper.

'Peter Sinclair, died on 27th March 1988 peacefully at his home in Marlow after a short illness aged 75. Born in Coventry in 1912, Mr Sinclair was educated at Ullathorne Grammar School and worked in the motor industry until 1939. He joined the army at the outbreak of war in 1939, was captured at Dunkirk and spent the rest of the war as a prisoner in Germany. On his return to Britain in 1945, he took the capital he inherited from his father's estate and became manager of the family investment trust he established and ran with great success. He married in 1948 and set up home in Marlow at Frieth House. Somewhat reclusive, Mr Sinclair rarely appeared at public functions, valuing his privacy and anonymity. A member of the congregation of St Peter's Roman Catholic Church, he privately supported the fund for the refurbishment of the church and its grounds. He leaves behind a wife and son. The funeral is to be held in private at St Peters' Church on Friday.'

I read this to Lisa, who was unimpressed. This was not much help, as I had told Lisa, censuses after 1911 were embargoed, so we'd have to look elsewhere. I wondered if his old school might supply us with any viable information, but Ullathorne Grammar School no longer existed, having disappeared during comprehensivisation in the 1970s. A quick search of the Friends

Reunited website provided us with little beyond a link to an Old Boys website for the school. This contained many texts and photographs from the relevant time, but there was no sign of Sinclair. Not even on the whole school photographs it displayed, which seemed strange. Sinclair senior might have missed one school photograph, but every one in his school career? It was almost as if he did not exist.

The only definite link we had for him was his son's comment about his war service, maybe Sinclair's military record might provide some useful information. Whilst chewing on cornflakes, I continued my search. Army records post World War One could only be accessed from the MoD if one applied in writing and regiment and number was needed, we had neither. Then I tried to see if lists of POWs could be accessed. They couldn't, however, I found that a complete list of British Army POWs held in Germany had been compiled and published as a book. Amazon had no copies available, but there was not time to order it anyway, but the Blackwell's on Charing Cross Road had a copy, though it was expensive. I told Lisa.

'You want to buy it?'

'Nope, it's alphabetical, so I thought I'd just pop in and peruse the book for free.'

'Cheeky!'

'Yeah, but cheap.'

'Okay, let's go then.'

We were interrupted by the ringing of the phone. Lisa answered and listened for a few minutes.

'I'm on leave, it's not really very convenient...' she said into the receiver. She then listened for a few moments before adding, 'I suppose I could make it this morning, if it's absolutely essential.' Another pause then, 'Okay, I'll be in at 10.00. Bye'

'Problems?' I enquired.

'They want me in the office.'

'I thought you were on holiday.'

'Apparently the job in Madrid is becoming more pressing and they want to discuss timescales with me.'

'I don't like it; you'd be very vulnerable, what better way to lure you into a place they can get to you. Look at what happened yesterday. Perhaps I'd better come too.'

'We've already decided that we're too visible together. There's a Police Station right opposite Seneschal's offices, I doubt they'll try anything there. At best, they'll try to tail me and I'll be watching for that.'

'I'm still not happy, I think it's too risky, but I'm not going to change your mind, am I?' Lisa shook her head. 'You better go in then, I'll go off to Blackwell's on my own. For god's sake be careful.'

Lisa and I parted to go to our separate destinations. The journey to Charing Cross was tedious, the bus spending time stuck in traffic and it took the best part of an hour. All the time, I was fretting about what was happening to Lisa. Once in the bookshop I forced myself to concentrate and searched the shelves in the history and military history sections to locate the volume I wanted. It was not there. I began to think I was wasting my time.

'Can I help you?'

I looked up startled, lost in my thoughts, I had not seen the assistant approach me. She was pretty, about nineteen, with dyed black hair and several facial piercings, yet she had a nice smile and an intelligent look in her eyes. I explained about the book I was looking for.

'Oh yes, I know the book. I'm afraid we only had the one copy and someone phoned this morning to reserve it. That'll be why you can't find it on the shelf. I could order you in a copy; it would be here in two or three days.' I looked disappointed.

'My problem is; I'm not sure if it's the book I actually need. I don't suppose it would be possible for me to see the copy, so I could make up my mind?'

'Normally, I'd have to say no, if the customer had paid for the book, it wouldn't be our property, but in this case, no money has been exchanged, so I don't see why not.' She reached under the counter and handed me the six hundred page tome.

'Is it okay if I sit over there and peruse it?' I asked, indicating a nearby sofa.

'Sure, knock yourself out. I'll be here when you've made up your mind.

Frustratingly, considering the duration of the journey to get to the bookshop, it took less than five minutes for me to find out what I wanted, and that included the time spent in checking and double checking I had got it right. I handed the book back to the girl.

'Thanks for your help, but I don't think it's exactly what I'm looking for.'

'Perhaps I could help you find the text you need,' she said, keen to make a sale. I felt guilty at misleading her.

'No, thank you for your help, but I think I need to reconsider how I'm going to proceed with my research.' The girl looked disappointed and I felt more guilty than ever and beat a hurried retreat from the shop.

Two hours after we had parted, I met Lisa back at the flat. It was clear from the flush of her cheeks and the set of her jaw that she was upset and angry.

'Okay, tell me.'

'I'm being lent on to go to Madrid now. Apparently the job won't wait and if I can't go then they'll have to send someone else.'

'So how's that a problem? You weren't that keen as it was.'

'No, that's when the not-so-subtle "If you don't go then we'll have to send someone else....of course in this financial climate, we're having to review staffing and may have to make cuts..." kicked in.'

'In other words, if you don't go now, you're out.'

'More or less.'

'Sounds like the work of friend Aylmer. He failed to get to me, so he turns his attention to you.'

'That's what I thought.'

'How'd you leave it?'

'I told them I couldn't go until James had been home next Tuesday, they seemed to be prepared to wait until then for me to make a decision.'

'They won't fire you. Aylmer's not that stupid, it's better to have you in the boat pissing outwards than the other way round. As long as you are with Seneschal, he has a measure of control over you; if you're fired, he loses that. But it's strange; this does not fit in with the thugs breaking into your flat to get to us.'

'I hadn't thought of it that way.'

'I'm beginning to suspect that there are two separate forces at work here, Mr X who is more direct and violent, and Aylmer, who is more subtle, a bit like Matt said.'

'You could be right, I was really careful that no-one followed me, I did all those things you see in spy movies, I even went into a ladies toilet, going in one entrance and straight out through one on the other side. I didn't see anyone. If it had been Mr X then I'm sure I would have been followed. Mr X wouldn't have missed a chance like that.'

'Be ready for Aylmer to come back with something even more attractive to buy you off; like they tried with me.'

'Do you think?'

'I'm sure, mark my words, I'm beginning to get a feel for how Aylmer works.'

'We'll see. Now what did you find out?'

'Well, thanks to my cheek in using Blackwell's as a reference library, I've added to the mystery. There was no Peter Sinclair of any rank held as a prisoner of war in Germany; the whole thing's an elaborate fiction.'

'You're sure?'

'Absolutely. The book I consulted listed all POWs in alphabetical order, so there's no chance of a mistake, unless the book is wrong and looking at the amount of research the authors have done, that's unlikely.'

'What the hell is going on then?'

'I don't know, but the more we research Sinclair, the less we seem to know. He seems to have spent his post-war life in the shadows and pre-war, it's almost as if he was born, then ceased to exist!'

Chapter 25

We carried on kicking ideas around about Peter Sinclair and his origins, without really getting very far. Lisa's comment about Mr X brought to mind my idea from the previous night, that had been temporarily driven out by fatigue.

'Did you find out anything about Peter Sinclair's mother?'

'Er, hang on.' Lisa consulted a sheaf of notes. 'Yeah, here we go, mother was Emma, nee Rogers. I got that off his birth certificate.'

'When did she die?'

'Dunno. I didn't think it that important.'

'It might not be, but if what I think is correct, it might just be vital.'

'No, problem, I'll look it up, I've still got plenty of credits on the ancestry site. When do you think she might have died and where?'

'I'm betting Coventry, November 1940.'

'Same as her husband?'

'Uhuh. My guess is they both died in the Coventry blitz.'

'Okay, what do you think is going on, then?'

'Just go along with me for a while, if I'm right, I'll explain all.'

It took Lisa less than ten minutes to confirm that my suspicions were correct. Emma Sinclair had indeed died on the same day as her husband, 14th November 1940.

'What was the cause of death?'

'It says here cause of death "Due to War Operations". What does that mean?'

'I think that was the standard entry for cause of death during the blitz.'

'So they both died together?'

'Yeah, it looks that way and last night, I found out that 14th November 1940 was the date of the blitz on Coventry, so that would all make sense.'

'So, I'm waiting for the great explanation.'

'Just one more thing, it may sound strange, but check for death certificates in Coventry for Peter Sinclair between 1912 and about 1920.'

'You're teasing me now! Come on tell me.'

'Bear with me, we're almost there.'

'Okay.' She tapped on the computer for a few minutes before saying, 'That's strange. Peter Sinclair, aged four, died 24th May 1916. I'm officially lost now, I haven't got the faintest what is going on...And don't tell me to wait any longer!'

'Alright, you've been patient. I presume you've never read Day of the Jackal?'

'No, go on.'

'Well, the author tells how the assassin, the Jackal, creates false identities by finding the grave of a child who died in childhood, who would have been about the same age as him. He then gets a copy of the birth certificate and uses that to get a passport with fake references. It could be done before they introduced all the checks they have now. It was a well-known trick in less legitimate circles.'

'So Peter Sinclair wasn't Peter Sinclair?'

'You've got it!'

'Then who the fuck was he?'

'Good question, I'm beginning to get an idea, but until we can dig up something new, I suggest we start writing up the story for the paper. I think it'd be a good idea to get the story out in the public domain as soon as possible, to ease the pressure on us.'

We spent the next few hours beginning to write up the story of William Howard Miller, starting with a description of the Reichstag fire and then reproducing his letter, describing his part in it.

'It's too long,' Lisa commented, looking at our draft, 'we need to cut it down. Jack reckoned the story needed to be in two or three episodes of about a thousand words each.'

'Okay, rewrite number one then.' We began to work our way through what we had written, losing words, whilst retaining the narrative of the story. Eventually, we gave up and watched television before heading for bed early, I still had not recovered from the previous night.

When I awoke the next day, there was a text message from Jane. 'We need to meet, please phone me.' I did as requested.

'Ian, I really need to speak to you face to face, there's something I have to tell you and I don't want to do it over the phone.'

'This sounds ominous. Could you meet me half way, I'm still in London.' I tried to sound phlegmatic, but my hands were beginning to shake and I felt hot. What new bombshell could she land on me? What would it be this time?

'I could meet you at Stansted airport, outside the departures entrance.'

'Okay, at 11.30?'

'Fine, I'll see you then.'

Lisa looked at me. 'What does the witch want now?'

'Don't talk about her like that....'

'Huh, witch wasn't my first choice, though it sounded similar. You can't let her walk all over you like this Ian. One minute she's walking out on you, the next she expects you to drop everything and go running to her. She can't have it both ways. Every time you speak to her you end up getting hurt all over again.'

'I know, but she's my wife and despite everything, I love her, even though I know I can't stay married to her after she's been with another man. We have to divorce now, because I could never forgive or forget that. Trust can't be re-established once it's been broken like that. I told you, there's no going back, it's just that going forward is so daunting, so hard.'

'Ian, I hope that if I marry, my husband will be as loyal and faithful as you.'

'Thanks, you make me sound like a Labrador or Alsatian.'

'No, Ian I really mean it, you can defend her even after everything. I just hope my husband will be as loyal.'

182

'You have doubts about James?'

'None, but he hasn't asked me, so I'm not counting my chickens before their hatched.'

'If he's worth it, he'd be stupid to let a girl like you go.'

She smiled at me affectionately. 'Go see her, but don't let her upset you any more.'

At exactly 11.30, I walked up to the departures door at Stansted Airport. I could see Jane already waiting for me. Jane. She was standing in the midday sun, her dark hair shining. She might have been over fifty, but I still saw the young woman who I first fell in love with, the woman I married two years later and the mother of my children. She had put on a little weight in the intervening years, but that filled out her face attractively, making her look far younger than her years. There she stood, sunglasses shading her eyes. My Jane. Soon to be mine no more. My mouth went instantly dry as I saw her and my eyes stung with unshed tears. I swallowed with difficulty.

'You're early,' I said.

'Yes, I was rather anxious.'

'Anxious, you? You've made all the running in this ....situation.'

'We can't talk here, let's go get a coffee.'

We forced our way through hordes of suitcase-burdened holiday makers, passing the departures door and going on through the arrivals door. Inside, we found a relatively deserted coffee bar and settled ourselves down in a corner with two unwanted coffees.

'Okay, what is it you wanted?'

'Ian, there's no easy way to say this, but I'm leaving Suffolk to move nearer Simon....' I zoned out of the rest of the speech as my mind reeled. Simon, bloody Simon, the boyfriend Jane had before she met me at University. The pain knotted in my gut. I could have coped with almost anyone else, but not bloody Simon. It was not just that I had always considered the man a total twat, though to be fair I had only met him once, nearly thirty-five years ago; but for Jane to go back to him seemed to negate the time we had together, almost as if she was expunging the Ian years as a mistake and going back to the time before me. Jane was still talking. 'I've found a job near him in Southampton, I haven't finally decided to move in with him, but it's a strong possibility. I wanted you to hear it from me, not second-hand through the kids. I'm going to tell them when I get back.'

I looked at her across the table; her eyes were as misted with tears as mine.

'Look, Jane, don't you think you're being a bit rash? This is all so quick; it's not like you not to look before you leap. I know we can't stay married, but I still love you and I don't want to see you get hurt. Are you sure that you're not jumping in with both feet because you're running away from something, rather than towards something? It's almost as if you're on the rebound. You've only been with him a few weeks, isn't this a bit precipitous? You'll be away from your friends, family and entire support network. You'll be alone, if it all goes wrong.'

'On the rebound? I'm hardly a teenager, Ian. We've talked it over. I'm aware that I'm taking all the risks and I've pointed that out to Simon. I've known him for thirty odd years.'

'No, you knew him as a youth thirty years ago, it's not the same,' I corrected. 'You're jumping into a relationship with someone you don't really know. It's no use saying you knew him in the 1970s. I'm not the same person I was then and nor is he.'

'We've talked it all through and I've found a job in Southampton, I gave my notice in yesterday. I move down there in a month.'

'I'll be honest with you, I think you're making a mistake and you'll come to regret it. You know that if…no, when it all goes wrong, I'll be here to help you pick up the pieces. I could never marry you again, but you'll always be my friend and I'll always love you.'

'I couldn't do that to you, Ian. I'm taking the chance and I'll have to live with the consequences if it doesn't work out.'

'I still think you're making a mistake and you should think about it more before you dive in head first.'

'I'm going Ian. I want to be happy and I hope you'll be happy too, eventually.'

The conversation went round in circles for half an hour, but there was no dissuading her, she had made up her mind and rash though the decision was, she was determined to stand by it. I kissed her on the cheek as we parted and it dawned on me that this could be the last time that we'd see each other on this footing. I drove the hour back to Hackney and walked into the flat, where Lisa was surfing the net in search of more information about Sinclair. She looked up as I entered the room.

'Hi, I think I've just found a picture of Sinclair senior from the early eighties. I'll just save it.' She looked at me more closely. 'Ian, are you alright? You look very pale and there's that empty look in your eyes again. She's done it to you again, hasn't she?' I haltingly told her the gist of our conversation. She regarded me with genuine pity.

'Oh Ian, I'm sorry, she's succeeded in dumping on you all over again. I agree with you, she's making a big mistake. You're right, she's behaving like she's on the rebound. How do you think Lucy and Rob will take it?'

'I really don't know. It seems a bit hard on Rob; she'll have gone by the time he gets back. It looks like I'll be taking him off to Uni on my own.'

My mobile began to ring insistently. I looked at the caller ID and was unsurprised to see it was Lucy.

'Hi Dad.'

'Hi love, what's up? Been speaking to your mother?'

'I have, what the fuck is she doing? She wants to move in with this Simon after just a few weeks, she'd be tearing me off a strip if I considered moving in with a guy after such a short time.'

'I know, love, I've told her that I think she's making a mistake, but there's no putting her off.'

'She wants me to meet him Dad, but I told her I wanted to talk to you first, I don't want to do it behind your back, I'll only go if you agree.'

'If he's going to be part of your mother's life, then you have to meet him. I'll be honest, I hate the idea of that twat meeting you, but she's your mum and you have to meet her partner. So if

185

it's my permission you're asking for, then I give it, albeit reluctantly.' I paused. 'Sorry, my comments were out of order.'

'Hey Dad, if that's the way you feel, there's nothing wrong with saying it. Get it out of your system.'

'Do you know if she's spoken to Rob?'

'Yeah, I had him on Facebook just now. He's not too happy about it all. He says he'll agree to meet Simon, but only if I'm there too.'

I smiled. 'That sounds like Rob. Always wants to have support when the going gets difficult. Give him my love.'

'I will, but perhaps you should talk to him.'

'Yeah, you're right I'll log on and talk to him when we've finished.'

'He's gone now Dad, you'll have to get on to him later. Are you alright Dad? I worry about you. I want to be there for you but this bloody dissertation is really dragging on. I hate the idea of you being alone through all this.'

'Don't worry about me love, I'll be fine and I'm not on my own, I'm still working with Lisa, she's been a great help.'

'Thank her for me Dad. I never really got on with her at school, but she's been a good friend to you throughout all of this.'

'I will; goodbye Lucy, take care.'

'You take care Dad, I'll speak to you soon, love you.' She hung up.

'Lucy.' I said holding up the mobile.

'Is she okay?'

'Somewhat unimpressed with her mother, but she's okay. She said to thank you for what you've done for me. She's grateful that I've got someone to support me through this shit.'

'Ian, it's been a pleasure. I'm just happy that I could be there for you.'

I looked at her. 'Do you know what?' I asked. 'You're wise beyond your years.'

'Wise? Me?' she laughed. 'I think all this is playing with your mind. No-one has ever accused me of being wise.'

'Well you are.'

186

'You didn't see me at uni, I spent half my evenings wasted, you should have seen the state I was in after Mayhem!'

'You still got a bloody good degree. I told you, you're a caring and wise young woman, and I'll always be in your debt. Maybe one day I'll have the chance to repay you.'

'Don't be silly Ian, you owe me nothing, I'm the one doing the repaying, for all those years of care at school… and all the tissues I used!

'Okay, we'll call it quits, now let's change the subject.'

Chapter 26

Owing to the time difference, I could not get Rob on Facebook until the following morning. He was not impressed with his mother's news and worried at what was going on at home whilst he was away. He was very concerned about me. Again he wanted to return to be with me, but I dissuaded him and told him about my work with Lisa, but left out the danger we were in. It reassured him that I had someone with me. Like Lucy, he knew Lisa from school, he was much younger of course and I think he had always had a crush on her. We chatted for a while and I arranged to meet him at Heathrow, when he returned as scheduled in three weeks.

Lisa came out from her room, looking less than her usual radiant self. Her eyes were red and swollen, she had obviously been crying.

'What's up, kid? Why are you so upset?'

'I'm sorry, Ian, I'm such a wimp. All that you've put up with and I get all weepy because James isn't coming home as we arranged.' I put my arm round her and hugged her.

'Hey, it's not the end of the world.'

'I know. It's just that I was looking forward to seeing him so much. He phoned me an hour ago and said that his boss needed him to work all next week in order to close the deal the week after. He said he could get the time off then.'

'Did he realise how upset you were?'

'Uhuh, I'm afraid I cried on the phone, then we had big row.'

'And you've been crying ever since. He'll be feeling as guilty as hell, you know.'

'Serves him right, the poohead!'

I laughed. 'Very grown up. Can I take back what I said last night about you being wise?'

'Thanks!'

'Look, give him a ring and make up. If he can't come to you, why don't you go to him? Get a flight to Prague and see your man. If he's that important to you, then show him; don't make the mistakes I made. Look at the bloody mess I'm in, you don't want to end up like me. Besides, you'll be safely out of the reach of our unknown bad guy. In the circumstances, it's probably just as well James isn't coming home, that could put him at risk too, unless he's going to go into hiding with us here. '

'You were always so good at putting me back together when I was upset and you haven't lost your touch. I'll go to Prague and surprise him, but only once we've got to the bottom of this.'

'Good girl, you know it makes sense. You're only young once, make the most of it.' She smiled at me.

'There you go again, sounding as if you're my granddad. You do realise that what you're telling me applies to you, too.'

'I've no-one to run to.'

'Not at the moment, but you need to make the most of your life. You will meet someone else and then you've got to go for it.'

'When and if that happens, I'll bear it in mind.'

'But seriously, we need to set a time limit on this, we're stirring up a hornets nest with this research, we need to find what the connection is between Miller and what's been happening to us soon. If we can't do it in the next few days, we're never going to and it'll be time for us to go looking for somewhere to hide until it's all blown over.'

'Okay, I'll agree to that as long as you take cover too, I'm not about to bail and leave you in the shit.'

'I've got an idea that ties all this together, which might expedite matters.'

'What?'

'I really don't want to say yet, there's no real evidence other than a hunch. I want you to play the devil's advocate to test my idea once we find some evidence. Now, let's sort out your trip.'

We went on the internet together and booked her tickets from Stansted to Prague on Tuesday morning. I offered to take her to the airport on my way back to Suffolk and then on to places unknown. After coffee, we went back to work on the story. My mind began to wander, could Sinclair really be who I thought? Was I jumping to hasty conclusions? I mulled this over in my mind worrying at the problem, whilst Lisa retyped the story again. Eventually we got it down to a length and a format that we were both happy with and Lisa emailed a copy to Jack. I was still niggled about Sinclair.

'You seem distracted,' Lisa said. 'Are you losing interest in all this?'

'Good God no! I'm just running over the Miller conundrum in my head.'

'Yeah, who the hell was he?'

'I'm not totally sure, but Sinclair senior went to a lot of trouble to change his identity.'

'Why so cryptic? Look, Ian, I'm in danger too, I've a right to be let in to the secret.'

'You're right. I've got no proof, but since he paid the care bills for Lisl Miller...'

'He's Miller?'

'It's a working hypothesis. We've had the whole thing the wrong way round. It wasn't Aylmer working through Sinclair to keep Miller hidden; it was Sinclair working through Aylmer!'

She laughed. 'That's wonderful; the father of the leader of the neofascist BNRA was a Nazi war criminal. This is dynamite! We could really sell our story now. In fact I'll bet it's just doubled or trebled the value of our story. Better still, it would destroy his carefully created image as a British nationalist'

'It's also not provable and would therefore be actionable for libel. We can't make any reference to it in the article, unless we have evidence to back it up, and it would have to be conclusive evidence. No newspaper would publish it, otherwise. It will have to be legally watertight. You've already told me how litigious Sinclair is where his image is concerned.'

'I suppose it also accounts for the break-ins and the threats.'

'Yep, we've crossed into very dangerous territory here and we can't do anything but to go on. We've already seen the violence of some of his supporters, especially Storm45. They don't hesitate to use force and I think they believed we knew more than we did. Now we've got to get the proof. It really is very risky.'

'But we've both said that someone needs to throw a spanner in Sinclair's works, now we've got the chance.'

'But at what cost? We don't have any evidence to support it, but if we have to try to find it and we'll need to be very careful that we stay under the radar whilst we try.'

'We have to go on; I will if you will, too, I can't do this alone. Remember what you said, all that's necessary for evil to triumph is that the good man do nothing.'

I sighed wearily.

'There's no stopping you and we have no real option anyway. We have to get Sinclair before he gets us, hiding might work, but bringing the truth to light and destroying him would be more effective, if we can do it. But there'll be a cost - what about Seneschal and the Madrid job?'

'Fuck them. I've got a few days respite, anyway, but I'm not being packed off to Madrid now.'

We spent most of the day trying to find some sort of provable link between Sinclair senior and Miller, but with no success - it was difficult to even decide on a way that we could prove it. There would be no DNA or fingerprint reference samples for Miller and Sinclair to compare, even if they existed, we did not have the knowledge or skills to be able to interpret the evidence to prove our theory.

There was no real way to proceed further, without evidence. The more I thought about it, the more I questioned my conclusions. I was a historian; I should be basing my theories on evidence not conjecture in the absence of it. Was I jumping to unproven and unprovable conclusions?

My reverie was disturbed by the phone Lisa answered, it was Jack.

'Jack has shown our article to his features editor, he's so impressed that he's changed the paper for this Sunday to include it. Jack says we are deeply unpopular with the guys who thought they had the paper largely ready for print. The journos whose work was bumped to make space for us are also very unimpressed. The editor wants the second instalment as soon as possible; he doesn't want to have such an impromptu state of affairs next week.'

'That's great. When can we expect the cheque? We could do with it, we've spent a fair amount in the pursuit of this story and I'd like to pay some back into the bank, before I start getting letters from my bank manager.'

'Not until after the second instalment I'm afraid.'

'Oh well, at least it'll piss Jane off and gain me some petty revenge.'

I decided to give up going round in circles on the Miller/Sinclair issue and decided to clear my mind. I rang Graham Price, who was now on holiday.

'Hi Graham, Look, I'm sorry to be asking favours again, but I've been doing some research that seems to have had some unfortunate repercussions. I think we could be getting into hot water here and I'd like you to be my insurance policy. I don't want to drag you into this, but I can't think of anyone else and as long as we keep it secret there's no threat to you.'

'I'm relieved to hear it Ian. What precisely do you want me to do?'

'I just want you to hold a copy of what we've found, as a sort of insurance. I'm going to email you the story and our conclusions, if you would read it and check my conclusions, then just hold on to it until I tell you otherwise.'

'Okay Ian, I must admit you've piqued my curiosity, I'd like to read your research. Send it now and I'll read it through. If I think you've missed anything or made too much of it, I'll let you know.'

'Thanks Graham, I'll send it now.'

'How're things going with Jane?' I told him the unexpurgated version of my messy break-up.'

'That's rough Ian, drop in and we'll have a few pints and see what we can do to cheer you up. The wife has some tasty friends who might be of interest to you; you know help you move on.'

'Thanks Graham, but I don't think I'm ready for that yet. I'll get back to you.'

'Okay mate, see you soon.'

I emailed Graham our story, played down our speculation about the Miller-Sinclair link. I wasn't ready to share too much of that with anyone but Lisa just yet. Within an hour Graham had phoned me back.

'Hi mate,' he said, 'I've read through the stuff you've sent me and I must admit I think your conclusions are perfectly valid, but there's one thing I think you've missed, not being a linguist.' He went on to tell me what he had found. Lisa raised an eyebrow as I hung up and looked puzzled when I broke into fits of uncontrollable laughter.

'The cheeky bastard, I can't believe the nerve of the man.' I gasped.

'What? What did Pricey have to say?' I was breathless with laughter, almost unable to speak.

'He told me what the word chabot means, as in Chabot UK Investments...' I paused for effect.

'Go on, stop teasing me.'

'According to Graham Price, chabot is the French for a type of fish.'

'And?'

'In English, that fish is known as the Miller's Thumb!' We both dissolved into laughter. This was not evidence, but it showed a link between Miller and Sinclair that added to our circumstantial evidence.

'He really did have the brass neck of the devil. It fits with him translating his name into other languages as he changed identities.'

'Yep, it really does fit his modus operandi. It's a pity we don't have more tangible evidence to support our conclusions.'

Lisa opened the laptop and pulled up the picture of Sinclair Senior she had found the day before.

'You cheeky bastard.' She said looking at the picture. 'I wonder....' She tailed off and began to peer at the photograph. 'Does it look to you as if there's something wrong with his left hand?' We zoomed in to look at the damaged hand in greater detail. There was certainly something wrong, but the picture pixelated before we could get enough detail to be sure. It certainly seemed that he appeared to be missing a little finger on his left hand, but yet again, there was an element of doubt, we lacked incontrovertible proof.

'How can we be sure it's him?' I asked.

'I saw a computer program at Uni that aged a photograph of you to show what you would look like when you got old. It was supposed to warn us off our life of excessive drinking and smoking. If we could find a program like that we could age that picture from Spain and compare it to this one.' I kissed her on the forehead.

'You are brilliant! If it is a reliable program, it would be a strong piece of evidence in our search.'

We spent an hour looking for the program on the net and eventually found a free but reputable one. We used Amy's printer/scanner and entered a scanned copy of Miller's face from the 1937 photograph; Lisa moved the slider to age the photograph by five years and printed the result. Next she aged the photograph by forty years and again printed the result.

I picked up the copies from the printer and compared the five year aged photograph with the face we had identified as Miller in the photograph from Auschwitz. This was the acid test, if it matched, then we could have greater confidence in the forty year aged photograph. It was a match. Hardly daring to breathe, I put the second print on the table, where we could both examine it. Lisa called up the photograph of Sinclair senior for comparison.

'It's not an exact match, but it's close enough for us to say that Miller and Sinclair are one and the same.' I said.

'Yeah, there is quite a similarity, but there are some differences, look here and here.' Lisa pointed to areas around the forehead and eyes of the aged picture.

'Mmmm, but the area around the jaw and the mouth are almost identical.'

'So that puts us back where we started, there is evidence that Miller was Sinclair, but it's not conclusive. Are we ever going to prove it?'

'I don't know. There must be incontrovertible evidence, the question is where? I suppose we could go back to Marlow and try St Peter's Church, there might be something in their records, but it's a long shot.'

'We're running out of time Ian, I go to Prague in three days and then I won't be able to put off Seneschal about Madrid; I'm going to have to go.'

'I know; the only good thing is you'll be safe, once you're out of the country you're less of a threat to Sinclair. You're right though, it's make or break, we're running out of time. Not all historical mysteries can be conclusively solved. After all we'll never know who killed Kennedy for sure. It's a problem, it's dangerous to go on, but equally dangerous not to.'

'It's so frustrating! We really need to get an answer to this. Now we're clutching at straws in Marlow.'

'Well I suggest we go to Marlow and clutch at straws tomorrow, it'll be better to go on a Saturday, if we're going to the church, they tend to be busy on Sundays.'

'Okay then, it's shit or bust tomorrow!'

Chapter 27

The light reflected off the Thames in the morning sunshine, making it shine like a river of ice, as we drove across the nineteenth century suspension bridge into Marlow. I parked the Saab outside the Premier Inn that stood close to the All Saints Church. We got out and walked down the High Street together.

'Where's the church?' Lisa asked.

'I think it's down here,' I said, turning into Station Road. 'If the map I looked up before we started out is correct, St Peter Street is down here on the left, the Roman Catholic Church where Sinclair was buried is down there. We shouldn't be able to miss it.'

'Okay, lead on.'

We turned back towards the River to find some of the oldest buildings in the town. Towards the bottom of the road the small gothic revival church was built of flint with strange square steeple beside the west end of the nave.

'The guide book says it was built by the elder Pugin,' I told Lisa. She looked blankly at me. 'The guy who designed the Houses of Parliament?'

'Oh!' she said without much interest. She frowned. 'Look at all these graves, where do you think Sinclair is buried?'

'Could be anywhere. The church looks all closed up, so we'll get no help there. Maybe we'd better go and start looking for his grave.'

It was a beautiful day for searching grave yards, but it did not take long for us both to get bored and frustrated, wandering through a seemingly random jumble of headstones.

'Fancy a coffee?' I asked Lisa.

'Yeah! I could kill for a Frappuccino.'

We walked up the High Street and found a Starbucks. Twenty minutes and two refreshing iced coffees later, we felt fit and ready to resume our search. We were walking down the street back towards the church, when I spied a black dressed clergyman a few yards ahead of us. The biretta on his head told me he was a catholic priest and the chances were he was associated with St Peter's church. I accelerated, pulling a mystified Lisa along with me. We caught him just as he turned the corner towards the church.

'Excuse me, Father.' He turned; he was about my age and build, with greying hair and friendly twinkling blue eyes behind horn rimmed spectacles. He smiled.

'Can I help you?'

'Are you the parish priest for St Peter's?'

'I am, Father Charlie Corrigan.' He introduced himself in a broad Glaswegian accent and held out his hand. I introduced Lisa and myself.

'We are looking for the grave of one of your former parishioners, Peter Sinclair, he died in 1988'

'Not one of mine, I'm afraid, I did not come here until 1992, shortly before my predecessor, Father Nathan, died.'

'Can you help us locate the grave?'

'Yes, if you come into the vestry, I'm sure the records will tell us where he was buried.'

He led us around the side of the church and unlocked the door into the vestry. The room was dark after the bright sunlight outside. Father Corrigan pulled a ledger from the shelf and began to leaf through it.

'Here we are, he's buried in the south-west corner of the graveyard, I'll show you.' He led us outside and across the graveyard. He stopped in front of a row of three graves with marble headstones.

'There you go, Peter Sinclair.' I looked at the graves. One was Sinclair himself; one was his wife, Alice, who had predeceased him by three years. The third headstone read Lillian Morrison, who died in 1959, presumably Sinclair's mother-in-law. I read Sinclair's epitaph. "Peter Sinclair, 1912-1988, beloved husband and father. Finally at peace."

'Highly appropriate, considering his tumultuous life,' I thought. Aloud I said, 'Thank you for your help, Father Corrigan. Do you know anything else about him?'

It's a pleasure to help and call me Father Charlie, everyone does. I hope you are not journalists; he has a famous, or rather, notorious son. I could not be party to anything of that ilk.'

'No Father, I'm actually a teacher. Lisa is a former student who's assisting me with some historical research. Mr Sinclair here has turned up as a peripheral, but interesting figure in our narrative. We're trying to put some flesh on the bones, if you'll excuse the pun.' I felt bad misleading Father Charlie, but needs must when the devil drives.

'Well, I never actually met him myself, but I understand that Father Nathan knew him very well, especially in later life.'

'Is there anything in terms of parish records that might throw any light on Mr Sinclair?' Lisa asked sweetly. It was interesting to see her work her charm on a celibate man. I smiled knowingly at her; she gave me a glare and ignored me.

'Yes, we have a full set of minutes for the parish community committee. I believe Mr Sinclair was an active member.'

He led the way inside the vestry again and pulled a series of volumes off a bookshelf. There were six of them and each was about two inches thick. I groaned inwardly, this could take forever, with little hope of us finding anything useful, we were really clutching at straws.

'There you go!' said Father Charlie. 'You can use the desk over there, if you want to go through them. Take your time; I've got a mountain of paperwork to get through.

I thanked him, handing a volume to Lisa and picking one up myself. The Catholic Church might no longer believe in it, but the next hour was purgatory. The committee's minutes were dull in the extreme, the detailed minutiae of a committee of worthy parishioners, who were seeking to make life better for the fellow members of their congregation. I garnered little useful information about Miller, beyond the fact that he was a major donor to the church roof restoration fund. To all intent and purpose, Peter Sinclair was a pillar of the community, far from the William Miller we were convinced he was.

'Will you excuse me a moment?' Father Charlie asked 'I have to go into the church and check we have enough hosts for mass tomorrow,'

'This is so far from the man we've been investigating; it almost seems we've got the wrong man. All of our evidence is circumstantial after all.' Lisa said what I was thinking.

'Yeah, he does appear to be a respectable member of the community, a far cry from our man Miller. I suppose he could have got religion in later life and turned over a new leaf when he created his new identity.'

'Now who's clutching at straws? We'll never manage to prove that. This is a bust. Can you think of any other avenues to follow, because this is a waste of time?'

'Nope, I'm totally out of ideas. It's a pity, but this is our final dead end. Probably just as well, we're running out of time and we've still got to write the second episode of the Miller story for the paper and then hope that when nothing else follows it, Sinclair will think that we don't know the rest of the story. If we keep our heads down, we might be lucky'

Lisa looked dejected.

'Are you giving up?'

'I don't see there's anything else to do, do you?' She shook her head.

At that moment, Father Charlie bustled into the vestry, carrying a flask of holy water that he placed carefully on his desk.

'Have you found enough, or do you find those records as boring as I do?'

'They're not exactly best seller material are they?' I smiled.

'Is there anything else pertaining to Mr Sinclair?' Lisa asked the priest.

'Nothing that would tell you about the man, but I have his library back at the rectory. He and Father Nathan were very close and he bequeathed his library to his friend when he died. When Father Nathan passed away, the books stayed in the rectory, they're still in my study today. Mind you, I've never really read them.'

Lisa and I exchanged glances, we each knew what the other was thinking; just when we thought we had reached the end, Lady Fortune threw us a bone of hope. Could Sinclair's book collection help us? It did not seem too likely, but it was the last hope we had, albeit a faint one.

'You can tell a lot about a man from the books he reads,' I said. 'Would it be possible for us to see them?'

'I don't see why not, you'll want a cup of tea after ploughing through all those dry tomes anyway. I'm parched, follow me and we'll see what we can do about both those things.'

Father Charlie led the way through the graveyard avoiding patches of unmown nettles, to the wall that encircled the south side of the churchyard. Set into the wall was a low wooden gate that led into an adjoining house. The path led through a well-tended garden to the rectory beyond. The rectory was a brick-built Victorian pile with a browny-orange tiled roof that was covered with patches of lichen. Father Charlie pulled a key out of his trouser pocket and unlocked the green painted side door.

'Come in,' he said. 'This place is rather a rambling heap, too big for one person, but it was built for the priest at the same time as the church. I suppose it was a matter of prestige and not being outdone by the Anglicans.' He raised his voice, 'Margaret! Margaret, it's only me.'

A small, middle aged woman appeared from what was clearly the kitchen.

'Margaret is my housekeeper,' he explained. 'Could you bring us three cups of tea through to the study please Margaret.'

'I'll bring them in presently.'

Father Charlie led the way through the hall and ushered us into his study. The large room was south-facing and bright, with a fine view down over the river. There was a Persian style rug covering the polished floorboards. One wall was lined floor to ceiling with mahogany bookcases, on which stood rows of books bound in fine brown leather. In the centre of the room was an antique desk and by the window stood a work desk. A smaller

200

bookcase containing a number of well-worn texts stood against the wall opposite the shelves. Father Charlie followed my eyes.

'Those are the books I brought with me. The shelves and books on that wall are the ones that Mr Sinclair bequeathed to Father Nathan. I'm ashamed to say that I've never really read them. A simple parish priest does not have too much time for that type of heavy reading.'

'Do you mind if we look at the Sinclair books, Father?' Lisa asked.

'Please feel free.'

At that moment, Margaret appeared with a tray on which stood a teapot, three cups and saucers, a matching sugar bowl and milk jug.

'I'll just get your lunch and then I'll have to be off, Father. Mother isn't at all well. '

'Don't you be worrying, Margaret, you get off to your mother and give her my best wishes for her recovery. Don't worry about lunch; I'm quite capable of making a sandwich.'

'Thank you, Father. There's cheese and ham in the fridge and some nice fresh bread in the pantry.' A minute or two later we heard the door shut behind her as she left.

'The poor woman, her mother is a sore trial to her. Now, shall I be mother?'

He poured the tea into the cups and handed them to Lisa and I, seated on a leather sofa in front of his desk. Lisa stood up and began to walk along the bookshelves, reading the titles of the books.

'I see what you mean about heavy reading Father. Some of these books look extremely dry.' She picked a volume off the shelf and opened it. 'This one is in Spanish.' She handed it to me. 'What does it say?'

'My travels through Estremadura with a donkey,' I translated. 'My Spanish is just about up to that.'

'That looks fascinating, not!' She put the book back on the shelf. 'There seem to be quite a few nineteenth century Spanish travel books in English too. It appears that Mr Sinclair had some affinity for Spain. There are some books in German too; they seem to be travelogues as well.'

'Mr Sinclair must have been quite a traveller,' put in Father Charlie. 'Would you like to stay for lunch, while you look through the books?'

'That would be very kind, Father. Lisa and I would like to look at the books without the distraction of having to find somewhere to get lunch.'

'You're welcome, it will be nice to have some company for a change, solitary meals can be a bit dull. I'll go make some sandwiches. Ham or cheese?'

Lisa chose ham and I chose cheese and Father Charlie left for the kitchen. Lisa and I began to peruse the book shelves.

'What precisely are we looking for?' Lisa enquired.

'To be honest, I haven't a clue. Anything really, a dedication or proof of ownership that refers to Miller. I don't know, just look.'

There were more than a few books there; I calculated that in all there had to be at least two hundred and fifty square feet of books. The top shelves were so high that Lisa struggled to read the titles. Eventually we agreed to search by height; I would take the upper shelves, whilst she took the lower ones.

'Sinclair's choice of reading matter reflects his life, with time spent in Spain and Germany. That fits with Miller, but Sinclair's behaviour seems at odds with Miller's,' Lisa declared.

'People change.'

'Not that dramatically, surely?'

I shrugged and continued to run my eyes along the shelves. In the distance I could hear Father Charlie whistling happily to himself. Lisa was gazing at the books at the other end of the case, when she suddenly halted and went back to the shelf she had just finished looking at.

'That's funny,' she said picking one of the slimmer volumes off the shelf. 'This one's leather-bound like the rest, but it doesn't have a title. All of the others have a title in gold.'

She balanced the book on her left hand and opened the brown leather bound cover. She turned the first page.

'Ian, look!'

She held the book out to me. From twelve feet away, I could not read the words, but the handwriting was very familiar - Miller's.

'What does it say?'

'It starts "This is the journal of Peter Sinclair, though I have not always been known by that name." '

We had found the next link in the chain and it might just lead us to safety.

Chapter 28

Lisa put the book down on the work table and we both eagerly leaned over it. The hand-written text was dated 31st October 1986.

This is the journal of Peter Sinclair, although I have not always been known by that name. Having reached my seventy-fifth year, I look back on my life with much shame and many regrets. I have committed many sins in this life for which I repent as the time for me to meet my maker approaches.

I will start my journal at the beginning and let my cautionary tale unfold. My name when I was born was William Howard Miller and I was born in 1909 in Maidenhead, where my father was an army officer; but I remember nothing of this, the first home I recall was in Pimlico, London. My beloved mother, Lisl, was German born and I grew up speaking German to her and English to my father and everyone else. My childhood was not unlike that of many people, until my father left for the Great War in 1916. I never saw him again; he was killed in the battle for Passchendaele Ridge in 1917. My mother and I were left to subsist on a meagre military pension. Thanks to the charity of my father's old regiment, I attended a decent school, but despite my abilities, without money, the prospect of university was a distant one. I drifted through many jobs in my youth, becoming bitter and resentful at my lack of prospects. My father had died a hero, yet his widow and son were left on the verge of poverty. It seemed at the time that this was the way that Britain rewarded the sacrifice of my father and his comrades. My bitterness drove me to seek redress for the wrongs done to me by joining the one political party who represented the interests of the dispossessed; I turned to the ideas of fascism. I drifted through the Imperial Fascist League and eventually wound up in Sir Oswald Mosley's British

Union of Fascists. My hatred for society led to my involvement in
attacks on Jewish shops and businesses.

'Like father, like son,' Lisa retorted. 'If he genuinely
regretted his misdeeds, you'd have thought he would have
brought his son up better.'

'You can't always blame the parents for the actions of the
child. There is such a thing as free will.'

'Huh! I tend to go with Larkin, "They fuck you up your mum
and dad, they may not mean to but they do…"'

'That's a bit harsh. Do I sense some issues here?'

'Yep, I'm just another screwed up kid from a split family. At
least you and Jane stayed together until your kids were grown up.'

'Well, you've turned out pretty well, despite that. Come on,
back to the story!'

In 1933 I came to the notice of the Party leadership, who sent
me as part of a mission to congratulate Hitler on his accession to
power…

'We know this bit, we've already seen it in Miller's own
words,' Lisa said.

'Okay, let's skip to after the Reichstag fire.' I scanned
through the next few pages to pick up the thread of the story.

I have often thought whether history would have been different
if I had not taken part, but I came to the opinion long ago, that my
part could so easily have been taken by another; that my actions had
no particular effect. The Reichstag Fire and its consequences would
have been the same, whether I had played my part or another
misguided soul had taken my place. The one thing that does weigh on
my conscience is the fate of poor Van der Lubbe; I was, in part,
responsible for his death. I still sometimes imagine the scene of his
execution and his decapitated body and I wonder if I could have
engineered a different outcome, had I not been so indifferent to his
fate.

Our reading was disturbed by the return of Father Charlie with a lunch tray, on which was a small mountain of sandwiches. He noticed my look.

'Margaret is always counting my calories and worrying about my weight, I thought I'd take advantage of her absence and enjoy myself and I felt guilty committing the sin of gluttony on my own, so I thought I'd corrupt you and Lisa into the bargain. What have you found there?'

'We seem to have found a handwritten autobiography of Peter Sinclair.'

'Does that help your research?'

'Too right it does. This is our biggest find since we started all this.'

'Well you're welcome to stay here and read it. Perhaps you'd let me read it, when you've finished?'

'Technically Father, it's your property, but I warn you, if you do read it, you might wish you'd been left in ignorance.'

'Now you've really piqued my curiosity, I'm keener than ever to see what you've found. But since you found the book, it's only fair that you two should read it first.'

We ate our sandwiches whilst partaking in light conversation with Father Charlie, but both Lisa and I were itching to get back to the journal. Eventually, Father Charlie left us to continue our reading.

On my return to England, I found myself much lauded by the leadership of the party, though I was sworn to secrecy about my part in the events of February 1933. I became disillusioned with the Party. To my eager young mind, they were achieving little, and social injustice and communism still continued to flourish. Attacks on Jews as the "enemy" gave me some perverted satisfaction, but change was not happening quickly enough for me. All I felt I had achieved was a criminal record for my part in a fight against communists in an Eastend pub. The Cable Street riot was a watershed for me. I saw the party humiliated by Jews and communists, whilst the police stood by, or at least that's how I saw it then. Moseley was a good leader, but

206

in comparison with Hitler, I thought him too moderate and respectable. When the Spanish Civil War broke out, I could not resist the call to fight bolshevism in a more direct way. I was a young, virile man and was anxious to take action rather than mouth platitudes. I volunteered in January 1937 and made my way to Spain, where I enlisted in the Nationalist forces. My early days were quite uneventful, as I spoke little Spanish and I do not think they really had a role for this strange Englishman. Thanks to my fluent German, I made friends with several of the officers in the Kondor Legion, one in particular, came from a town near where my grandparents had lived, poor Karl, he was killed flying on the Russian Front in 1942. Thanks to him I became friends with many of the Luftwaffe officers flying in Spain. I always had a gift for languages and my Spanish improved rapidly. In the course of the next few months my halting Spanish improved to the point where I was fluent. By June 1937 I had proved myself with the Nationalist army at Guadalajara and commanded a platoon in the army that captured Bilbao. My promotion was rapid; by 1938 I was a captain in charge of my own company. I fought through the battle of the Ebro, being one of the defenders in the hills overlooking Gandesa. It was there, amidst the barbed wire and trenches ,that I began to understand what my father had gone through before his death in the Great War. The horror of trench warfare had an immense effect on me, I saw friends and my men die in the most terrible ways, for which I blamed the attacking Republican forces. I came to truly hate the Republicans and their supporters, though not nearly as much as my men did, the internecine struggle of civil war seemed to bring out the worst in them and their hatred for their own countrymen today defies my understanding, though at the time it was something I felt I shared with them. Our chance for revenge was not long in coming, when my company and that of Commandante de Vega were ordered to carry out a reprisal raid into Republican territory. Unfortunately, Sancho de Vega, yet another friend, was shot through the throat by an anarchist sniper and died shortly afterwards, even before we had completed our crossing of the Ebro River. It fell to me as the senior officer to assume *command of the expedition. I ordered de Vega's company to hold the river crossing and my company advanced into Republican territory. The mood of the men was volatile, our losses on hill 481 had been heavy and they lusted for vengeance. Ten miles or so into enemy territory we found the anarchist commune at Montegrillo. Under cover of darkness I moved my men into position to storm the village at first light. We met little or no resistance and the village and its inhabitants were soon in our hands.*

'Let's see how he justifies his actions at Montegrillo,' said Lisa.

'Shhh, don't disturb our concentration.'

This is where I come to the first of my great regrets, for the events that ensued are a subject of great shame and disgust to me, but at the time I considered my actions totally justified. How I wish that someone could have stopped me, no matter by what means, for then at least my conscience would be clear.

Having the people of Montegrillo in my hands, I decided to set an example that our enemies would not forget. As the Bolsheviks' great hero, Lenin said the purpose of terrorism is to terrorise, and I intended to make our enemies very afraid. To try now to excuse my actions by saying I was angry and in shock after the loss of so many friends and comrades in the battle, would be wrong. I know now that my actions were both immoral and criminal and I am sure that my immortal soul will have to atone for those sins when I come before the throne of the Almighty. To my eternal regret I commanded my men to carry out all manner of unspeakable atrocities on those poor people. In my rage, I ordered that every male over the age of ten be made to dig their own graves and then I had them shot. As if that was not enough, when my men asked what to do with the women, I quoted the words of our General, Queipo de Llano, who had said 'Our brave Legionaries and Regulares have shown the red cowards what it means to be a man. And, incidentally the wives of reds too. These Communist and Anarchist women, after all, have made themselves fair game by their doctrine of free love. And now they have at least the acquaintance of real men, and not milksops of militiamen. Kicking their legs about and struggling won't save them.' Even today, all these years later, the words are burned into my brain. I can never forget that murder, rape and mutilation were all committed not just at my orders, but with my active encouragement. As I walked around the village I saw the bodies of the men I had ordered to be killed and heard the screams of women and girls as they were brutalised by my men at my instruction. Even the children did not escape my wrath - I released the surviving children, but only after I had the right hand of each boy cut off. It was only when my own son was born that I came to fully appreciate the full horror of my behaviour, but at that moment I did not perceive the inhabitants as people, but as vermin, to be exterminated. I had no more thought of them than I would have had for a nest of ants.

We left the bodies of the inhabitants in the smouldering ruins of the village and retreated back across the Ebro, where our exploits were lauded by General Queipo de Llano. I even gained promotion to Commandante, though some of the professional soldiers regarded me with a haughty disdain. I saw no further action in the war and the inaction palled. On 25th January 1939 I returned home to England. I remember the date so well because it was the last time I was to see my beloved mother.

'I don't believe it,' said Lisa, 'but I'm beginning to think he is genuine in his regrets. I almost feel sorry for him, having to live with that on his conscience.'

'I shouldn't feel too sorry for him just yet; remember the worst of his crimes are to come. Many people find religion as they get older and enter God's waiting room, looking to atone for their sins. It doesn't mean they were not criminally culpable for what they did when they were young. Anyway, let's get back to the narrative.'

A friend from my B.U.F. days found me a job in Portsmouth for the next few months and on my return to London, I found myself under arrest. I had brought home with me from Spain the trusty machine pistols that had saved my life more than once. I had shown them to a number of my former acquaintances from the BUF, and I can only assume that one of them was also a police informant, I can think of no other way they could have known. I was at first remanded to Wormwood Scrubs, but later my lawyer succeeded in gaining bail for me. Having spent little in Spain, I had saved a deal of money and was able to post bail for myself. When my barrister warned me that I faced a long custodial sentence, I gladly decided to sacrifice money to ensure my freedom and stay out of gaol; I secretly slipped out of the country bound for France, without the opportunity to see my mother. I had no idea that the circumstances of my return would make it impossible for me to see her again.

By now it was getting on for late afternoon and Father Charlie came into the study.

'How's it going?' he asked.

'We're not even half way through yet, Father,' Lisa replied.

'What is this all about? I'm dying to know.'

I hadn't the heart to lie to Father Charlie again, so Lisa and I filled him in on the whole story, from the Self diaries through the Miller letters and what we had subsequently found. He looked at us in amazement when we told him of the links to Richard Sinclair and thus to the BNRA.

'I have to tell you that the knowledge contained in this book could be very dangerous to possess.'

I described to Father Charlie the problems we had encountered in pursuit of Sinclair/Miller: the threats, the break-ins and the bribes.

'A most pernicious organisation, I would very much like to see them stopped. They don't just present a political threat to this country, but a moral threat too. Evil has to be confronted; you can't run away from it, it has a way of catching up with you. But that begs a serious moral question, should the sins of the father be visited on the son? Can a little evil be done in the cause of the universal good?'

'I see your dilemma, Father, and technically, the journal belongs to you, so we cannot publish anything without your approval. If you don't want us to continue, we'll bow to your decision,' I told him, hoping he would decide in our favour. I did not relish spending the rest of my life with the threat of Sinclair's thugs hanging over me.

'I really don't know. It's getting late; perhaps you could return tomorrow after I've looked through the journal a little. It's my busy day, but if you come about ten, I'll give you my decision. If I decide to let you use the journal, then you can work here, I'll be in the church most of the day.'

'We'll go now Father. We'll return tomorrow, I hope that you will allow us access to the journal, even if you don't want us to publish, because we've come so far now, it'd be unbearable not to find out the end of the story.'

Then, frustrated, we left.

Chapter 29

That evening, we found it difficult to focus on writing the second episode of the article. It took much longer than we'd expected. It was well after midnight before we had an acceptable version that we could send to the paper.

'Do we change it if Father Charlie agrees to let us publish the journal?' I asked. 'This sort of thing is rather more in your domain than mine.'

'No, if we can run with it, we'll know by tomorrow and when we send this in on Monday. We could give him the outline of a third episode and hope he's interested.'

'I should think he'll have our hands off.'

'Yup, we might make a bit of a killing out of this, but we'd have to share it with Father Charlie or the Church. But that's not as important as destroying that poisonous bastard Richard Sinclair, because that's what these revelations will do. To say nothing of saving our own skins.'

'Yeah, but Father Charlie has a point, does the end justify the means?'

We left it at that and called it a night. The next morning I was up early to get a copy of the Sunday paper that was running our article; it was quite a kick to see our names in print as the authors. Of course, it also left us open to further reprisals and I thought belatedly that it might have been wise to have published under a *nom de plume*. After a quick breakfast we departed for our appointment with Father Charlie.

The day was cool and overcast as we pulled into Marlow. We pulled on to the rectory drive and got out. Father Charlie must have been looking out for us, because he came to the door even as we walked up the gravelled path.

'Good morning, Father,' I greeted him. Lisa smiled nervously.

'Hello, come in.' He stood back and waved us into the hall. 'You know where the study is, make yourselves at home, I'll be there in just a minute.'

The short wait was an agony. Any moment now, we would find out if all the work we had put in over the past weeks would be for nothing, in which case we'd never learn the end of the story. That would be unbearable after all we had achieved. Father Charlie came into the room and sat behind his desk.

'I won't keep you in suspense. I've thought very hard about this and I've even prayed for guidance, something I haven't done in a while. The answer is; I still can't make up my mind.'

Lisa looked bereft and said, 'But Father, we've run out of time, we've only got until Tuesday, then we'll both have to run for cover…' she tailed off as the priest held up a hand.

'I hadn't finished. I was about to say that I couldn't make my mind up about publication. I have no problem with letting you complete your reading of the journal. I still have not completed it myself. I reached the part where Miller had been recruited into the SS in Occupied France. The one thing that came across to me was that Miller had much to answer for, but he seemed to be truly repentant. I can only hope for the sake of his soul, he confessed to Father Nathan and was absolved. I have to go back to the church to prepare for mass. Will you be alright here? There's coffee and tea in the kitchen. Help yourselves.'

'Aren't you worried that we might just take the journal, Father?' I asked.

'I've always prided myself that I'm a good judge of character and my instinct is I can trust you. I have every confidence.'

'Thank you, Father, we'd never betray your trust. We do appreciate your kindness in letting us finish the journal. We will abide by whatever you decide about any publication,' I said, while thinking, 'No matter what the consequences.'

'Right, I'll be off then; I'll be back after midday mass. Perhaps you'll have finished by then and you can tell me the finale to the story.'

He handed Lisa the leather-bound journal and we sat down at the work table to continue our reading.

I had only been in France for a matter of days when war broke out. I was torn between my mother's people and my father's. I decided I owed little to Britain and immersed myself in life in Amiens, where I had found work. The blitzkrieg attack in the spring of 1940 left me in an invidious position, a British citizen behind German lines.

Within days of the French surrender on 22ⁿᵈ June, I was arrested by the French police and handed over to the German military authorities. For several weeks I was imprisoned in Amiens, but in July I was transferred to an ilag near Paris, we were not informed of where, but I later found it to be at St Denis. Life in the camp was easy, if somewhat tedious, but conditions were reasonably good and rations were supplemented by Red Cross parcels. There was plenty of time for sport and such pastimes, but I felt out of place, it seemed to me that one way or another I would have to choose between my English and German halves. I became increasingly isolated from my fellow inmates and my contempt for their misplaced optimism became manifest. My so-called comrades distrusted me because of my fluent German and 'unpatriotic' outlook and I found myself an outcast. In some ways I was, for I could not see how Britain could win the war, it was only a matter of time before the Luftwaffe destroyed the RAF and Britain would fall as the rest of Europe had.

The real change for me came when John Amery came to the camp in late August, trying to raise a unit of British volunteers for the Waffen SS. I had no intention of joining, Amery seemed as misguided as my fellow inmates, but in a different way. I doubted his ability to organise such a unit and doubted his leadership abilities even more. However, his visit sparked in my mind a plan to extricate myself from the camp. I had got to know one of the officers attached to the camp, a wounded Luftwaffe Oberleutnant, Hans Weber. Hans had been attached to the camp administration until he was deemed fit enough to return to active service. Amery's visit had reminded me that I still technically held the rank of Hauptsturmführer in the SS; this presented me with an opportunity to get out of the camp and also to join the side that was certain to win the war. I prevailed on Hans to send a letter I had written to my old friend Sepp Dietrich. For a few weeks, I heard nothing, until out of the blue I was summoned to the Commandant's office. He told me that he had received instructions from none other than Gruppenführer Reinhard Heydrich, the Deputy Head of the SS. Within the hour, an SS officer appeared with a uniform for me, not in the black I had worn previously, but in grey-green, complete with badges of rank, black squares with three diagonal silver pips and two silver stripes on the left collar, to balance the silver SS lightning flashes on the right. I was released into his custody. The very next day, I was taken to Sepp Dietrich's headquarters.

'William, my friend,' he greeted me. 'How are you? Please sit.'

'I'm well Sepp. Thank you for rescuing me from that infernal camp.'

'It's not me you need to thank. I could have ordered your release on my own authority, but that may have had repercussions later and would have certainly been a lengthy process. I spoke to Heydrich, who has a very high opinion of you and he ordered your release and commission into the Liebstandarte immediately. If you will accept the post, you are to act as my aide, until Heydrich has considered how best to use your talents.'

'I would be honoured Sepp.'

'In that case the officer waiting outside will show you to your quarters.'

I jumped to my feet and saluted. 'Jawohl, Herr Obergruppenführer!'

'Thank you, William, you may go.' I turned to leave when he barked at me. 'Hauptsturmführer Muller! You are incorrectly dressed!' I looked at him in confusion.

'I am sorry Sir, this was the uniform provided.'

Sepp exploded into a gale of laughter. 'You are incorrectly dressed because you are not wearing the medal that the Führer has awarded you. Hauptsturmführer Muller, in the name of the Führer, Adolf Hitler, for your services to the Reich, I present you with the

Order of the German Eagle.' He placed a red ribbon, bordered with white and black lines over my head. The white cross with eagles between its arms made a stark contrast to the grey-green SS uniform. 'It is normally worn on your left breast, your batman will see to that. Congratulations!'

I held out my hand, but Dietrich ignored it, enveloping me in a huge bear hug.

'The Reich does not forget those who performed meritorious service. Now get along to your quarters and I'll see you later. We can discuss old times and what your new duties entail.'

I saluted and turned smartly to march out of the room.

For the next eight months, I served as Dietrich's aide, ensuring his orders were dispatched and generally that the administration around him ran smoothly. I accompanied him to Greece, but knowing my reservations about actually fighting against the country of my birth, he carefully ensured that I was kept out of active service. They were happy times and I developed an intimate and lasting bond with Sepp.

In the late spring of 1941, I was called into Sepp's office. As usual he offered me a chair and slid his silver cigarette case across the desk to me. As I lit the cigarette he looked at me.

'William, my friend, I regret that the time has come when we must part company.'

'Why Sepp, are you being transferred?'

'No, you are. Orders arrived today that you have been reassigned to the RHSA in Berlin. There is a transport flight leaving for Berlin in two hours and you have to be on it. The day after tomorrow, you are to report to Heydrich at the RHSA offices in Berlin.'

It was with regret that I took my leave of Sepp and hurried to pack and catch the flight to Berlin.

Two days later, I was standing in Heydrich's office in Berlin. I was surprised by the warmth with which I was greeted. I had always regarded Heydrich as somewhat of a cold fish, but he embraced me, kissing me on both cheeks.

'Please sit down, William,' he said. I took the offered seat.

'The Reich has much to thank you for. Thanks to your actions in 1933, the Party was able to consolidate its position. Your name is even known to the Führer, but we will come to that later. I understand from Sepp Dietrich that you wish to serve the Reich in the war, but would prefer to avoid taking action against the English because of your parentage. Ordinarily, I would have doubts about any Englander who came with such an offer, but in the light of your previous service to the Reich, I have no such reservations. Sepp has also been very complimentary about the way you have fulfilled your duties. I should like you to become my adjutant, working here at the SD.'

I was stunned; I had not expected anything like this. I stared at Heydrich's long-nosed aesthetic face, lost for words.

'Well man, do you accept?'

I jumped to my feet, standing to attention. 'Jarwohl, Mein Gruppenführer!'

'Good man.' Heydrich smiled. 'My clerk outside will ensure that you are comfortably billeted and I'll expect you here at 9.00 tomorrow morning.'

I was housed in a former hotel, only a mile from SD headquarters. The hotel had been confiscated from its former Jewish owners in 1938 and commandeered by the SS as accommodation for officers posted to Berlin. I was assigned a suite of grandly decorated rooms, for my personal use. It was all a far cry from my childhood in London.

It took me a month to become fully familiar with all aspects of my duties. In that time I saw Heydrich four or five times a day, with the exception of weekends which he insisted on spending with his wife and children. On those days I worked on alone in my office, ensuring that everything ran smoothly. As Heydrich's adjutant, I came in to contact with many of the party leaders, including Goering, that fat buffoon in his fancy white uniform bedecked with gold braid; Goebbels, a small rat-like man and most of all Himmler, the bespectacled coldly ambitious Reichsführer of the SS. On one or two occasions I also met the Führer himself.

217

Within a few weeks of my elevation to the SD, I found myself transferring with Heydrich to Prague, when he became Reichsprotektor of Bohemia and Moravia. My work remained largely the same, only the surroundings changed. Heydrich had a separate staff to deal with the governing of the Czechs, my role remained concentrated on the SD. In late October 1941 Heydrich called me into his office.

'Sit down Muller, you may smoke.'

'Thank you Herr Reichsprotektor. How may I be of service?'

Heydrich laughed. 'That's what I like about you Muller, always straight down to business. This could be a crucial task. With our invasion of the Soviet Union, we have spread our forces a little thinly. I think that there is a real danger of planned resistance breaking out in our rear, orchestrated by communists and other political opponents.'

'What General Mola called his fifth column?'

'Exactly, I sometimes forget that you fought in Spain.'

I did not believe that, Heydrich never forgot anything.

'I think that the crushing of this opposition, and especially its leadership, will, in the near future, be essential. As yet, no-one in the leadership has seen the need; I want you to prepare a plan for the crushing of opposition in our rear areas. I know you can be ruthless, I have read about your career in Spain. I want you to give full rein to that ruthlessness. You may requisition such staff and resources as you think necessary, but I want your plan presented to me within four weeks. I will also expect regular updates on your progress. Untersturmführer Freund will take over your day-to-day duties for the time being.'

This was a huge task and there was not much time to achieve it. I put together a team of SD and Gestapo officers and for the next weeks we worked fifteen hours a day, seven days a week. By the time the month was up, I had a plan I was happy with to put to Heydrich.

'This is good, Muller,' he said. 'I think there are areas that still require a little refinement, but in essence, this is exactly what I wanted. The Führer has come round to my way of thinking and in a

218

week, he plans to issue a decree, it will be called the Decree of Night and Fog. This will order the rounding up and execution or imprisonment of all opposition and resistance. I will pass on to him your idea that we shed the shackles of international agreements and deal with opponents in our hands in a more...permanent manner. Your work will mean that we can start immediately the decree is proclaimed, without the need for delay.'

I was later to learn that the purge of opposition after the decree was to lead to the arrest of seven thousand resisters and their families and the deaths of nearly four hundred by execution. That is without counting the unknown number of those imprisoned in concentration camps. People were seized in the middle of the night and simply disappeared, never to be seen again. That was my work and another sin for which my immortal soul will have to answer. All I considered was how I could please my masters in achieving the Führer's goals, with no thought as to the consequences for the people involved.

Lisa stopped reading and looked at me.

'He's doing it again, confessing to have committed the most horrendous crimes, but he's sorry now.'

'Yeah, there are a lot of things you do in your youth that you regret in later life.'

She smiled at me. 'Do tell.'

'Wild horses wouldn't drag out of me some of the things I did in my youth.'

'Ian, I never saw you as such a rebel!'

'Okay, Father Charlie is coming back, so you can stop winding me up.'

Father Charlie crossed the lawn with a cheery wave and came into the study through the French doors.

'How's the research going, my merry bookworms?'

'Slowly Father, but it's very interesting,' I said.

'I've taken the liberty of telling Margaret that you'll be staying for lunch and she tells me it'll be ready in a few minutes, so if you'd like to come through to the dining room, you can carry on with the journal after we've eaten.'

Chapter 30

Sunday lunch with Father Charlie was an impressive affair. Margaret treated us to a roast beef dinner, with Yorkshire pudding, roast potatoes and all the trimmings. Father Charlie was good company, too. First, he made us tell him about our progress with the journal, then he amused us for the rest of the meal with ecclesiastical anecdotes. Despite my eagerness to return to the journal, I found myself enjoying the meal and time flew by. In due course Lisa and I, now replete, settled once more to Peter Sinclair's journal.

As a reward for my contribution to the Decree of Night and Fog, I was promoted to Sturmbannführer. My duties continued to be that of adjutant and confidant to Heydrich, who I had come to look on as a close friend. There was no sign of the characteristics of the 'Butcher of Prague' as he had been named, I always found him to be solicitous and amiable. There was a dichotomy between his public and private personas. On many occasions I was invited to join his wife and children and was treated as a member of the family.

At the beginning of January 1942 I accompanied Heydrich to Wannsee, where he chaired a conference of all parties involved with the resettlement of the Jews. The aim of the conference was to decide what was to be done with the Jews within the Occupied Territories, now that the planned resettlement of the Jews in Siberia had been delayed due to the stalling of our attack on the Soviets. After the first day it was clear that there was no decisive opinion in the meeting. I drew to Heydrich's attention letters from Greiser, the head of the administration of the Warthegau province of Poland, to Himmler asking permission to 'deal with' the Jews sent to the Lodz ghetto, who were unable to work and who he could neither feed nor house. He complained that an epidemic of spotted fever and starvation made it inhumane to continue to crowd Jews into the camp. He had

220

succeeded in getting Himmler to assign to him *Sonnerkommando Lange*, an SS group led by Herbert Lange, who had developed techniques of gassing in a large van using carbon monoxide. I supplemented this with copies of reports from Lange at the concentration camp of Chelmno, where he had begun large-scale killings the previous month.

'It's a good idea, Muller, but the whole scheme is too small scale to succeed,' Heydrich said, showing me a sheet of paper that estimated that there was the problem of some twelve million Jews across Europe that needed to be addressed.

'Obergruppenführer,' I said, 'have you read the reports from Hoess at Auschwitz Camp? He reports the efficaciousness of Zyklon B gas in an experiment where four hundred Russian prisoners were gassed in a makeshift gas chamber in an underground armoury.'

'I see your point. Put the two ideas together and we have a possible solution. I believe Hoess is already constructing a huge camp at Auschwitz-Birkenau; we could amend the plans to include gas chambers and some means of disposing of the bodies. Yet it would be a mammoth undertaking. I'll see what the conference thinks of the idea tomorrow.'

Thus in essence, I became, if not the father of the Holocaust, then one of the minds that helped to fashion it, a heavy burden to carry for the rest of my life. Now, not a day passes that I do not regret bringing those ideas to Heydrich's attention in my eagerness to please him. The rest of the Wannsee conference is a matter of historical record; there, thanks to my prompting, the decision was made to exterminate a race of some twelve million souls.

Life in Prague continued in what had become its routine way. I dealt with matters for Heydrich and spent weekends with his family, who I came to regard as my family. Heydrich became a kind of elder brother to me. He sent me to Auschwitz-Birkenau to report on the construction of the camp with its new gas chambers and crematoria. Not being content with the progress, he left me there to oversee and expedite the construction, by ensuring that Hoess got all the resources and co-operation he needed.

I was still at Birkenau when I heard that Heydrich had been wounded in an assassination attempt on May 27th. A partisan had attempted to spray his bulletproof car with a machine pistol. When the pistol jammed, Heydrich had ordered his driver to stop and drew his sidearm to arrest the assassin, so typical of him. As he exited his car, a second partisan threw a bomb into the vehicle, wounding both Heydrich and himself. True to type, Heydrich had pursued his assailant despite his wounds, but had become weak from shock and sent Klein, his driver, to pursue the bomber. Klein had been wounded in the ensuing gunfight and the culprit had escaped. All this I learned in a phone call from Lina, Heydrich's wife, who assured me that he was not seriously wounded. He had a broken rib and had lung and spleen damage, but the surgeons who had operated on him were confident he would make a full recovery. Two days later, Lina phoned again - infection had set in caused by the horsehair stuffing from the car seats that had entered his body in the explosion. The prognosis was not good. I set off at once in my staff car. I arrived in Prague three hours later and went straight to the hospital. Heydrich was feverish and pale. I stayed with him an hour, then at his request escorted Lina home to the children. The next day, doctors told us there was nothing else they could do, the septicaemia was too advanced. The following day Himmler flew to Prague to visit Heydrich. In Himmler's presence he said goodbye to his children and later that day, after Himmler had left, he slipped into a coma from which he never recovered. He died two days later with Lina and I beside his bed. In death his face took on an ethereal beauty I had never noticed in life. I took Lina home and sat with her as she informed the children that their beloved father was dead.

I was filled with a deadly rage at the death of my 'brother', a sensation I had not felt since Spain. I vowed then and there to extract vengeance for my dead friend. First I had a final service to perform. I escorted his body back to Berlin and was one of the pallbearers who carried his coffin to his final resting place in the Invalidenfriedhoff. I stood comforting Lina, whilst his eulogy was read by Himmler. At the end of the ceremony the Führer himself spoke to Lina to offer his condolences.

In my absence from Prague, the assassins had been located in the vault of St Cyril's church, where they had held out against repeated attacks and committed suicide when their capture became inevitable. My chance to fulfil my vow to avenge Heydrich had gone. Nevertheless, I flew back from Berlin straight after the funeral.

The Führer had ordered widespread reprisals for Heydrich's death. He ordered the execution of 30,000 random Czechs and told the SS to "wade in blood" to find his killers and their associates. He was persuaded by Governor General Frank to moderate his response, yet I believe some 14,000 people were arrested and sent to camps. The Gestapo unearthed a link between the village of Lidice and one of the assassins. The Führer ordered "teach the Czechs a final lesson in subservience and humility" and I was glad to arrange it.

I accompanied the SS reprisal squad to Lidice, technically Hauptsturmführer Max Rostock was in command, but outranking him, it was my orders that prevailed. On my orders all of the inhabitants were rounded up. Males over fifteen were locked up in a number of farm buildings, whilst the women and children were incarcerated in the school. In batches of ten, I had the 173 men and boys executed by machine gun fire. Such was my rage that I commanded the execution detail personally. When I was finished, seventeen rows of bloody corpses lay on the ground, some with shattered skulls and others with intestines and other organs hanging out and I felt satisfaction. The women, I had removed to Ravensbruck concentration camp. The children went to Chelmno, with the exception of a few very young children, who were sent for re-education in German families. I cared not that this was the same as a death sentence. Finally I ordered that engineers bring up explosives to raze the village to the ground. It was in the course of this that I was hit in the hand by shrapnel and doctors were forced to amputate what remained of the little finger on my left hand. Hardly a glorious episode, but I was nevertheless awarded a silver wound badge. Now I regret those actions, my only defence before God will be that I was lost in grief for my friend. Today it seems like insanity had gripped me and robbed me of all rational thought, leaving only a visceral desire for vengeance.

After Lidice I took the leave that been accruing for the past year and spent the time in Berlin with Lina and the Heydrich children, to whom I was Uncle Willi. At the end of my leave I was sent back to Auschwitz-Birkenau as an adviser to Commandant Hoess. I was to spend the next two years at Auschwitz. Strangely, it is my time there that weighs lightest on my conscience, as I was not involved with the killing. My task was to ensure that the economic opportunities were exploited to the full. Commanding the administration of what the inmates called Kanada, I was responsible for ensuring that all assets were returned to the Reich, from high value items like gold, jewels and currency to items for recycling such as spectacles. I was sure that there was a degree of corruption amongst the men under my command, but try as I might, I could prove nothing.

In late 1943 rumours of corruption reached the ears of the authorities and Morgen, an Obersturmbannführer from the RPKA, arrived to investigate. I have no doubt that he thought that I was involved, for he spent hours questioning me. Eventually, only two of my men were arrested. Despite his efforts, Morgen failed to garner any evidence against me, but I felt sure that what he could not find, he would fabricate. Knowing he kept all of the evidence in the hut he was using as the centre for his investigation, I ensured that nothing would come back to haunt me, thanks to a judicious piece of arson. Although nothing could be now proved against me, my reputation was seriously damaged by his allegations. I was incensed after all my service to the Reich and decided that if I was to be accused and treated as if I had committed these crimes, then I may as well feather my own nest. I began to retain items of high value that were easily hidden and transported; diamonds and other precious stones were particularly useful in that respect. In the following months I accumulated a fortune in precious stones. Today I admit that my actions were morally dubious, but as the true owners were dead, it still does not feel like theft. Of all my crimes, this is the one that *bothers my conscience least. These actions did allow me to care for my family and in the period after the war, I have taken the money that I have amassed from the prudent investment of those valuables and I have anonymously donated a far greater sum to Jewish charities. I hope that goes some way to making amends.*

Father Charlie put his head round the door of the study.

'I don't want to disturb your reading, but I'm going to say evening mass. Feel free to make yourselves a drink while I'm gone.'

'Is it that late already?' Lisa asked. 'We'll never get to the end. We're just getting to the good part, how he managed to get away with all this.'

'Mmm, he does seem to be a walking war crime. There seem to be few atrocities that friend Miller did not have a hand in. I love the way that mere theft does not bother his conscience. I should think not, it's the merest trifle in comparison with two counts of mass murder and involvement in planning genocide.'

'I know what you mean, I'm getting a bit tired of all the hand-wringing, "Oh I'm so sorry for my crimes, forgive me." Some things are unforgivable. Come on, let's take a short break for a drink, it'll help our concentration and in the long run will speed thing up.'

'Okay, ten minutes then it's back to the death-throws of the Third Reich!'

'Right, I'll go make some tea then.'

Chapter 31

Our break lasted fifteen minutes, then it was back to the story. With tired eyes, we continued to read:

I remained at Auschwitz until early 1945. With the war now going against Germany, a number of senior army officers attempted to assassinate the Führer with a bomb at his Rastenburg headquarters. The SD were ordered to root out the traitors and Kaltenbrunner, Heydrich's successor, recalled me to Berlin to help with the investigation. The main protagonists in the plot; von Stauffenberg, Olbricht and von Haeften had been overzealously executed by General Fromm and died without being questioned. On the Eastern front, General von Tresckow had chosen to commit suicide in no-man's land with a hand grenade. On the orders of the Führer, the SS were to spare no efforts in identifying and bringing to justice all of those involved in the conspiracy. Himmler passed the law of sippenhaft, the relatives of those involved in the conspiracy were also to be held responsible and punished. This was my task for Kaltenbrunner, I was to identify and arrange for the arrest of the relatives of the accused conspirators. I did not personally carry out the arrests, but followed my orders in identifying and having transported to camps people like von Stauffenberg's wife and brother and von Tresckow's wife. For once I have few regrets for my part in these events. If I had not followed my orders then another would have done so.

'The old excuse, I was just obeying orders. That's what all the war criminals tried to use as a defence,' I exclaimed in annoyance.

'I see your point; he does exactly as he's ordered, perhaps even willingly, then he tries to wriggle out of the moral consequences.'

'Sorry for disturbing you, it's just that he really annoys me, always seeking to put the best complexion on his actions. "I was grieving, I was furious, I was ordered." It makes me sick.

226

Anyway, back to the journal, we must be getting near to the end of the story.'

It was clear to everyone but the Führer, that the war was lost. With the Russians pressing from the east and the British and Americans crossing the Rhine in the west, I began to plan how to extricate myself from the mess that was Germany. I realised that I would be a wanted man once Germany fell and began to plan my escape. I was not alone in this; many in the SS began to seek to escape the retribution of the Allies. The "Organization Der Ehemaligen SS-Angehörigen", the organisation of former SS members or Odessa was already helping prominent SS officers to escape the Reich. I did not want to spend my life in South American exile like so many of my colleagues. I had the resources to start a better life and I realised that it would be easy for me to disappear into the chaos of the collapsing Reich and reappear in a new identity, a British one, which would get me out of Germany. Unlike members of the Waffen SS, I had never had my blood type tattooed on my arm - it had not been necessary, as even in my time with Sepp, I had been nowhere near combat, thus there was no physical way to identify me. It was simply a matter of the paperwork that would allow me to disappear. Consequently, Odessa procured for me forged identity papers and a British Army uniform. So William Miller, or Wilhelm Muller as I was known, disappeared and Corporal Reg Clayton of the Royal Army Service Corps, prisoner of war, took his place.

'What's that about tattoos?' Lisa asked, 'I don't get it.'

'Members of the Waffen SS, effectively the SS army, had their blood group tattooed inside their left arm, to ensure they had first call on supplies of blood if they were wounded.'

'Charming! Sorry to have interrupted your concentration, I didn't know if it was important.'

In the dislocation following the collapse of Germany, there were many former prisoners of war roaming around, thus I hid myself in

227

plain sight. I was picked up by the Army, who fed me and issued me with a new uniform. Things were too chaotic for identities to be checked against military records and within a matter a days I had been repatriated to Britain. It would not be possible to maintain the guise of Reg Clayton in a civilian society of birth certificates, passports and all the red tape of the state. Once in England, I heard about the destruction of Coventry, which offered me the opportunity to change my identity again. I visited the city posing as a bereaved prisoner of war searching for relatives. I found the grave of Peter Sinclair, who had died in infancy. Had he survived, he would have been my age. Alongside him were buried his mother and father, he was the ideal candidate. I obtained a copy of his birth certificate and Peter Sinclair was reborn. The jewels I had looted from Auschwitz were slowly sold off for me to obtain the capital to finance my new life. My one regret was that I could not see my beloved mother. William Miller had to remain dead. I took care of her anonymously; it was too little, but it was all I could do for her. No-one knew my identity and I had to preserve that secret. Even my wife never knew of her husband's previous life.

Now, in old age the sins of my past weigh heavily on my conscience. I have returned to the Church of my youth. In an attempt to atone for my sins, I told everything to my friend and confessor Father Nathan Donovan. This text is the result of my talks with him, a way of me coming to terms with my guilt.

Peter Sinclair 31st October 1986

'So that's it then,' Lisa said. 'It's all a bit of an anti-climax.'

'Yes, I feel a bit deflated. It seems strange to have reached the end of the story…or is it? Look, there is another page here.'

Turning the page, I showed to her another addition on the page after the signature:

Postscript
Today I told my son, Richard, the secret of his heritage. He expressed some surprise at my confession. I explained the full horror of my appalling actions during two wars. I was amazed at Richard's

reaction to my disclosure. Far from condemning me, he applauded my wartime record, expressing a fiery hatred for Jews and communists. My late wife and I did all we could to ensure that his upbringing would produce an educated, liberal, humanitarian. In many respects he reminds me of myself at his age. It seems that blood will out and the hatred I carried in my early life still runs in the blood of my son, though for less reason. In my discussions with him, he extolled the virtues of Hitler and decried me for abandoning the politics of my former life. Despite what I had told him about my own experiences, he vehemently denied the holocaust had happened, claiming it was a mixture of fabrication, anti-Nazi, pro-Zionist propaganda and exaggeration. It seems hard to credit that my educated son could deny the veracity of events that I witnessed with my own eyes.

Richard has expressed political ambitions which I shall do my best to suppress. He has all of the charisma of the Führer, but is far better educated and in many ways, less politically naïve. I genuinely fear for the fate of Britain should he ever enter politics. I have committed many sins in my life, but I sincerely believe that my son is capable of worse. For now, I will try to direct his energies into business, but with the restless energy he displays, I fear business will not hold enough attraction to make him permanently eschew a political career. I can only hope that someone will prevent him from making mistakes of an even greater magnitude that mine.

P.S.   27ᵗʰ January 1988

'That's a damning indictment of Richard Sinclair, considering his father's record,' said Lisa.

'It could do enormous damage to Sinclair and the BNRA if it became public knowledge. If Sinclair suspects the existence of this journal, you can see why he would go to any length to keep it secret.'

'The revelations about his father would be damaging enough. Now we know for certain why there have been so many attempts to stop us.'

'Yes, but can you imagine the damage that would be done, if his father's opinion of him became public?   With his father's background, the idea that Sinclair was too extreme for him would certainly hole him beneath the waterline.'

'You do realise how dangerous this information is? Sinclair would stop at nothing, and I mean nothing, to prevent this going public. If we were in danger before, then it just increased tenfold. It really is a matter of publish or die.'

At this juncture, Father Charlie returned from evening mass, enquiring about our progress. We gave him a brief outline of the end of the journal's story. Finally we showed him the postscript. He put on his glasses and read the last page, frowned, then reread it.

'I think this puts a whole different complexion on me allowing the publication of this journal. I believe from the postscript that Peter Sinclair would want his confession to be published, if it stopped the political ambitions of his son. So if you want to publish, you have my blessing. You can take the journal with you as evidence to support your story.'

I thought about this. 'I think it would be better if the journal remained in your care, Father. I've taken enough notes for us to be able to write the final part of the story. We have already suffered enough threats because of our findings; this could make us even more vulnerable. Sinclair would go to any lengths to get his hands on it. He knows about us, but you are an unknown, so the book will be safer with you. We may need to produce the journal as proof of our article; if you have it, we know where to find it. You are our failsafe.'

Father Charlie looked up at me. 'Agreed!' he said.

It was late afternoon when we got back to London. Both Lisa and I were stunned by Sinclair's revelations. My mind was in a whirl but there was more to it than just Sinclair, the empty feeling inside me and the fear of the future was returning. My time investigating the enigma that was William Miller had given me a purpose and shielded me from the hopelessness of reality. I had been living in a protected bubble. Now we had reached the end of our journey, it would soon be time for Lisa and me to part. Once we published the story, I would have to return to the existence that I hated and feared, alone. Again the prospect of a solitary life raised its ugly head and there would be no Lisa, no Miller, nothing to shield me. Reality had to be faced. For the first time in weeks the hopelessness of my situation overwhelmed me.

Working with Lisa had given me focus, it had given me something to live for, now once more I remembered that I had lost everything and there was simply nothing left to lose.

Lisa looked at me, 'You okay? You've got that thousand yard stare again.'

'Uh? Sorry. Come on, we can't wait for me to get my act together, we have work to do. We need to get the final drafts of the articles written, you're off to Prague in a couple of days, remember?'

Despite having a head that felt as if it was stuffed with cotton wool, I managed to retain enough focus to play my part in the writing. By early evening, we had completed our first draft.

'I can't face rewriting it again today! I can always postpone my flight if we don't get it all completed tomorrow,' Lisa stated.

'No you won't. Until this hits the streets we are in greater danger than ever. In fact it would be better if you went earlier, not delay your flight.

'So this is it Ian, we've almost finished?'

'Looks that way.'

'It's strange, you've become such a big part of my life, I'm going to miss you. This project has dominated my life for the past few weeks and I feel at a loss now it's coming to an end.'

'I know exactly what you mean, but we both have to return to our real lives. You have James waiting for you and I…well I have to return to whatever my future may be.'

She regarded me with sympathy. 'You'll be alright Ian, I promise. You'll rebuild your life; it'll just take a bit of time, that's all. You're a strong man, hang in there and it'll get easier, I promise. It did with Dad and I know it will with you.'

'Yeah, I'm sure you're right. Perhaps if I try to pick up the pieces and persuade the world I'm okay, I might manage to persuade myself.'

'I really appreciate all you've done to help me and I'm going to take you out to dinner to thank you, come on.'

'Okay,' I said, putting my words into practice and hiding behind a brave and cheerful façade to mask the emptiness I felt.

It was still light as we walked to the tube station at Bethnal Green and took the underground up towards Charing Cross. After the problems we had with the tail two days before, I was more vigilant than ever looking for suspicious characters. I notice a tall, well-built young man in a denim jacket who had got on the tube at the same time as we did. As the carriage lurched he lost his balance and grabbed at a pole for support. As he did so, the sleeve of his jacket rode up over his wrist to display the same lightening flash tattoo I had seen on the thug in Covent Garden the week before.

'Shit!' I hissed.

'What?' Lisa enquired.

'That guy over there...no don't look...he's got a Storm45 tattoo. They must have been staking out all of the Tube stations in the area around your flat, hoping to locate us. And they have.'

'You can bet your life he's summoned the cavalry. What are we going to do?'

'I really don't know. I can't see the police believing we're being threatened by thugs set on to us by one of the highest profile politicians in the country. All we can do is head for the West End and hope that some opportunity to lose him comes up, before his mates arrive.'

We changed lines on the underground, Lisa deliberately trying to keep to the deeper lines where there would be no mobile phone signal for our tail to summon help. I sat racking my brain for a way we could lose him, but came up blank; Sunday evening in London was not the best time. What we needed was a big football crowd to lose ourselves in, but there were no matches at that time on Sundays in summer. Lisa sat staring out of the window at the station we had reached, a look of concentration on her face. We exited the tube at Leicester Square and as we travelled to the surface on the escalator, Lisa broke into a grin.

'I've got an idea. Follow me.'

I used the reflection in a shop window to check on our pursuer. Somehow he must have managed to summon help, because he had been joined by two hefty skinheads. Our odds had just got a lot worse. I pointed to the reflection to alert Lisa.

'Oh crap!' she said. 'Come on, hurry.'

She led me along the road towards Leicester Square. Our pursuers were closing on us rapidly as we turned into the square. It was crowded, heaving with a throng of mainly young girls thronging round the cinema.

'How did you…? What's going on?'

Lisa grinned at me, 'When I saw an advertisement for the movie in the tube, I remembered reading that the premiere of that latest vampire movie was tonight. It was always going to be crowded with teenies trying to catch a glimpse of the star. Not that I blame them, he is cute.'

'I thought you were taken.'

'A girl can look,' she pouted.

'Yeah, this crowd's all well and good, but unless we find a way to delay them, those thugs are too close for us to be able to lose them, even in this crowd. I don't know how we're going to manage that, they're only fifteen yards behind us.'

'Watch and learn.' Lisa grinned at me again and stalked right up to the nearest policeman on crowd control. I tagged along, wondering what she was planning. She surely was not going to enlist the aid of the policeman; we had agreed that they would never believe us.

'Excuse me, Officer.'

The constable turned. He was about Lisa's age, the old adage about policemen looking younger than ever crossed my mind. When he saw Lisa, he suddenly became very helpful. That girl really did have an amazing effect on the men about her.

'Can I help you. Miss?'

'Yes, could you tell me, is Panton Street this way?' Lisa turned and pointed straight at our pursuers, who froze for an instant, then turned around, scattering and trying to blend into the crowd.

'No Miss, it's over there,' said the policeman, nodding in the opposite direction, right into the thick of the crowd. 'But you'll never get through....' He tailed off as Lisa plunged into the crowd with me in her wake.

Lisa forced her way into the crowd, then veered to her right, pushing her way through the more thinly packed periphery of the mob. Lisa dragged me out of the crowd and across the road. A quick glance behind showed we were alone. She led me into a big Edwardian fronted hotel on the southern side of the Square. We entered the plush reception area and crossed into one of the bars. However, this was no time for us to have a drink and we exited from the bar into another street that led us away from the Square. Walking so fast we were nearly trotting, we hurried down the street until we reached the Charing Cross Road. At once, Lisa flagged down a black cab and we dove in through the rear door. Lisa gave him the address in Bow and we were away out of the reach of our enemies. We remained silent for most of the journey, both of us lost in our thoughts of what might have come to pass, had it not been for Lisa's quick mind.

'We were lucky there,' said Lisa, as she unlocked the door.

'Not lucky, you saved us. Thanks.'

'We're in serious trouble, aren't we?'

'Yeah, big time. You need to get out of the country now, we can't wait until Tuesday.'

'But what about the article? We haven't finished.'

'Leave the draft with me. You phone the paper and tell them we've got a sensational third episode; I'll email a rewrite for you to amend in the Czech Republic and when you're happy with it you can send it on to the paper. You know where to find me when the payment comes through.'

'Are you sure? I really don't like the idea of bailing and leaving you in the shit.'

'You needn't worry, I'll be picking up some clean clothes from home, and then I'm out of here to places unknown.' I picked up the laptop and booked Lisa on the first flight from Stansted to Prague the following morning.

'It's a bit expensive; can't we get a refund on the other ticket?' Lisa asked.

'Bugger the cost, my credit card can pick up the tab. We're really out of our depth here and I need you to be safe.'

'Okay, but I'll pay you back.'

Exhausted, we both went to our separate beds, though neither of us got much sleep.

Chapter 32

Early the next day I turned the car northwards up the M11, to drop Lisa at Stansted on my way back to Suffolk. We parted outside the terminal; she kissed my cheek and promised to be in touch soon. Then she was gone, leaving me to return to my wrecked home and wrecked life. The three remaining weeks of the holiday yawned like an eternity before me. I actually looked forward to getting back to school. A sad state of affairs, I thought, when all I had left in my life was my job. I had phoned my friends with whom I intended to seek refuge, but they had not answered; more than likely they were on holiday. I decided to go home and think about my next move. I was sure I would be okay at home for twenty four hours whilst I sorted myself out. It was not as if I had much to lose anyway, even if Sinclair did catch up with me.

'Come on,' I said to myself, 'pull yourself together, you can do this, you have to do it.' But it was so, so hard.

I drove home in silence, I could not face any music, lyrics about love or loss could have been the final straw. Three quarters of an hour later I pulled the Saab onto the drive of my home. Unlocking the front door, I went in. The clean-up people sent by the insurance had done a good job, but the house seemed rather Spartan, with so much of the damaged furniture having been junked. I made myself a black coffee, as there was no milk and sat down to contemplate my future. Giving up, I went upstairs and lay on the bed. I had slept poorly last night and besides, sleep provided a short escape from my problems.

I was awakened by an insistent knocking on my front door. I looked out of the bedroom window to see a well-dressed man in his thirties at the door. He was a long way from the thugs who had followed us the night before, he looked more like a Mormon evangelist.

'Hang on; I'll be there in a minute,' I called out of the window. I opened the door, squinting as the afternoon sun shone in my eyes. The door suddenly exploded inwards, sending me reeling. After kicking the door, the man stepped inside and closed the door behind him.

'What the fuck do you think ...' I was cut off as he gripped my throat in his right hand, pinning me to the hall wall.

'You have seriously inconvenienced a friend of mine, Mr West,' he said in a cultured voice. 'The article in Sunday's paper really was a mistake on your part and there will be repercussions for you and Miss Mann, when we find her. Now, the paper said there was going to be a second part next week, I'm here to dissuade you from writing it.'

'It's too late,' I croaked through the grip on my throat. 'The follow up article was emailed last week, there's nothing I can do.'

'How unfortunate!' He swung me into the corner, turning me and punching me hard over my right kidney. The pain took my breath away, shooting right across my back and dropped me to my knees. A foot pushed me down on to the ground and a shiny, black, hand-made shoe kicked me hard in the ribs, knocking any remaining breath from me. The two agonies, my back and ribs competed for supremacy, leaving me in a state of virtual paralysis, unable to even cry out.

'Well, I suppose if we cannot stop the article, my friend would want to see it in advance, forewarned is forearmed. You must have a copy of the article, where is it?'

I could not have answered him, if I had wanted to; and I did want to. The pain that I was feeling after only two blows meant that I would have been only too happy to co-operate, rather than have the beating continue. My pride made me want to hold out, but common sense screamed at me to give in.

Unconsciously, my eyes flicked to the hall table where I had left the folder that contained the coming Sunday's article and my notes from the Sinclair journal. My assailant followed my eyes and stretched out his right hand to pick it up. As he did so, his jacket sleeve and the cuff-linked shirt sleeve rode up to display a tattoo on the inside of his wrist, a runic lightning flash letter S, with the numbers 4 and 5 in the angles of the 'S'. Storm45, I had seen that tattoo too often recently for me to mistake it. I looked up from the floor to examine his face more closely. I had seen him before, he was the man I had seen directing the Storm45 thugs that day in Covent Garden. He leant down towards me.

'We'll be in contact, Mr West, when my friend has examined these papers. We might be paying you another call, Miss Mann too. Such a pretty girl, Miss Mann, the same as your daughter Lucy in Manchester, my colleagues would so like to meet them...'

Leave them alone, you bastard!' I gasped.

'So impolite, Mr West, when I have been so courteous.' Then he kicked me again. By the time the red mist of pain had cleared, he had gone.

I lay on the floor and gently examined my ribs. They were painful, but I did not think anything was broken, only bruised, but that did not make breathing any easier.

I lay on the floor for half an hour before I tried to raise myself. I crawled upstairs to the bathroom, where I found some codeine tablets. I sat on the bathroom floor, breathing shallowly, waiting for the tablets to kick in. Once the pain had subsided to mildly excruciating, I pulled myself to my feet and descended the stairs. I was moving like an octogenarian, but at least I was moving. I pulled out my mobile and dialled Lisa's number. She answered at the second ring.

'Hi Ian, what's up?'

'You have to stay in Prague, don't come home, stay with James.'

'What do you mean stay...'

'Listen to me Lisa. I've just been paid a visit by Storm45. Amongst other things, serious threats were made against you and Lucy. You have to stay there until it's safe.'

'What about you, are you okay?'

'I've been better, but I'll survive.'

'I'm coming home now!'

'No you are not! For Christ's sake Lisa, see sense. I've just been given a kicking, and from my attacker's tone of voice, there is something worse planned for you. Stay there where you are safe.'

'Alright Ian, but what about you? I'm not leaving you to face this on your own. Why haven't you gone into hiding?'

'Things fell through, I've got one or two things to see to, then I plan to get the hell out of here. I'll let you know when I'm out of harm's way.'

'Ian, I'm frightened, be careful, please!'

'I'll be fine; I'll see you, kid. I'll ring you when it's safe to come home.'

'Do take care. Bye.'

I had managed to reassure Lisa, but there was no fooling myself, I was frightened too.

Holding my injured ribs for support, I crawled back upstairs for my wallet. I made a call and conducted some urgent business, then I phoned Lucy.

'Hi Dad.'

'Hi Lucy. Do you still have a standing invitation to visit your 'in-laws' in Spain?'

'Sure, we've had an invitation to go at any time, since they retired there last year. Why?'

'I want you to go – now. There's a flight at seven tonight.'

'Dad, what's going on? You're frightening me.'

'Stay frightened. Go to Spain and disappear until I phone you.'

'Stop being so cryptic, Dad, tell me what's going on?'

'You were right about crossing Aylmer and Sinclair being dangerous, the research I have been doing has all blown up in my face and I want you safe until it all blows over.'

'But I've still got my dissertation to finish.'

'Take it with you.'

'I don't have the money to pay for the flight...'

'I bought your ticket a few minutes ago; it's waiting to be collected from the BA desk at Manchester Airport. Look Lucy, this is no joke, you are in serious danger. I've had a visit from a Storm45 thug, who made explicit mention of you and Lisa; it doesn't take a genius to work out what they were threatening. I want you safe out of the country. I'll call you when things have died down. You and Rob are all I have left and I couldn't cope if anything happened to either of you. Rob is safely out of anyone's reach and I want you the same. Promise me.'

'Okay Dad. I'll ring them now and tell them I'm coming.'

'Thanks Lucy. I love you.'

'I love you too Dad, please be careful.'

'I'll do my best. Bye.'

I hung up. Now at least the only things that mattered to me were beyond Sinclair's reach. The next thing would be to find somewhere to hole up until I found a way to extricate myself from this situation with my skin more or less intact.

I packed some clothes in a case and I winced with the sudden stabbing pain that seared through my injured ribs, as I tried to swing the case up off the bed. With difficulty, I wrestled the case down the stairs and dragged it out through the door. Despite the case not being particularly heavy, it still took both of my hands to wrestle it into the boot of the Saab. The time it took cost me dearly.

A black BMW with tinted windows screeched to a halt, blocking the drive. Two men got out of the passenger side doors and came towards me. One was my assailant from earlier in the day. A little over six feet, with blonde hair cut expensively, a long face out of which peered blue eyes, he wore an expensive Italian suit and the shiny, black, hand-made shoes, with which I was all too familiar. He was accompanied by a character that seemed to be a cross between a Neanderthal and a gorilla. Had he possessed a neck, he would have stood at over six feet tall, but he did not seem to have one. He was roughly square, with massive shoulders that seemed to be as wide as he was tall. He wore jeans and a tight black tee-shirt, the sleeves of which were rolled up to fully expose bulging biceps. His dark hair was cropped close to his skull and small piggy eyes peered out from under a mountainous brow ridge. I turned back to the house in a vain attempt to escape. One huge hand caught hold of my arm in a crushing grip and swung me to face the urbane thug who had assaulted me earlier.

'I thought we were friends, Mr West, why try to run away from me?'

240

'It could be something to do with my aching ribs since your last visit.'

'Oh come now, that was a love tap compared to Karl here, if you upset him. And struggling like that will upset him, despite its futility.'

'What do you want? I got your message from the last visit.'

'Ah well, that was a warning, now it seems that my friend himself wants to see you personally. You are very privileged.'

'I'm ecstatic. Who is your friend?'

'He's a very important man. You'll know him when you see him.'

'Tell Sinclair that if he wants to see me, he can come here, not send his Storm45 thugs to fetch me.'

'So you do know more than you should.'

'I would have thought it was clear from the papers you stole from me, so don't play games.'

'I'm not playing games; I have not seen the contents of the folder that you so kindly lent to us. Only my superior is privy to their contents. That is why he would like to speak to you.'

'I'll say it again, if Sinclair wants to speak to me, he can phone me and make an appointment.'

'Very amusing, but I'm sorry, it doesn't work like that, Ian. I may call you Ian?'

'Do I have a choice?'

'Not really, nor do you have a choice about accompanying us. Either you get into the car, or Karl here will pick you up and put you in the boot. The choice is yours.'

I gave up and allowed myself to be escorted to the rear seat of the BMW, crammed in beside the monolithic Karl.

Chapter 33

The car sped off down the road. I watched the familiar surroundings flash by outside the tinted windows. I tried hard not to show the fear that was gnawing away inside me. I had been severely shaken by my encounter with the suave, nameless thug seated in front of me. I was a teacher, totally unused to this sort of thing and the unknown element was as frightening as the physical threat. The car pulled up at traffic lights in the busy town centre.

'This is my chance,' I thought. If I could get out of the car, they surely couldn't kidnap me in front of so many witnesses. My hand moved surreptitiously to the handle set into the door. I yanked it back and threw my weight at the door. Nothing happened, except for the pain that shot from my injured ribs. The door remained shut and the car pulled away as the lights changed.

'Please, save yourself the trouble, the child lock is on that door, it can only be opened from the outside. I really would prefer it if you would stop treating me as if I were a mindless thug, Ian. I would wager that my degree is as good, if not better, than your own and probably from a better university.'

'If that's the case, what are you doing caught up in this?'

'That's a long story. I studied politics at university, rather like your daughter.'

'Leave her out of this!'

'As you wish. Anyway, suffice it to say that my involvement relates to a passionate philosophical commitment to a certain political credo. I want to see my country regain its past greatness. I like to see myself as a patriot.'

'Samuel Johnson was right, then.'

'Don't be offensive, Ian. Patriotism is not the last refuge of the scoundrel; it is an essential duty and noble belief.' He turned in his seat and I could see the fanaticism in his blue eyes.

'If that's the way you seek to justify your actions, far be it for me to challenge your beliefs; especially when I'm sitting next to this Neanderthal of yours.'

'Now, now Ian, you wouldn't want to hurt Karl's feelings, he might get upset. That is if he had any idea what the term meant. Thought is not Karl's strong point.'

'I'd never have guessed,' I sneered sarcastically.

'I admire your guts, Ian. Not many people in your predicament would have the balls to answer me back like you are doing. I respect that.'

'You mistake apathy for courage. The only things I value are beyond your reach, I have nothing else to lose.'

'Oh you do Ian, you have your life.'

'I said of value. If you had done your homework thoroughly, you would know that my life was destroyed when my wife left me. There's nothing frightening about you threatening to kill me; not when I've seriously thought about doing it myself. I don't want to face the life that stretches out in front of me, so go on, do me a favour. In fact, if you're clever enough, everyone will believe that I killed myself.'

'Come, come Ian, surely there are things that you value.'

'Yes there are, Lucy, Rob and Lisa, but they all have their own lives and they're all beyond your reach, so you have no hold over me.'

'Interesting. We must resume this conversation at some future point.' He turned back in his seat, leaving me to contemplate what was in store for me in the immediate future. What I had said, I thought was bravado, but the more I thought about it, the more convinced I became. I had nothing worth living for but the protection of those I loved, and it was something worth dying for, if that was what was necessary.

The journey took half an hour. From the dual carriage way, we took an A road for a time, then turned off along a narrow country lane. Finally, the car turned left onto a track that ran through a small wood towards a cluster of isolated farm buildings. I estimated that we must have been in the vicinity of the Suffolk/Norfolk border. The BMW bounced along the track, lurching into potholes and more than once, I was bounced into the immoveable bulk of Karl, with an ensuing stab of pain from my ribs.

I looked at the farmhouse itself as we pulled into the farmyard. It was a well maintained, red brick two-storey structure, topped by a brown tiled roof that was streaked with moss. Around the farmyard stood low buildings of the same red brick construction, closing the remaining three sides of the farmyard.

'We're here,' announced my captor unnecessarily as the car slowed to a stop. He opened my door. 'You can get out, but don't do anything silly like trying to escape. Firstly, that would be a waste of time and secondly, it might tend to make Karl testy. We wouldn't want that, would we?'

I held up my hands in submission. To tell the truth, curiosity was becoming as strong an emotion as fear. I really wanted to hear what Sinclair wanted, for I was sure it was Sinclair that I had been brought to see. I did not think that they simply wanted to kill me. It would not have been necessary for them to take the risk of bringing me all the way out here, when I could have just as easily been killed in my own home. I was ushered in through the door of the farmhouse.

'This place belongs to a supporter. He has lent it to us for a few days as a "retreat". It's quite isolated; I doubt there's another human being within three miles. So your meeting will not be disturbed. I'm sure you will find that most reassuring.'

I did not, but refrained from saying so. He turned in the doorway.

'Wait here please, Karl,' he said to the behemoth, who waited passively, arms folded, blocking my only exit from the building. 'Do step this way, Ian, your host is waiting for you.' He opened the door into a comfortable living room. Seated in an armchair was the figure I had expected to see, Richard Sinclair.

'Thank you, Nick, if you wouldn't mind waiting outside so that I can talk to Mr West privately.' The well-dressed thug nodded in acknowledgement and closed the door behind him.

'What the hell do you think you're doing?' I blustered. 'I thought you were supposed to be a respectable politician, not some sort of gangster who arranges kidnapping and beatings.'

Sinclair looked up at me and sighed.

'Can we cut the crap, West? Sit down. I've read your notes and it's clear you have a good idea about my origins and I understand from Nick that you have some insight into what we are trying to achieve and how we are doing it.'

'If you mean that the way even your Nazi war criminal father was concerned that your ideas and beliefs were too extreme even for him, then yes. You are trying to perpetuate the biggest con in British political history, seizing the balance of power by carefully understated racism; appearing to be oh so respectable, whilst you use those Storm45 thugs to help you achieve your ends!'

'You have been busy. Look West, I'm first and foremost a businessman. What will it take for you to hand over the journal and just go away? One hundred thousand? A quarter of a million?'

'Do you seriously think I'm that stupid? You're not going to simply let me walk away with your money, in exchange for the journal.'

'Why not? Once I have the journal, you cannot harm me. You could no longer prove anything, and no paper would print the story for fear of legal action. I have a reputation for being somewhat litigious. It's a useful way to make sure that editors are...sensitive to my feelings?'

'And what if I tell you to stuff your money?'

'That would be a real mistake.'

'I've already explained to your lackey. I'm not scared of you, I don't care if I die, I've been toying with the idea of suicide, and it would just make up my mind for me.'

'Unfortunate things might happen to those you hold dear. It would just go to show what I have been saying in my speeches about the failure of the government to maintain law and order.'

'Again, I told your minion that all the people I hold dear are beyond your reach. My son and daughter are abroad in parts unknown, as is Miss Mann.'

245

'And your wife?'

Jane, I had not thought about Jane. I had successfully moved everyone else beyond Sinclair's reach, but due to our split, I had not thought about her. If he really threatened Jane, then I would collapse like a house of cards. Despite everything, I still loved her. She might not want me, but I had to protect her. The only thing I could do was bluff.

'Go ahead. The bitch left me and has run off with another man. She's destroyed my life and is about to take my home. You'd be doing me a favour.'

'Really? Perhaps if we arranged an accident for your wife, you might...'

'Forget it! I wouldn't go out of my way to harm her, but I don't care enough that your threats to her will make me cave into you.'

'Perhaps not, but there is still your daughter, Lucy, and Miss Mann. They have to return to Britain some time; I doubt they'll remain in hiding forever. Your allegations might damage my political prospects, but I assure you, I will avenge myself. You really would not want to know what would happen to the young ladies if I had them picked up and handed over to Nick's Storm45 lads. Some of them, I believe, could be categorised as sadists. They're such attractive young women; it would be a real pity. The choice is yours.'

'I don't have the journal; I only had access to it.'

'You surely don't expect me to believe that? That bloody journal. I cannot believe that the old man could be so weak. He had blood in his veins once, but it turned to water as he got older. That old fool Father Donovan didn't help, feeding him all that bullshit about confession and saving his immortal soul. When my father told me about his past, I was proud of him. He was a warrior who had done what was necessary to defend the things he believed in. Who cares if a few anarchists or Czechs were killed? Who cares if some of the property of a few dead Yids in Auschwitz came into his possession?'

'One and a half million is rather more than a few.'

'I thought you were supposed to be a historian, West. Yet you've fallen for that Zionist claptrap about a holocaust. The Holocaust didn't happen. Yes, a few Jews died in camps, they were not used to real work, but the Holocaust was the invention of the Nazis' enemies to blacken their name. The idea has been perpetuated by Jews to morally blackmail the world ever since.'

I looked at him with contempt. This was a long way from the moderate, reasonable Sinclair. This was the man his father had feared.

'I should have known that holocaust denial would be part of your credo, a part of history to be rewritten. What's the matter; is real history so inconvenient for you that you have to espouse that bullshit? Strange that you never mentioned it in your speeches or interviews.'

'I'm not going to debate my political beliefs with you, West. I want that journal. Where is it?' I just looked at him. 'Nick!'

'Yes sir?'

'I want you to uncover where Mr West has secreted his daughter and Miss Mann. When you do, you will tell me where they are and unless Mr West co-operates, your boys can have them to play with. Go away and find them.'

'Yes sir, I don't suppose it will take long. We should have some leads by morning.'

'Right, lock Mr West upstairs, he can spend the night contemplating the fate of his womenfolk if he does not give me the journal.'

I was hustled out of the room and half pushed, half marched up the stairs.

'Oh dear, Ian, it looks like you've succeeded in upsetting the boss, I cannot tell you what a bad idea that is.'

I was forcefully shoved into an unfurnished bedroom and I sprawled on the floor. The door was locked behind me and in the fading light I could see that the window was too small to facilitate an escape. I was trapped.

Chapter 34

I barely slept that night. Sometime around midnight I heard the BMW pull away down the rutted track. Doubtless, Sinclair was off to more comfortable lodgings. The pain of my ribs, combined with the discomfort of the floor and my fear and apprehension, to ensure that the night was long and sleepless. I paced the room trying the door handle; I opened the window and tried unsuccessfully to squeeze through. It was no good, there was no escape. I sat on the floor, trying to think of a way out of my predicament. How could I protect Lucy and Lisa from the vile threats of Nick and Sinclair? I was not worried for myself, but I was scared for those in my life who meant so much to me. My mind went round in circles, if I gave Sinclair the journal, what were the chances that he would keep his end of the bargain? Was there any way I could fashion a deal that would keep Lucy and Lisa safe? Why had I got involved in all this? Had Sinclair bought my bluff about Jane? Only this last question seemed to have an answer. He had ordered Nick to trace the girls, but he had made no mention of Jane, she would be free to pursue her new life without me.

As dawn broke, I gave up trying to sleep and sat on the floor with my head in my hands. Only then did I drift off into a light doze for an hour or so. The sound of the door unlocking roused me. I looked up to see the golem-like Karl standing there.

'Downstairs!' he said in a curiously high pitched, almost strangled voice.

'Good morning Karl, talkative as ever, I see.' He scowled at me and I decided that provoking him was probably not a wise course of action.

He escorted me down and thrust me into the living room. Once again, Sinclair was sitting in the same arm chair, only this time he was flanked by Nick, who stood close to the open window.

'Sit down, West. I trust you have had ample time to reconsider your situation. Nick here has just been reporting on his efforts to trace Miss Mann and your daughter. I thought you might like to hear what he has to say. Go ahead Nick.'

'We have not traced their exact locations just yet; it's just a matter of time. Miss West left Manchester airport at 7.30 last night bound for Malaga, there are a lot of hotels in the area, but we have men following up leads as we speak. Miss Mann was a far easier matter; she flew out of Stansted at 11.15 yesterday morning on a flight to Prague. I have discovered that her boyfriend is currently working there, so it's a reasonable assumption they are together. I expect to uncover her exact whereabouts by midday.'

I said nothing, trying hard to keep the terror from showing on my face. I thought I had been so clever in moving them out of Sinclair's reach, but I had seriously underestimated the length of that reach. I could not believe that he had tracked them down so quickly. My options were becoming more limited by the minute. Sinclair was looking at me with a smug expression.

'Well Mr West, nothing to say?'

'Alright, you win; I've not got any choice. I'll take you to the journal, but I want guarantees about Lisa and Lucy's safety.'

'What? You don't trust me?'

'What choice do I have? You hold all the cards. I'll just have to accept that you are a man of your word.'

'Excellent! I told you yesterday, I have no need to harm anyone once I have the journal and the rest of your research. Once the journal is in my hands, you will be able to prove nothing. If you try to tell anyone, you'll be dismissed as a left-wing crank. So first of all, the journal, where is it?'

'I'd have to show you. It's in the safe keeping of a third party. I can't see him tamely handing it over to you. I'll need to be there to persuade him.'

'And where is this person?'

'The Thames valley, I'm not prepared to be more precise than that.'

'So close to home, unbelievable! You can drive me there this morning.'

'Do you seriously expect me to chauffeur you around, whilst you are threatening the people I love? Dream on.'

'I do not propose to take Nick, Karl or anyone else. The fewer people, even my people, who know the contents of that journal, the better. So it will be just you and me, Mr West. Since I cannot keep an eye on you and drive, my choice is simple. Either you drive, or you travel locked in the boot and I drive. What will it be?'

Once again, I was beaten, and I knew it.

'Just to ensure that you stay honest, Mr West, I will be taking a little insurance.' He pulled a squat, bulky semiautomatic pistol from his jacket pocket. I recognised it from US television shows, it was a 9mm Glock. That would give him something like seventeen bullets at his disposal. One would be enough.

'Aren't you taking a risk carrying that? It'd ruin your image as a respectable politician, if you were found in the possession of a firearm.'

'The benefits of public life, no policeman would think to stop and search me. Karl, yes; but me...not likely. So I'll take the risk. Wait for me in the car please, West, I would like a word with Nick.'

I was escorted outside by Karl, past the open window of the lounge towards the BMW. As I stood by the car waiting, snatches of conversation drifted from the window.

'.......When you locate.....Mann, deal with the problem.'

'.....West girl?'

'Do as you please.....let your boys.....good time....deserve a reward but wait for my instructions...after I deal with West'

'The bastards!' I thought, 'They're still going after the girls!' I was on his hit list too, but I did not matter, I put little value on my life. After all, what did I have to live for? My mind raced, there had to be some way I could save the girls from the depredations of these animals. But if there was, I could not think of it.

I got into the driving seat. I thought of driving away and going to the police, but they'd never believe me. Besides, the keys were not in the ignition. I adjusted the mirror and waited for Sinclair to join me. Sinclair tossed me the keys as he got in to the passenger seat.

'Turn left out of here, then take the lane for a mile.'

I drove as instructed, the BMW bouncing uncomfortably and making the seatbelt pull painfully against my injured ribs. Following Sinclair's directions, we reversed the journey that had taken me to the farmhouse.

'Are you prepared to tell me where the journal is now?'

'What, while you hold a gun on me?'

'The gun's in my pocket. I hope you will co-operate and it will not be needed.'

'But the threat's still there.'

'Certainly it is. I am too close to achieving my political dream to allow anything to stand in my way. The latest opinion polls suggest that we could even finish second in the election, surpassing even my highest expectations. No-one will be able to form a government without our support. We will be in a position to force the other parties to adopt key areas of our policies.'

'You can forget the party political broadcast, I'm not voting for you. No-one else would either, if they saw the man behind the image and knew his true agenda.'

'But you cannot deny that I have taken a minority party and brought it into the main stream of politics. I have attracted voters to right-wing ideologies in a way that no-one has since Mosley, and possibly even surpassing him. This country has been a slumbering giant for too long. We have allowed our culture and achievements to be derided and despised. Once I have power, we will rebuild; the alien cultures that have pushed out true British values will be marginalised. It will all change once only true Britons will have full citizenship.'

'Your very own Nuremburg Race Laws. When do you ban marriage between Britons and other races to preserve the purity of the bloodline?'

'I will not bandy words with you. My dream for a British Britain will become reality, despite the cynicism of left-wing, liberal intellectuals like you!'

All the time Sinclair had been ranting on, I had been trying to think of a way out of my predicament. As we pulled along the slip road on to the dual carriageway, it came to me. It was the ideal answer for someone who had nothing to lose.

Within a few minutes, I saw ahead a familiar bend in the road; I knew what was on the other side. I pressed down on the accelerator and the car's speed began to increase. My palms on the wheel began to sweat and then the shakes set in.

'Slow down!' Sinclair instructed. I pressed the accelerator down harder; the speedometer crept up to eighty five miles per hour.

'I said slow down!' he repeated starting to pull the gun from his pocket.

'Forget it! You can't shoot me unless you want an accident at this speed. You made one big mistake...' All the time, I was straining my eyes, searching for the final piece of my plan. Then I saw it. 'I heard your orders about Lucy and Lisa; it's not going to happen. You miscalculated, you forgot one key point, you should never take on a man who has lost everything, because he has nothing left to lose. You underestimated me, and that makes me a dangerous opponent, Sinclair!'

With that, I jerked the wheel to the left. As the car veered off the road straight towards the tree that stood outside the estate offices, everything went into slow motion. I will never know whether it was the adrenaline that flooded my system, or the fear, or simply that was my mind was racing, but everything around me slowed to a crawl. Pressing the accelerator to the floor, it would only be a matter of seconds before I wiped myself out and took Sinclair with me.

Over the roar of the engine, I heard a terrified scream from the seat beside me as Sinclair finally understood my intention. The tree was only yards away. With a thump, the front wheels of the BMW mounted the grass verge. With only seconds to impact, images flashed through my brain. It was not, as is popularly claimed, my life flashing before my eyes, but images of Rob as a baby; Rob as a young man with his winning smile; Lucy as a scary two-year-old and the attractive intelligent woman she had grown into and finally Lisa, always Lisa, the young woman who had gone from being an ex-student to my closest friend. I didn't want to die. I had things to live for, I had people to live for, I hadn't appreciated that until it was too late, or was it? My right hand wrenched the steering wheel to the right, whilst I groped between the seats with my left. Where was it? With the nearside headlight just feet away from impact with the tree, my searching fingers found it; the seatbelt release. The nearside wing of the BMW collided with the tree and Sinclair's belt broke free. One second he was there, arms thrown up in front of his face screaming and then he was gone, snatched away by an unseen hand. I just had time to see him disappear, before the airbag exploded in my face, blotting out everything. There was the scream of twisting, tortured metal and I felt the car spin like a Catherine wheel as the rear of the BMW swung out to my right, then the car began to roll. I recall being buffeted by the side airbag deploying and then everything dissolved into darkness.

Chapter 35

A dim light interrupted the darkness; I struggled to open my eyes and emerged into the dazzling light of a hospital ward. I felt as if I had been run through a threshing machine. My face felt tight and sore and my head felt like someone was playing football with my brain. Breathing hurt, my ribs felt like a red hot iron was being run through my chest. My left leg was stiff and immobile. I felt grim, but I was alive. As I forced my eyes open, I saw a distraught Jane sitting beside my bed.

'Ian? Oh thank God!' She pushed the button that brought nurses running to my bed. A doctor was summoned and examined me, asking a whole series of questions that varied between the banal, "What year is it?" to ones that I could not answer.

'You're a lucky man, Mr West, you have some cracked ribs from the seatbelt, some contact burns on your face from the airbag, a dislocated left knee and a slight concussion. From the paramedics' description of the car, you got off lightly.' He ordered painkillers for my ribs and head, then left the nurses to dispense them. When we were alone again, Jane bombarded me with questions.

'Ian, what were you doing driving Richard Sinclair? Are you all right? I've tried to phone Lucy, but she's not at her flat.'

'One thing at a time,' I groaned. 'My head is thumping so badly I can hardly think. What are you doing here?'

'I'm still your wife, Ian. Despite everything, I still love you. I wouldn't ever want anything to happen to you.' She hesitated, then continued, 'Ian...I've got to ask...you didn't...'

'What?'

'Do it deliberately?'

'Of course I did.'

'Oh Ian, have I really reduced you to the state where you not only try to commit suicide, but kill someone else in the process. I never thought you could be so selfish.'

'Sinclair's dead?'

'Yes, he was dead when the police arrived; he was thrown right through the windscreen out of the car and must have died instantly. Why are you smiling?'

'Because it worked; I saved Lucy and Lisa and even managed to survive, myself,' I thought, but said nothing.

We were disturbed by a uniformed policeman, who wanted to take a statement about the accident. I told him that Sinclair had been holding me at gunpoint, forcing me to drive his car and I had lost control because he was making me speed. He looked sceptical, but wrote down my statement nevertheless and left mumbling about a further CID interview later.

'Ian, what did you mean about it being deliberate? You just told the police it was an accident.'

'Because he was threatening Lucy and Lisa with rape or worse at the hands of his thugs and because I don't fancy a prison term for manslaughter.'

'But why was Richard Sinclair threatening you?'

'It's a long story and the drugs are making me too drowsy to tell it now. You can get hold of Lucy at her boyfriend's parents' place in Spain. Tell her it's safe to come home and ask her to pass on the same message to Lisa.'

'I might have known that Mann girl would be behind this somewhere.'

'Look Jane, I appreciate you being here for me, but you gave up any rights you had over my actions when you walked out on me. Please pass on the message to Lucy. I'm too spaced out to tell the full story now, but I promise I'll give you the full picture tomorrow. I just need to sleep now.'

'Okay Ian, you're right, I have no right to criticise. I'll make the call to Lucy, but I want the full story in the morning.'

She left and I fell into a drug-fuelled sleep that saw me through the rest of the day and the succeeding night, only punctuated by the occasional topping up of the painkillers from the night staff.

The following morning, Jane appeared by my bedside shortly after breakfast.

'I phoned Lucy as you asked, now keep your side of the bargain.'

'Okay, here goes, you have to accept that this seems pretty far-fetched...'

Before I could launch into the story, we were interrupted by a tall, balding man in a suit. His saturnine features made unlikely that he was a doctor.

'Mr West?' I nodded in reply. 'Chief Inspector Warren.' He flourished a warrant card. 'I read the statement you gave to the uniformed officer last night and I have a few points I'd like to clear up. Perhaps we could have a few moments...ah... in private?' He said looking pointedly at Jane.

'This is my wife, she stays; she needs to hear the whole story as you obviously do too.'

He glanced around at the empty beds on either side of me; the only inhabitant of the bay was a young man, the victim of a motorcycle accident, who had yet to regain consciousness.

'Alright, your wife can stay, but this interview stays strictly confidential until I indicate otherwise. Agreed?' Both Jane and I nodded our consent.

I ran through the whole story, starting with Lisa's discovery of the Self diary, through the story of William Miller and then his links to Richard Sinclair. I explained how this could all be supported by Lisa, Father Charlie and the documentary record. Finally, I concluded the story with my abduction at the hands of Storm45. The only thing I left out was the deliberate nature of the crash, though I could see from the look in Jane's eyes that it all made sense to her now.

'You really expect people to believe this, Mr West?' asked Warren.

'With the exception of the last part about the abduction, it's all provable and I can provide corroboration. I told you the story was far-fetched...'

'Well, as it so happens, I do believe you, Mr West. Let me explain, I'm not with Suffolk Constabulary, I'm Special Branch. We've been investigating the activities of Storm45 and suspected a link to Sinclair, but we were unable to prove anything. Your statement was brought to our attention and I had the wreckage searched and lo and behold they discovered the Glock you described in your statement. It was covered with Sinclair's fingerprints. So in fact, you're in the clear as far as we are concerned. We'll mop up the Storm45 members that we know of and just let sleeping dogs lie about Sinclair, now that he's dead.'

With that, Warren excused himself and left, promising to be in touch later to clear the publication of our findings about the Miller-Sinclair story, but he left me in no doubt that the part of the story involving Sinclair and Storm45 was strictly off limits, unless I particularly wanted an in depth investigation of the crash. Warren had clearly put two and two together and suspected that the accident was far from accidental. When he had departed, Jane sat on the edge of my bed, glanced at her watch and looked into my eyes.

'Ian, I'm sorry to have to leave you here, but I've got a job interview tomorrow and I need to go.'

'Southampton?'

She nodded with tears in her eyes.

'You better get going then.'

'Lucy should be home tomorrow, so you won't be alone. You'll be alright?'

'Does it matter? You go on and get on with your life; I'm your past, look after your future.' She leaned over and kissed me on the cheek, then walked out of my life for the last time.

Epilogue

I was out of bed in a wheelchair, when Lucy and Lisa arrived the following day. They had arranged to meet at the airport and had come straight to the hospital, pausing only to buy flowers and balloons with which they decorated my bed and locker.

Lisa arrived with the news that James had taken the opportunity of her visit to Prague to propose to her. She had, of course, accepted. Lucy insisted on getting the full story and then visited Father Charlie to read the Miller journal for herself. She helped Lisa and I write the final instalment for the newspaper, ensuring that the story was angled to have the maximum political impact. Warren contacted us to ensure that no mention was made of the BNRA-Storm45 link; that was strictly prohibited.

Without the charismatic leadership of Sinclair, support for the BNRA fell away in the polls. The newspaper revelations about Sinclair, father and son was the final nail in their coffin. By the time the election came, their standing was so low that they failed to win a single seat.

I was released from hospital within a few days, Lisa insisting that I recuperate at her Hackney flat. This met with the complete approval of my daughter.

Since then, Jane and I have filed for divorce. She seems happy in her new life. I still miss her, I always will, but I no longer feel so totally bereft. I don't know what the future holds, but I know that I have so much to lose, so I'm getting on with my life.

Author's note

Historians are still debating who was responsible for the Reichstag fire. The version that I have recounted here, including the parts played by Karl Ernst, Adolf Rall and Hans Gewehr has been offered as an explanation and the description of the fire does owe much to the account of eyewitness Sefton Delmer, which can be found in full on the internet. Did the Nazis do it? When asked later Karl Ernst replied, 'If I admitted it I would be a bloody fool; if I denied it, I would be a bloody liar.' So make up your own mind. What is indisputable is that the fire paved the way for the establishment of one of the most brutal, tyrannical and inhuman dictatorships the world has ever seen.

Although there was no village of Montegrillo, the atrocities I have described there are similar to those committed by the Nationalists elsewhere in the Spanish Civil War. Believe it or not, the words used by Miller/Molinero encouraging his men to commit rape, really were spoken by General Queipo de Llano.

There was an internment camp established in 1940 at St Denis near Paris, but there is no museum, the camp is long since gone.

The concentration camps of Auschwitz and Birkenau still remain as a memorial to those who were so barbarically murdered in the Holocaust. They are a terrible reminder of what mankind is truly capable of, if unrestrained by morality. For those who wish to understand the true origins of the Holocaust, I would recommend Ian Kershaw's excellent *Hitler, the Germans and the Final Solution*. The Holocaust Archive in Krakow is, however, a product of my imagination.

Elsewhere, historical characters and the places described in this novel do, for the most part, really exist.

Stuart Allison
Sufffolk 2010

2073480R00138

Printed in Great Britain
by Amazon.co.uk, Ltd.,
Marston Gate.